His Brother's Legacy

Mary Jeanette Valdez

For James,
Thank you for your patience and support even when characters are running through my head.

Cover art by Rachel Scribner

His Brother's Legacy

Prologue: England 1772
Chapter One: Boston
Chapter Two: Damn British
Chapter Three: A Love Story
Chapter Four: The Irish Girl
Chapter Five: A Change in the Wind
Chapter Six: Timothy
Chapter Seven: A Soldier's Call
Chapter Eight: A Letter from Home
Chapter Nine: The Cruel Hand of Fate
Chapter Ten: Unwelcome Visitors
Chapter Eleven: Strange Visits
Chapter Twelve: Piece by Piece
Chapter Thirteen: Decisions
Chapter Fourteen: A Parable Rewritten
Chapter Fifteen: Jealousy and Faith
Chapter Sixteen: Resurrection
Chapter Seventeen: Frustration
Chapter Eighteen: Old Trunks and Muddy Camps
Chapter Nineteen: Ninevah
Chapter Twenty: A Broken Man
Chapter Twenty-One: A Long Night
Chapter Twenty-Two: The Attic
Chapter Twenty-Three: Discovery
Chapter Twenty-Four: Either…Or
Chapter Twenty-Five: The Effects of Irish Whiskey
Chapter Twenty-Six: By Morning Light
Chapter Twenty-Seven: The Search
Chapter Twenty-Eight: Camp
Chapter Twenty-Nine: Accusations
Chapter Thirty: Departures and Returns
Chapter Thirty-One: By the Light of Day
Chapter Thirty-Two: Diversion and Attack
Chapter Thirty-Three: Starting Over
Epilogue
About the Author

Prologue: England 1772

"To England!" Major William Weathers yelled thrusting his mug above his head. "May she continue in all the glory that is due her and may those ignorant, thieving, two-faced colonials not live to see her glory."

His toast ended in roars of 'aye's' and 'amen's'. Stepping down from the bench, a bit more wobbly than usual, William swallowed the drink as his good friend John, bright cheeked and unsteady, paid for another.

Steadying himself on the shoulder of the man next to him, John stood. "I just want to tell my dear friend William that he will be sorely missed," he announced, his words slurring as he spoke. Others in the room 'aahh'd' at his display of emotion, but John held up a hand, quieting them. "I also want to say that if there is anyone who can tame the savage colonial woman it is Major William Weathers. I can only hope that he doesn't leave a little piece of him behind." The tavern erupted in laughter and John stumbled back to his seat, nearly missing it altogether.

"Thank you, John. That was too kind of you." William said, thanking him and rolling up his sleeves, the tavern growing warmer because of all the well-wishers crowded inside. He took another drink and, for a moment, a bit of heaviness fell upon him as reality broke through his foggy brain. William was set to leave tomorrow for Boston. Hearing so many stories of what it was like there, he didn't know what to expect. He knew it was going to be difficult being an English soldier in a city known for its ill treatment of agents to the Crown.

There were reports of fights breaking out daily between the colonial men who penned themselves the Sons of Liberty and the Crown's soldiers. Tax collectors were tarred and feathered, strung up on polls, humiliated in front of hundreds for simply performing their duty. Then there were the stories of the natives. If it wasn't bad enough that you had to watch your back around the colonials, you had to be doubly sure to watch your head around the natives. It had been said that there were cannibals just waiting to scalp and devour anyone that wandered into the forests. Exaggerations he was certain, but all the same it was a frightening prospect.

None of this mattered to William, though. The army could throw him into a forest thick with natives, or a street full of colonials begging for his blood. The only thing that worried him was running into one person…Edward Weathers. He had never forgiven his older brother for leaving England. It had crushed his mother and ruined the good name of his father.

George Henry Weathers, William's father, had served in the English navy for almost thirty years. He often filled his sons' heads with tales of the sea, leaving William to wonder how many of them were true. While their father's stories of pirates and sea battles never impressed his youngest son, they found a captive audience in his eldest, Edward.

When George Weathers finally retired from the navy he began a private shipping business with the colonies. He imported rice, tobacco, cotton, furs, anything that would make a profit, and profit he did. Soon he was able to build a second ship, a third, and then a fourth as well. George Weathers quickly began to amass a small fortune and built a large estate south of London, away from the hustle and bustle of the city.

As soon as Edward was old enough, he began to travel with his father. Edward loved the sea, the different ports, the adventure, but a rift was forming between father and son. It seems Edward saw too much of the world at too young an age and began to form his own opinions about how the world should be run. He fell in love with the ideas that were forming across the ocean in the colonies, reading the works of John Locke and Thomas Payne. After their father's death, Edward made the decision to take the ships and his inheritance, and move the business to the Southern colonies.

William knew that Edward still wrote to his mother, but he never asked her about him. There was no need. He had kept up with his brother's business through government friends. It seemed that Edward Weathers had become a well-known smuggler watched closely by the English navy. His ships made frequent trips to France and the West Indies, but had never been caught with anything illegal…yet. William knew it was only a matter of time.

To further anger William, Edward was no longer just the owner of a shipping fleet and possible smuggling ring, but was now Captain Edward Weathers of the Continental army. William had no desire to see or speak to his brother and had decided long ago that if he and Edward were to meet on the battlefield, England, not family, would come first.

The loud voice of Douglas Mather, a one armed man, injured in a battle with the French, interrupted his musings. "No doubt the women will be dying for a real man and anxious for some English blood." Douglas laughed.

"I can assure you, Sir, that it's only English beauties for me," William said with a smile, trying to enjoy his party and box away his anger.

Two more friends entered the bar and found William surrounded by well- wishers, empty glasses, and those who had simply wandered in from the London streets hearing word of a celebration. The door to the tavern opened again, but this time, a man, windblown from his hurried ride, entered. His face was pained and he tried to catch his breath while he asked the bartender a question.

Seeing the rider enter, William's conversation had stopped. Everything in the room disappeared as he watched the bartender nod and point in his direction. Looking to where the bartender motioned, the man caught William's eye, shook his head soberly, confirming what William knew when he saw him enter. She didn't have much time left and he had to go to her…now.

Standing quickly, William caught himself on the table, his head spinning. Like a well-trained soldier, he pulled himself together, made his apologies, and hurried to leave.

The horse's hooves pounded the dirt road as William rushed towards his family's home. His aunt had sent word to him in London that his mother would not recover this time. The best doctors had called on her, but there was nothing more to be done. William tried not to think of the scene he was to come upon, but continued forward towards home.

After Edward's departure, nothing had been the same for William. With his father dead and his older brother gone, William had been left to pick up the pieces of his broken family. The late Mr. Weathers had been very loyal to the King and having a son join the rebellious traitors across the ocean was an embarrassment to the family. The only good to come out of the news was that his father was buried before he could know. It was Mrs. Weathers who was sent into a downward spiral. Without her husband and beloved oldest son, she could no longer function. Falling into a depression, she abandoned the things that used to make her happy. She no longer spent time in her garden, but let it fall to ruin. Frequently ill, she didn't have the strength or desire to get well.

Soon the pressure of trying to live up to his mother's ideal of his older brother took its toll on William. He had tried his hardest for three years, but could no longer stand watching his mother turn into a ghost, mourning Edward's leaving and knowing that he would never be the one to please her. Seeing the estate safely in the hands of his uncle, he joined the army.

He wanted to be as far from the ocean and ships as he could possibly get, but he could never get away. Now he was being sent to the colonies, perhaps to redeem his family's name, perhaps to die for his country. Either way, it was evident that his life was not his to control and never would be. He would always be making up for Edward's decision, always the second son, always at someone else's call, and always plagued with guilt for feeling the way he did. That was why William raced towards home now.

He arrived at the immense, red brick English country house just before sunset. In the five years he'd been away he had tried to make it home at least twice a year. This time the house and grounds had changed more than they had before his last visit. The gardens were overgrown and the shrubbery brown. His mother, who had been known for her talent with plants, had finally given up trying.

William couldn't count the hours he had spent as a young boy on his hands and knees in the dirt helping her plant flowers. It wasn't that he enjoyed the work, he certainly didn't, but it appeased his mother. She let everyone within hearing distance know that she didn't trust the "help" with her garden. So, as always, being the dutiful son, William dug in the musty dirt, while Edward sailed the seas with his father.

It didn't bother him that his father spent so much time with Edward; it simply irked him a bit. As a young man, William hadn't found it fair, but wasn't going to complain. He figured the time would come when he got older that his father would take him to sea. Then, he would be able to join in the jokes with his father and Edward, be greeted when he returned with celebrations, and his mother would cry over his safe return. For now, he knew she needed him, and he didn't want to let her down. It seemed, even at that young age, William was the sturdy one of the family.

"William, put the foxglove over by the gate," his mother would order, sending William to the other end of the garden, plants in hand. The flowers, overgrown from the good care she had given them, tickled his nose and made him sneeze.

"Be careful," he was reminded. "You must handle them with care." William apologized, gently placing the flowers by the gate. He would then stand, brush some of the hair from his eyes, and wait for instructions. As he rode past the now brown and dying garden, he couldn't help but see the symbolism.

There were three carriages in the drive. One he recognized as his aunt's, the other as Reverend Shaw the local vicar's, and the third, he assumed, was the doctor's. He walked into the house slowly, the walls cold and lifeless despite the familiar furniture and paintings. The vases, usually full of fresh-cut flowers, were empty and the house was stale, in desperate need of being aired out.

Taking in the dark, wood paneling of the main hall, William sighed. This was where it had happened. This is where he'd last spoken to his brother over ten years ago; he'd been seventeen, Edward twenty-five.

He had just returned from a ride and from the faces of the servants, he knew that something was wrong. He could hear the shouting once he'd entered the main hall, and there was no doubt whose voice it was. William recognized the crying of a woman's alto voice and Edward's rich baritone raised above it.

George Weathers' will had been read just a week before, and William was not surprised to hear his mother upset, that's what her life had been since their father's death. The tone in her voice now, though, was full of anger, and there was no mistaking that.

"Edward, you can't be serious!" Rosemary called, following her oldest son as he stormed out of the sitting room and up the stairs. "Think about what you're doing!" Her voice was desperate now. "You would leave me? Leave your brother? Run off without a thought or care for us?"

Edward tuned quickly on the stairs, pulling her up short. "Goodness, Mother," he said, rolling his eyes. "I'm not abandoning you."

Rosemary dabbed her swollen, red eyes with her kerchief, catching sight of William standing silently in the entryway. "William!" she called out, rushing back down the stairs to him. "William, tell your brother he cannot leave us. Tell him it's too soon. Tell him..."

"Please, mother." Edward shook his head joining her on the landing. "You act as if you will be left alone," he put a hand on her shoulder. "William is here, he will..."

"You're leaving?" William interrupted.

Straightening himself to his full height of a good inch over six feet, Edward smiled broadly. "I'm moving father's shipping business to the colonies. It's all settled. Father had been thinking for some time about setting up a few ships there. I spoke to his associates and decided to take the chance and risk it. Nothing here will be changed. I'm using my part of the inheritance father left to do this." His face beamed with pride and Rosemary knew there was no talking her son out of his plans. He was too much like his father, too much the carefree adventurer. Hiding her face in her kerchief, she broke into a new bout of sobs and hurried upstairs.

William, too stunned to react, suddenly felt like an outsider in his own family; he'd never heard anything about this before. "The colonies?" They were the only syllables he was able to speak at the moment.

Edward nodded, excited words tumbling out of his mouth. "The colonies are where the money is, William. Business is growing there in leaps and bounds and we need to have a piece of it."

Edward waited for some sort of reaction, but there was none. Laughing uncomfortably, he tried to plead his case. "Surely you understand, William. I'm twenty-five years old. I need some adventure in my life!" Edward was growing frustrated, why did no one understand? Why was this even an issue? He was a grown man who needed to get on with his life.

"And you've been waiting for father to die so you could do this? Take your inheritance and run?" William's words hit Edward hard.

"Of course not," Edward countered, hurt that his brother would even think such a thing. "Father was going to send me to set up the firm in South Carolina anyway. He wanted this to happen." He paused uncomfortably. "It's just worked out better this way now that he's gone."

"Oh, Edward, that's ridiculous," his mother laughed angrily. "Your father wouldn't want you to have anything to do with those rebels across the ocean," she sniffed. "You fall in with their lot, and you will become lost!"

"That's why we need you here!" William shouted, unable, at seventeen, to understand what his older brother was going through.

"You don't need me here," Edward sighed, running a hand through his sun-streaked hair. He'd been over this with his mother earlier and it was growing tedious. "You're almost a man, William. It's time for you to take your place now. Besides, Uncle Richard is here to help with anything you need. You are more than capable of running the estate on your own. Father's will set up everything and neither of you will be in want for anything."

William shook his head. "You can't do it. You can't just pack up your things and go."

"The decision is already made!" Edward shouted, tired of discussions. "I'm going, and you and Mother are just going to have to accept it." Turning, Edward stormed up the stairs, slamming doors along the way.

William shook off the memories as his aunt, holding a kerchief to her face, hoping to hide her tears, greeted him in a quiet voice. "William, you made it. I was afraid you wouldn't be here in time."

"How is she?" he asked anxiously.

"Not well. She's asking for Edward, but I didn't have the heart to tell her he's not here." She took his hands in hers. "Perhaps seeing your face will bring her some final comfort," she said with a weary smile.

William could hear the raspy breathing as he opened the door to her room. Picking up his Bible, the vicar stood, giving William the chair next to the bed.

"She is ready to go," he told William in a quiet whisper. "Her soul is prepared."

Saying nothing, William nodded. Shaking his head, the doctor also stood, giving William a sympathetic handshake as he followed Reverend Shaw out the door. Sitting down slowly next to the woman who had raised him, William took her frail hand in his.

"Mother? I'm here now," he said quietly.

Rosemary Weathers turned her head towards his voice, raising it slightly. "Edward is that you? Did you bring the baby?"

William frowned. "No, mother. It's me, William, your youngest."

She smiled a bit. "I've read each of your letters hundreds of times. I'm so glad you came back to me."

Sighing, William was barely able to find his voice, humiliation rising to the surface. "It's William, Mother."

She grasped his hand, her grip almost nothing. "Oh, William's fine. He's run off to join the army. He wants a military life like his father, but you've come back to me now," her voice quivered, barely above a whisper. "I can't wait to meet your Margaret." She seemed to attempt a laugh, but it only came out as a strange sort of hiss. "Don't tell your father, but I don't even mind that she's Irish."

William frowned, furious that Edward was putting her through this, hurt that she couldn't even see that he was right there with her.

"Edward," she said resting her head back on her pillow. "I know why you left, and I think your father does too, even though he won't say it."

"Father's dead, mother," William choked out. "Remember? He died ten years ago." He tried to speak softly to her, but could feel the blood in his veins beginning to pound.

For a moment her eyes cleared as if she were trying to accept the truth. William hoped she would understand, but when she spoke, he knew she had lapsed again. "Are you staying in England, Edward?"

Finally, with no choice left, William decided to play along. "No," he said, shaking his head, trying to control his anger and disappointment. "I'm sorry, but I have to go back."

Nodding, she closed her eyes. "I understand. Your life is there now."

William sat there for a while, watching her fall back to sleep until she let out a final raspy breath. Wiping away a tear, he kissed her cheek, surprised at how warm it still was. Standing, he composed himself and stepped into the hall, greeted by the anxious eyes of his aunt and the somber faces of the doctor, the vicar, and the servants as he shut the door behind him. "She's gone," he said and left to return to his ship, cursing his brother with every breath.

Chapter One: Boston
Boston, Massachusetts, Fall 1774

Major William Weathers stepped onto American soil one of the most hated enemies many colonists had ever known. Instead of stepping onto the land and seeing a country full of possibility like thousands before him, William stepped onto the land overwhelmed, feeling nothing from his fellow men but disgust, anxiety and apprehension.

Since the quartering act had been amended in June to include taverns and inns, he was to stay at the boarding house of a colonial family with another officer instead of living in barracks or a tent on the large grass commons with hundreds of others. It was something he was not looking forward to. He would rather be with his fellow soldiers as one big company, but it wasn't his choice. These were his orders and he would follow them. It was his duty, as so much else in his life had been. Duty. Honor. Nothing else.

With his coat and colors worn proudly, tricorn hat in place, brown hair pulled back in a cue, he straightened his shoulders, standing up as tall and proud as he could. He knew from the beginning that this would be a difficult assignment, had read the reports on the feelings of colonists towards the "lobster backs" as they called them. Feelings of anger and distrust had come to a forefront years earlier, and things had only gotten worse since then.

The boarding house and tavern he was to stay in was supposedly located off of King Street, close to the harbor and just down the street from a make-shift command post. Stopping there first, he picked up his orders and checked in with his superiors. A fellow officer, Lieutenant Kelley, was kind enough to walk him to the Welch's home and give him a little insight into the man he would be sharing his rooms with.

Lieutenant Kelley, having spent the past three years in Boston, and having a good idea of what William should expect, informed him of just that while they made their way down the cobblestone street. "Unlike most families, the Welch's haven't given us too many difficulties. They are of course rebels and, as such, won't be enthused about having another English soldier with them. Most colonists have refused to quarter our men, but the barracks are full, so they have no choice. We offered the Welch family a small compensation for their services and they suddenly became," he paused, "less patriotic than before and were somewhat more willing to house a couple of officers. You might prepare yourself for a little bit of trouble though. Noise at all hours to try and rattle you, cold breakfasts, that sort of nonsense. They know better than to try anything else, though. The law states that they are to provide you with food, shelter, goods, whatever it is you need."

"Hugh Pearson," William said abruptly stepping aside in fear of an oncoming carriage that threatened to run them over. "They said I would be rooming with a Colonel Hugh Pearson. Who is he?" William couldn't help but feel a little conspicuous in his bright, red uniform. While there were other soldiers along the street, he didn't miss the side-glances and suspicious looks people gave him as they went about their daily routines. He was taken aback a couple of times when insults were yelled by passersby, and it didn't take long for William to realize they were speaking of him.

"You'll get along fine with Colonel Pearson, one of the most upstanding men in the King's service. You'd think the man a saint with the morals he holds himself to," Kelley laughed a bit. "Some have said that he prays for forgiveness before and after battle, and if he kills someone, he's been known to pray with them during their dying breath," Kelley threw him a look. "A bunch of hog's wash if you ask me, but what can you do?" he shrugged.

They came to a two-story, red brick boarding house connected to a tavern. "The Welch's own the tavern as well," Kelley explained. "You will be allowed free service anytime."

Turning to William, Kelley reached out to shake his hand. "Well, I'll leave you, God save the King and all of that. If you need anything, don't hesitate."

William nodded as the official looking Lt. Kelley was swallowed by the crowd. He took a moment to get a good look at his surroundings. A nip of autumn was in the air, and the entire block made up of reds and yellows and browns, was a striking difference to the green English countryside he had left. Walking up the worn, brick sidewalk, William knocked on the weathered, wood door in front of him. He heard some muffled yelling, and some stomping until, finally, the door swung open with abrupt force.

"Ah, it's another one. I suppose you're here to stay as well." The old woman was short and thin, only coming up to William's shoulders, limp gray hair pulled back into a bonnet, and the lines on her face were proof enough that smiling was a rarity. Her shoulders were stooped from years of hard work meant for someone twice her size. Looking over William, she sighed. "I suppose they would send us another well-fed chap who'll require plenty of meat. This will be great for business," she mumbled.

William wasn't sure what to say. It seemed odd, but he was slightly intimidated by this gruff little woman.

"Well, come in," she ordered. "If the English come by and see you standing there in the street they'll have me strung up on the gallows." William ducked as she ushered him inside the house and shut the door, blocking out the sun.

The house was dim, uncomfortably warm, and smelled of mold and beer. He could hear the mumble of conversations and the clinking of glasses from the tavern next door.

"You keep your weapons with you," the woman ordered as she walked in front of him, all business. "If you leave them lyin' around I can't promise whose hands they'll end up in. Breakfast is at seven, lunch at noon, and dinner six. I know I'm obliged to feed you, but if the food is gone then you'll have to go next door and be fed along with the other customers, few of them as there are. You rotten English are always finding ways to bleed us dry."

She led him through a large kitchen with a roaring fire in the corner, where a young man was bustling around filling bowls with some sort of stew and a girl was chopping something that had been alive at one point, but what it had been, William was uncertain. He ducked again as she led him up a small staircase to what he assumed was the attic. While he was fairly tall, he had never felt conspicuously so until now. Not certain whether it was the brightness of his jacket in the darkened house, or his manner of bearing, but he decided maybe it best to slump his shoulders just a little bit.

Mrs. Welch paused before they entered. "Now don't think you're going to be living in high style just because you're English. They say I have to give you a place to stay and that's what I'm doing," she warned. "I have six other soldiers taking up the other rooms, so this is what you get."

William entered the tiny attic after her. It was cold and wet. The dank, moldy air was not going to be pleasant to live in. What he wouldn't give to be back in his cozy London barracks again. Unfortunately, he was here, and there was nothing more to be done about it.

Above him, the beams of the house were exposed and the sun shone in through a couple of holes in the roof. Looking at the ceiling, he wondered how he was going to last the winter in this place. He had been told the winters here could be brutal. She must have guessed what William was about to ask.

"Timothy will be patching the roof on Saturday. The Colonel," she said sarcastically, knowing that she had no intention of fixing it, "made a stink about it last week when it rained. Claimed it caused him to catch cold. Vengeance from God is what I call it. Your bed is there." She pointed without ceremony to a single straw mattress on top of a broken wood frame. "I don't expect you have many clothes with you, but when you need 'em washed give everything to Ginny…everything except that jacket. Heaven strike me down if anyone in my house ever touches a redcoat's uniform. I'd rather wish for boils on my hands than touch one."

She turned to William. "Well, that's it. No disrespect meant to his Majesty, but I hope you die at the hands of one of our good Continental fighting men."

With that she slammed the door shut and William ducked under a shower of dust and dirt that fell from the ceiling. Swearing, he took off his coat, looked at the dust covering its back and shook his head. Frustrated, he brushed it off as best he could, stretched himself out on the bed and imagined himself elsewhere.

He was trying to clear his head when the attic door was flung open and his roommate, the picture of an English gentleman, Colonel Hugh Pearson, entered.

"A new arrival," Pearson said loudly, strutting over where William stood to greet him.

"Major William Weathers, Sir. It's a pleasure to meet you."

Pearson smiled, taking the gesture of politeness, as a compliment. "Thank you, Major. Fresh from England are you? Well, I'm sure you will become acquainted with the ways of colonial life soon enough. Pardon my appearance," he said, drawing attention to his muslin shirt and dark red vest. "I don't normally leave without my uniform jacket, but I figured once in a great while wouldn't hurt anything." He let out a sort of laugh, put on his jacket and primped himself in the cloudy mirror.

Extremely well built, gray eyed, and handsome, Pearson certainly looked the part he was playing. His features were chiseled and squared, a gift from his Saxon ancestry. Even so, there was just something about him that didn't sit right with William. William was also tall and well built, but unlike Pearson, whose handsome features seemed to have been cut from a Roman statue, William's thick dark hair and blue eyes gave him a softer, natural charm.

"Have you eaten yet?" Pearson asked. "No?" he answered when William shook his head. "Well, the first thing you will learn here is to never miss a meal, especially if Miss Ginny is serving." Following Pearson's lead, William put his jacket back on, dusting a few remaining specks of dirt from the arms, holstered his pistol just in case, and followed Pearson down the narrow staircase.

William had learned a long time ago that silence was sometimes best. His father had taught him to always look over a situation before saying anything, something his brother Edward had never mastered. Edward always rushed into things head first, ignoring the consequences of his hasty actions. Their father had always said to let the other person speak first and reveal their motives. That way you know where you stood and could avoid saying something you might end up regretting. William decided it would be best to follow that advice in his current situation. He didn't know quite what to think about the brash man he was following down the stairs.

They missed lunch so, as Mrs. Welch had warned him, they went to the small tavern connected to the house since it was almost half-past one. There were only a few customers eating and drinking, but the quiet buzz of conversation was quickly muffled when the two soldiers entered. William couldn't help but notice a couple of angry faces following them as they found a table. Taking a seat, he cautiously laid a hand on his pistol for security.

Aside from the small compensation they received from the government, quartering soldiers had not been good for the Welch Tavern. The place had once been a hotbed of activity because of its close proximity to the harbor, and could serve hundreds a day. It had functioned not only as an eating establishment, but an inn and meeting house as well. Now, with the presence of the English, the Welch tavern was lucky to feed fifty, and most of them English soldiers. Mrs. Welch constantly grumbled about the failing tavern, spouting that Mr. Welch would turn over in his grave if he saw what his pride and joy had become.

No sooner had they made themselves comfortable than the conversations picked back up again and a young woman of about eighteen brought half a loaf of bread and two mugs of beer to their table. The buxom girl was extremely pretty with rosy cheeks and light brown hair tied back in a green ribbon that almost matched the color of her eyes. Small freckles dotted her nose and lit up her face giving her the appearance of a doll. Smiling politely to William, she then immediately turned her attention to Pearson.

"Major, you must meet the lovely Miss Ginny, the prettiest colonist you will ever see," Pearson said, smiling at her. Ginny's cheeks blushed a bright pink as she tried to ignore the compliment. "Miss Ginny, this is your new border. Major, what was it again?"

William nodded politely. "Major William Weathers."

Ginny smiled slightly, turning her attention back to Pearson again. "It's your favorite today," she said, bouncing off towards the kitchen glancing quickly back at the Colonel with a smile.

Looking about the room, William caught the eye of a young man standing against the wall watching the scene, a deep frown on his face. Scowling, the young man watched as Pearson drank from his mug, oblivious to what was going on around him. With a silent curse, the young man went back to serving his own customers.

"I've found that not all colonials are bad," Pearson said, bringing William back to their conversation, "simply misguided. These 'Sons of Liberty' fill their heads with all sorts of mindless nonsense." Pearson took another long drink of ale, setting the empty mug aside. "They simply need to be shown that the King will not stand for such silliness. You'll learn soon enough," Pearson assured him with a condescending smile.

William nodded his agreement as Ginny returned with two plates of roasted chicken and vegetables. Setting down William's plate first, she then focused on Pearson's, lingering just long enough to catch William's curiosity. Smiling sweetly at the Colonel she left, but not before William noticed a slip of paper sticking out from under the bottom of Pearson's plate. The Colonel must have known it was there because, at the same moment, he slipped the note into his pocket, thinking no one was the wiser.

Looking up, Pearson gave William his most charming smile. "What part of England did you say you were from?"

Chapter Two: Damn British
Ten miles outside Charleston, South Carolina

"Damn, damn, damn, damn, damn!" Edward shouted, storming into the kitchen. "Damn!" He roared, slamming a door just for good measure. "Bloody 'ell! Buggered navy blighters! Damn!" Standing in the middle of the kitchen, he ripped the post-rider's letter to pieces.

Margaret, working with Abigail in the kitchen tried not to laugh even though it brought her great enjoyment when her husband got angry. Over the years he had tried very hard to rid himself of his strong English accent and take on a more "American" sounding one. When he got frustrated, though, that would fly out the window and all his h's would disappear as well as any r's at the end of his words, pleasing her immensely after all the grief he was always giving her for never having lost her Irish lilt.

"Damn!" Three-year old Matthew shouted proudly, following his father's tall boots as he paced the room. "Damn!" Matthew yelled again happily. Margaret Weathers and two house-workers stared at the child, shocked.

"Matthew!" Margaret said sternly, going to the little boy. "We do not say that," she scolded, picking him up. The boy's lower lip began to tremble and tears welled up in his eyes. Margaret turned to her husband, giving him a stern look. Oblivious, he poured himself a cup of coffee and quickly drained it, a deep frown on his face.

"Edward, did ya hear what your son just said?" she asked, but her husband was lost in his thoughts. "Edward! Did ya hear what

I asked?" shouted Margaret, her faint Irish accent becoming stronger, her voice angrier.

He looked over at his wife. "I have to see Sam," he said, and without discussion began to leave.

Margaret threw a glance at Abigail who was busy kneading some dough, her dark face full of laughter, trying her best to hide her amusement at Mr. Weathers' behavior.

"Edward!" Margaret shouted before he left the kitchen.

"I'm sorry, dear," Edward said, turning and placing a kiss on her forehead, storming out, his frown still in place.

Shaking her head, Margaret looked at Matthew, adjusting him on her hip as he clung to her neck. "I think we should let your father be."

Abigail wiped her hands and brought Matthew a cookie as Margaret sat him down at the table. She then addressed Megan in the highchair. "Men are curious creatures, Miss Megan. That's your first lesson in life." The tiny blond-headed babe smiled as if she understood.

Edward's carriage carried him swiftly to the Wallace plantation. Let in by one of the slaves he barged into Samuel's study without being announced. Sam, a short, barrel-chested man in bifocals sat at his desk reading a large ledger book in front of him. Looking up, he watched as Edward stormed in and promptly kicked the large desk with his boot. Stepping back and taking a deep breath, he kicked it again.

"I take it this isn't a social visit," Sam said, watching Edward wince. He was a strong man, but even Sam thought that looked painful.

Too distracted to turn around, Edward poured himself a glass of whiskey, drained, it and spoke cautiously. "Frances was being followed by an English vessel. The cargo was seized when they boarded." Turning slowly to face Samuel, Edward ran a hand through his hair.

"How much cargo?" Sam asked cautiously, not really wanting to know the answer.

Edward paused for a moment, not wanting to say the words. "All of it."

Sam stood, Edward motioning towards the desk in an invitation for Sam to take a kick as well. Frowning, Sam shook his head. Unlike Edward, he was able to control some of his baser instincts.

"Of course nothing can be traced back to us because the manifest showed the ship was from Portugal on a trip to the Spanish controlled islands off of Florida," Edward explained as if it made things better.

"Do you have the letter?" Sam asked quietly.

"I tore it up," Edward admitted sheepishly.

"All that cargo," Sam groaned, sitting back down. "This isn't good Edward," he told him straightly, and then repeated the words. "This isn't good."

"I know." Edward sighed, flopping into the chair across from Sam, his long legs stretched out before him. "We'll make it up, though. It will take a while, but we will."

"There's a war coming, Edward," Sam said rather harshly. "If the English put any more restrictions on shipping we'll be ruined."

"But not if we can fend them off," Edward countered, sitting up a little straighter. "Come on, Sam. We're not going to be broke, nowhere near it. You only lost £4,000. I lost £6,000. You said last week that there was more than £30,000 in the smuggling account. It's more of an embarrassment really." Edward tried to find a bright spot in the poor outcome of their latest voyage.

"How far out are the other two?" Sam asked, thinking the situation through.

"Barring any further difficulties," Edward said hopefully, "the Fair Rosemary is ten days out with about £5,000 of cargo total, and the Rebel Spirit is due back in a month with £4,000."

"That almost covers it," Sam said, thinking. He looked back at Edward. "What do we do now?"

Sitting back, Edward smiled, a familiar glint in his eye. "We try again."

Chapter Three: A Love Story
The Weathers' farm

A month after the ship had been boarded, more bad news had hit the Weather's family with the death of Margaret's uncle. Edward, as unofficial head of the family had spent the past two days meeting with lawyers and other business associates. Trying to decide the best way to divide up the land, pay off debts, and make certain his widow would be cared for in a custom she was used to was a much harder feat than he had anticipated.

He found Margaret in baby Megan's room rocking the child to sleep, her eyes closed, humming a gentle lullaby. Standing in the doorway, he watched her for a time, an angelic sight to behold. He knew those were the words that every husband should say, but to him, the words were not just lip service.

It was a well-known fact that Edward had married one of the most beautiful women in South Carolina. Constantly, he was reminded of the fact by friends and strangers alike at parties, dinners, or any other time they were in public. Edward, of course, noticed the side-glances she received from other men, but never worried for an instant. He knew that Margaret loved him passionately, not to mention that no man would be stupid enough to want to face him on the dueling field.

It was times like these, when she was simple and at ease, that he adored her most. He never knew a mother could love her children the way Margaret loved theirs. While he knew his mother had cared deeply for him, he'd never been close to her as a child. He had been fed by a wet nurse, than tended to by nannies, sent off to school, and finally taken to sea. His parents had been affectionate to him and his brother when they were home, but there was something special about the way Margaret cared for the children.

When most people in England and Europe said society should do things one way, Margaret did the opposite. She didn't pawn her children off on nannies or slaves. She changed their diapers, wiped their spit-up, bathed them, fed them, and cared for them when they were sick. Perhaps it was because she had never known her own mother and was raised from infancy by her father that she cared for them the way she did. Edward often wondered if she was trying to make up for what she had never known as a child.

Finishing her song, Margaret gave the sleeping child's soft curls a gentle kiss. She stood up carefully, laying the sleeping baby in her crib, giving Edward a tired smile when she saw him leaning against the door frame. Covering the baby with a blanket, she went to where Matthew was asleep on the trundle bed in the corner. The little boy had been insisting on sleeping in his sister's room lately so that he could come get his mother if she cried.

Margaret bent over and gave the little boy a gentle kiss. "My big, brave protector," she whispered.

Slowly she shut the door behind her, careful not to let the latch click and undo all her hard work putting the baby to sleep. When she was certain the door was closed, she turned to Edward.

"Is everything settled?" she asked in her musical Irish accent that still sent his heart racing after all these years.

"Yes," he told her, his voice cautious, knowing what he had to say would be difficult for her to hear. "Your aunt has arranged for passage back to Ireland next week. Michael is going with her. He's going to start a new firm in Dublin. He has no desire to run the plantation and no head for it either. He said he would rather watch after his mother." Edward leaned against the wall and ran his hand along the molding. "Are you sure you don't want me to take over the fields?"

Margaret sighed, taking his strong, arm, impressed that the man was still so muscular. At over six feet tall, Edward was an imposing figure and Margaret clung to him as a rock both physically and emotionally. "It's just too much, Edward," she answered. They walked down the stairs to the kitchen for some tea. "We have enough to care for here," she said, trying to look at things realistically. "I just don't see how we would be able to handle your ships and a five hundred acre plantation."

Abigail was waiting for them. She had kept Edward's dinner warm and set it in front of him at the table when they came in.

"Thank you, Abby," he said, letting the warm tea restore some of his energy after a day of dealing with lawyers.

"I agree with you," he finally said. "I asked Sam to handle the sale of the land and your aunt finally agreed to free the house slaves. Sam will handle the placement of the field hands as well and take care of the paperwork."

Margaret nodded. In the short time she had known and lived with her Uncle Seamus and his wife, she had grown extremely fond of her uncle. Even though her father had been soft spoken and her uncle too boisterous for his own good, she felt closer to her father when she was around her uncle. With his death, though, there was no more connection, and it left Margaret feeling slightly off balance, as if an important piece of her was missing.

Seamus had carried the same Irish pride, the same kindness as her father. His death, two weeks earlier, had come as a shock and had affected her more than she thought it would. Her uncle had been the only relative willing to take her in after her father's death when she was nineteen. He had cared for her like she was his own daughter and made sure that she never wanted for anything. Even though she had Edward and the children, Margaret couldn't help suddenly feeling orphaned and alone.

Edward, always able to sense what she was feeling, reached across the table and took her hand. "I will always be here. You know that don't you?" he whispered, his kind and loving words bringing tears to her eyes. "I would never leave you wanting, or alone."

"I know," she sighed, not wanting him to see her upset, but unable to shake the pain she was feeling. "I'll see you upstairs."

Abigail smiled sadly as she watched Margaret's small figure leave the kitchen. Giving Edward a nod, she spoke with wisdom. "She will be alright," the woman assured him. Edward thanked her and worked on finishing his dinner.

Margaret, still very much with the appearance of a young girl at the age of twenty-seven, had never thought of herself as a beauty. She didn't have the traditional looks possessed by the women in the classic paintings she'd seen in books as a child. She was too small in the wrong places and had just a bit too much in others. Her blond hair was always the topic of conversation from the women in the village. They said that no good would come of her, that she would end up being too proud and she would end up in a world of sin.

Growing up in such a small village, which was really no more than a cluster of small farms, Margaret had never attended dances, or spent time in the larger cities to learn the latest fashions. After coming to the colonies, she eventually became more comfortable in her skin. She attended teas and parties, slowly learning how society worked, picking up on the do's and do not's.

Edward wasn't the first to fall for her thick golden hair, rich brown eyes, and pale Irish skin. There had been plenty of gentlemen falling over themselves to dance with her, or come into good graces with her uncle. Edward was, however, the first to win her heart.

Edward first met Margaret in 1772 after she had been in the country for a only month. He had spent most of the previous seven years since leaving England at sea, dropping anchor all over the Atlantic, but doing most of his business with the southern colonies.

His newly built ship, The Legacy, was on its second voyage, docked in Charleston for a brief layover while some repairs were made from a storm that had caught them by surprise. Leaning over one of the ship's yard arms, Edward held his knife between his teeth and pulled the flowing white sail towards him. The sail had been ripped on the last leg of their trip from the Gulf of Mexico, and since a bad case of food poisoning had struck several crewmembers, Edward, owner and captain of the ship was gladly helping with some of the repairs. Fifty feet above the deck of the ship Edward and two of his sailors gave the sail one last pull.

"I found it!" Edward called to the two men balancing on the arm with him, taking the knife out of his mouth and examining the gash in the heavy cloth. "It's too wide to stitch! Let's go ahead and lash it to the arm! I'll see about ordering a new sail while we're in port!" Edward swore at the bad timing. He just couldn't seem to get the upper hand. Lifting his eyes to Heaven, he asked, "Can't just one thing go right?" Frustrated and meaning no disrespect, he figured it couldn't hurt to ask.

They tied the sail to the yard arm and climbed down the ratlines to the deck. Francis Toppin, Edward's second in command, had been watching the progress above and waited for the final decision on the sail's fate.

"How does it look?" he asked Edward nervously.

"It'll need to be replaced," Edward replied, jumping to the deck, stretching his back, stiff from being bent over the sail.

"Can we have a new one made in two weeks?" asked Francis worried about their timetable. They had two weeks to unload this cargo, reload and head back to France. He knew that if Edward didn't time it just right, the next trip across the Atlantic and back would be miserable in the bitterly cold north wind. They had been in Charleston merely a week and Edward had already complained daily that they were wasting precious time.

Edward sheathed his knife and went to get a cup of water from one of the barrels on deck. After a couple of long gulps he wiped his mouth with the back of his hand. "What time is it?" he asked.

Perplexed, Francis answered, "ten o'clock," before returning to business, "Perhaps if we tell them it's a rush order…" He stopped when he realized Edward was leaving in a hurry. "Edward, where are you going?"

Without stopping, Edward hollered back to him, "I'm sorry, Francis. I have to go. I'll see about the sail while I'm out." Francis watched, confused, as Edward flew over the last couple of steps and ran towards the crowd of people mingling on the pier.

Edward couldn't believe it was so late; his only hope was that he hadn't missed her. For a week now he had been seeing the same young lady by the shops on Concord Street. He had been reading one of the popular political pamphlets when he'd first noticed her across the street from where he stood. Even the ideals of revolutionaries didn't set his blood rushing like she had. He didn't know what it was that had caught his eye, but whatever it had been, all the angels in Heaven must have played a part.

She'd had on a simple dress of pale yellow cotton with a fashionably wide skirt and sleeves that opened at the elbows with lace ruffling on the end. He wasn't one to care much about women's fashion, but knew he would never forget that dress. The way the lines of the dress outlined her figure, the straw sun hat with the long yellow ribbon that fell down her back. Her golden hair, tied in a perfect knot at the nape of her neck. He never saw her face, but the next morning he saw her again.

This time she was in the company of an older woman, her mother, he assumed. While the older woman marched forward, the young lady lingered behind, glancing in shop windows then hurrying to catch up with her before she lost sight of the other woman in the crowd. That day he saw her clearly for the first time. Her face full of life and sweetness, her golden hair, pink cheeks and red lips making her dark brown eyes exotic and adding a depth to her face that not many women possessed.

Each day he became a bit more brave. One day he crossed to her side of the street and waited for her. She stopped to look in the window of a milliner's shop just a few feet away from where Edward stood, so close he could have reached out and taken hold of her hand. He was tempted to do just that, but held himself back. It might have been his imagination, but he swore he could smell roses. Only a breath away, he was entranced.

He studied the expression on her face while she looked at the hat in the window, noticing that her pale skin had been lightly kissed by the southern sun, her cheeks flushed, warmed by the exercise of keeping up with the older woman. She looked away from the window and, for an instant, Edward caught her eye. He smiled at her, but she quickly lowered her head for modesty's sake. Following behind her a few feet, he watched them climb into a carriage. Stopping behind a mule drawn wagon, he tried to do his best to act natural.

Keeping his eye on the carriage, he couldn't help but notice her peek her head out of the window and look over the crowd. The driver, climbing into his seat at the top of the carriage, looked over the crowd curiously, wondering what his young mistress had been looking for. Edward, not yet wanting to be discovered, made himself scarce in the crowd.

Today Edward had a plan. He wanted to learn her name, but feared that now it was impossible. Since he had lost track of time he hadn't been able to change clothes, and was hot and sweaty from working with the torn sail all morning and wearing only a simple pair of breeches and a white shirt with its sleeves rolled up. He was certainly not dressed to meet a young lady and so he reminded himself to make sure and keep his distance.

Frustrated, he hurried to the block of Concord Street where she normally walked. He scanned the people milling around the different shops, searching every face on the street, hoping to see her. Worried that he had missed her, he dashed in front of a group of people to cross to the other side of the street.

Margaret had to walk swiftly in order to keep up with her Aunt Bonnie, her tight corset not helping. Every morning they made the same trek. They would leave their house on Broad and make their way to Concord Street where they would meet Patrick and the carriage. Occasionally, her aunt would stop for a few necessities she needed in one or two of the shops, but she never allowed them to wander about looking at gifts or linger in any of the clothing shops.

"Our morning routine is for our health, not for mindless window shopping," her aunt repeated to her. "Your uncle may wish to waste his days lounging around in his wealth, but I will not let our prosperous fortune make an old, fat woman of me."

Margaret constantly found herself dawdling behind when she caught sight of something exciting in a store window. There were so many new things she hadn't seen before and longed to just have a few minutes to look. She had only been in the colonies for a month, and was still trying to adjust to the dramatic differences between the bustling harbor city of Charleston and the rocky fields of Ireland.

On this particular morning she was paying more attention to the passersby than to the shops. Since coming to live with her uncle and his wife, every evening was filled with dinners and dances and parties. Through the attention of others, the looks and whispered conversations of the women, the longing faces of the men, she began to realize that she was really very pretty, although she would never dare to admit it. "A woman should be all things modest and humble," she would remind herself. Something she had always heard growing up.

When her uncle ordered her new dresses made for her, the seamstress continually went on about what a beauty she was. With her fashionable gowns and a new found self-confidence, Margaret became increasingly aware of the young men in her company. There was one man, though, that she couldn't shake from her thoughts. She had seen him, just for an instant, on the street the day before last, but that hadn't been enough. He had been tall, handsome, and, from the amount of sun on his face, she figured he had to be a sailor, the kind of man that they wrote adventure stories about. Although she knew it was probably impossible, she hoped that maybe she would see him again.

In the remote case that they might cross paths again, Margaret had worn her most becoming dress. It was rich blue with a cream lace bodice and navy trim. She had picked out the perfect bonnet, with a navy ribbon and white flowers that tied at the side of her chin. Without appearing too forward, she tried to get a quick glimpse of any man who looked like the sailor she had seen. Slowing her pace for a moment as they passed a tailor's, she found herself lost in a small crowd of people, her aunt nowhere in sight. She struggled to the front of the crowd only to be stopped again by a man cutting foolishly across the street in front of her. The man, not watching where he was going, barely missed being hit by a carriage.

Swearing, Edward picked himself up off the dusty street in front of the horse that had nearly trampled him, more annoyed then scared by the distraction. Brushing off the dirt, he let out a heavy sigh, the driver of the carriage still cursing as Edward walked toward to the sidewalk. He managed to throw back a couple good insults and slapped his tri-corn hat on his pant leg, hoping to get most of the dust off. His day was not going well. He set his hat back on his head and looked up in front of him, thinking his heart would burst. Standing directly opposite him, her dark eyes staring directly into his, was his young lady.

Embarrassed, Edward gave her a crooked grin. The girl smiled, about to speak when a woman's voice called out nearby.

"Margaret O'Connor, come along!"

Looking behind her at the sound of her aunt's voice, Margaret turned quickly back to the handsome man in front of her. Foolishly, Edward tipped his hat and ran. He had accomplished his mission. He'd made an idiot of himself, but he had learned her

34

name and something else as well. The older woman's accent was unmistakable and he knew his heart was lost for all the trouble it was going to cause him.

"Good God," he laughed, running back towards his ship, ecstatic and shaking his head at the irony of it all, trying to catch his breath. Looking up to the Heavens, feeling like a giddy school boy, he thanked God for the odd encounter. With a smile on his face, he was constantly amazed at his maker's sense of humor. "She's Irish?"

Chapter Four: The Irish Girl

For three days Edward tried to decide the best way to meet the young woman. He knew her name, but didn't have enough connections in the city yet to be properly introduced. His crew was given leave for Saturday so he took the opportunity to sit in a small tavern on Hasell Street and keep his ears open for anything he might find useful in his search. He was thinking about giving up when a familiar carriage stopped in front of a vendor's cart. Recognizing the driver immediately, he quickly paid his tab and hurried across the street, hoping for something, anything, more he could find out about the girl.

Patrick McCauley, driver, butler, all over man of the house for the O'Connor family, was a lucky man. While some would say that God was watching out for him, he preferred to think that it was his ancient Irish heritage that kept him out of trouble. At the age of fifteen he got in a scrape with another boy, and if it hadn't been for a torrential rain storm that came up suddenly and forced everyone indoors, he probably would have been dead, or beaten to a pulp.

Another time, he was planning to go after a pair of English boys that were causing trouble in town. When going to fire his musket, he learned that he hadn't loaded it properly. Staring into the face of the boys' father, he prepared his soul for death, only to be recognized as one of the gardener's nephews and spared a very painful end. In truth, it was his many connections made in the pubs of Dublin that gave him a leg up on his competition, but Patrick preferred a more supernatural version.

When his family's farm went belly up, he met a fellow whose cousin knew of a man named Michael, whose brother, Seamus, was planning to move to the colonies and buy some land there.

After numerous introductions and a few pints, it was decided that Patrick would serve as butler and general man about the house for Seamus' family. He was put on the family's payroll and had been sitting pretty ever since.

From the moment Patrick started working for Seamus O'Connor, Seamus' luck began to change. It wasn't that he'd had bad luck; it was just that things were always a bit of a struggle for him. After he hired Patrick on, all of that suddenly changed. His investments tripled, his fields brought in record crops. He was even able to gamble some and come out on the winning side. Because of this, Seamus trusted him implicitly. In other words, when Patrick said, "jump", Seamus asked, "how high?"

Patrick was engrossed in a newspaper full of anti-English sentiments when the man approached him.

"Excuse me, Sir." Edward put on his most polite, most un-English sounding voice, and bowed slightly. "About three days ago you picked up an older woman and a young lady. Could you tell me where they live?"

Patrick eyed him suspiciously. "And why should I be tellin' you of me employer's affairs?" His Irish brogue was thick, but Edward had no trouble understanding him after having sailed with all sorts of Scot, Irish and Welshmen.

Edward had to think quickly. "The young lady dropped something that I believe belongs to her." His words stumbled out clumsily and he only prayed it didn't sound as bad as he thought it did. "I am sure that she would greatly appreciate getting it back."

"Well then, t'is rather fortunate you fount me. If you hand it to me, I will make certain that young Miss Margaret receives it," Patrick answered with a grin, proud of his quick thinking. He had noticed the young man keeping a close eye on the wee Margaret several times and he knew the look of a man desperately in love. He didn't want to make it too easy on the lad, though; a man in love needed a challenge.

"That's the problem," Edward said, trying to sound concerned. "I don't have it with me," he confessed, "but I would be happy to return it to her myself, to avoid having to trouble you any more than necessary," he added quickly.

Patrick smiled at the lad's cleverness. "Well," he rubbed his chin, drawing out the young man's torture. "I just left 'em at the dress makers. They'll be there fer a wee spell. I s'ppose t'wouldn't hurt if ye called later this afternoon. The family should be home."

Edward smiled broadly. "Thank you very much, Sir. Thank you." He hurried off, but turned back after walking a few feet. "Where?"

Patrick laughed. "The family's city home is on Broad Street. O'Connor's the name. You won't miss it. It's the only house with an Irish cross hangin' on the door." Edward thanked him again and left for a second time.

Margaret tried to stand still as Mrs. Duget pinned the hem of her dress. She had been standing there for over half an hour and was getting restless. It was hot. Still not used to the humidity of the South, Margaret would rather be anywhere than where she was. While she found her new home exciting, she still missed Ireland, and would give just about anything for a cool breeze at that moment.

Her father had died only four months before. He'd been everything to her and she could only think about him in short bursts or else she was afraid she might fall apart and never recover. After he was buried, it was up to her aunt and two uncles to decide what to do with their dead brother's nineteen-year-old daughter. Seamus O'Connor, his oldest brother, owned a plantation in the colonies and it was decided amongst them that it would be best for her to cross the Atlantic and start over with his family. Her uncle left soon after the decision was made and two weeks later Margaret and her Aunt Bonnie were boarding a ship for Charleston, South Carolina.

Stretching her neck to the side, Margaret slouched back slightly. Receiving a gentle nudge in the ribs and a stern look from her aunt, she straightened herself and tried to concentrate on her reflection in the mirror. She adored the color of the dress, there was no denying that. It was dark maroon with a white lace petticoat that peaked out underneath the heavy, velvet material. The combination of colors made her skin creamy and milky white and brought out the red in her lips.

Margaret smiled to herself, proud of how nicely it formed against her bust, giving a hint of cleavage that made her feel very feminine, and just a tad naughty. She enjoyed the luxury of the new dresses. It was just the many tiresome fittings she'd been attending that she couldn't take any more. She appreciated everything her aunt and uncle were doing for her, everything they were giving her, but she just wanted a rest. Honestly, she didn't think she could take one more introduction, or bare listening to anymore of her aunt's friends going on and on about how her life had changed so, and how the poor dear was so lucky to be away from Ireland.

The bell on the shop door rang and a mother with two school age boys entered. Her aunt went to greet them, and Margaret rolled her eyes, sensing another introduction coming. She was constantly astounded by how polite her aunt was to others when at home she was distant and cold to Margaret and Uncle Seamus. As predicted, Bonnie O'Connor made the introductions and Margaret smiled at the woman politely. She raised a hand to wave, but received a sigh when Mrs. Duget tugged at her skirt.

Margaret glanced to where her aunt was busily chatting with the woman who had entered, feeling the woman watching her. They were always polite, but she knew what they were thinking after one woman had been brave enough to say it to her face. "Couldn't find a decent man in Ireland?" the lady had said with a snake-like smile. "You had to come all the way to the colonies." She shook her head with mock sympathy. "Pity."

She knew the women, especially the mothers with single, eligible daughters saw her as a threat, but Margaret didn't really care. She hadn't had many friends in Ireland and she didn't need any here. Pulling out her courage and that Irish pride her uncle was always talking about, she pretended that it didn't matter to her, pretended as if all of this was nothing new to her.

In fact that hadn't been the truth at all. Margaret had grown up as isolated as one could be in the small village of Lachlan, one that is difficult for even natives of Ireland to find on the map. Everything had been old. Everything had been slow, and it made a quaint world for a young child to grow up in, but Margaret hadn't minded. She had been spoiled by the older ladies living in the small rows of elderly farms, especially those women whose children and grandchildren would not be seen again having left for more prosperous opportunities elsewhere.

With all the homemade dolls she could want, she learned to cook watching her many grannies over the fires and old stoves. She listened to their stories, and to their many, many words of wisdom. At times she felt a curiosity, but at others she knew was lucky to be where she was. Windows were always open and if one was bored, you simply had to walk next door to find a friend and someone to talk to.

Margaret had been perfectly content with her life. She didn't know anything different and, for her, it was ideal. She'd grown up in Heaven and wouldn't have wanted it any other way. Unfortunately, she couldn't inform every new person she met of this. So, she decided to let them think what they wanted to.

Margaret had met too many people to remember since she had arrived, but only the sailor she had seen twice near the harbor, and couldn't get out of her head, was the one she really wanted to meet. She sighed, deciding that since it was Saturday the docks would be fairly quiet so there was no use in inventing an excuse to walk by and see if he was there. She wouldn't even know where to find him if she could sneak away, knowing that after the long ordeal in the dress shop her aunt would be in a hurry to get home. She let out a little sigh, disappointment setting in.

Mrs. Duget stood with a grunt. "It should be ready on Wednesday, Mrs. O'Connor."

Margaret nearly bounced off the raised platform where she was being fitted for the gown and rushed to the dressing room. Bonnie thanked her while Margaret changed and they stepped outside into the heat of the morning already like an oven when it hit her skin. She waited in the warm sun while her aunt talked with another older lady arriving at the shop, but Margaret was hungry and growing sleepy as she waited. A yawn threatened her and Margaret forced a smile as she was introduced to the elderly woman whose name she would never remember. The women turned and began another conversation about the rising price of tea.

"Auntie, do you mind if I wait in the carriage?" she asked politely.

Bonnie dismissed her with a nod of her head and turned back to her conversation. Margaret spotted the O'Connor carriage and made her way to where Patrick was waiting for her, scandalous papers in hand. Ever since arriving in the colonies, Patrick had found a hobby of reading any and all pamphlets that were anti-English. The family knew that if Patrick had time on his hands, he would be reading his papers, and cursing the English under his breath. Seeing Margaret coming his way, Patrick jumped down from his seat, opened the door, folded down the step, helping her in.

"How are the English today, Patrick?" Margaret teased.

"The same," he said with mock sadness. "Raisin' our taxes and bleedin' us dry. How was the shop today, wee Maggie?"

She gave him a wary look. "It was very long and very tedious, Patrick. Don't get me wrong, the dress is beautiful, they all are," she added, not wanting to sound ungrateful. "I just can't stand perfectly still for hours on end. Does she always have to stay so long?" Margaret asked, looking out the window for her aunt, fanning herself with the bonnet she had removed. It was hot outside, but inside the carriage it was stifling.

"She's been takin' it easy on you," Patrick said, leaving the door open to allow a bit of a breeze. "Why, I've seen her chat with those society folks for o'er half an hour. Fer a woman who says practic'lly nothin', she can certainly make up for't." Patrick shook his head. "Don't worry, you'll be home soon. There's a roast waiting and your aunt won't allow it to go dry simply because she had something to say."

"Good," Margaret said leaning back in the seat. "All I want to do today is take a long nap."

Patrick smiled. "I don't think that's going to be entirely possible this afternoon." He leaned against the carriage window with a sly grin. "You see, a young lad was askin' about you t'day. It appears you dropped somethin' on the pier a couple a days ago and he wanted to return't."

Confused, Margaret thought for a moment. "I didn't drop any…" she shot upright.

Patrick gave her a wide, knowing grin. "So, you did notice the young sailin' lad followin' you."

"He's coming? Today?" Margaret's face beamed with excitement and was just as quickly replaced with concern. "But, Patrick, we don't know anything about him."

"We McCauley's come from a long line of ancients and I can tell a lot about a man at first glance." Patrick lowered his voice a bit. "He's a good man, I can guarantee that."

Margaret looked out the window to see her aunt waving her good byes, and Margaret sat back smiling, trying to ignore the butterflies in her stomach. Patrick held the door open for Mrs. O'Connor and Margaret couldn't believe how much better her day was going to be.

Chapter Five:
A Change in the Wind

Along with the plantation they owned, the O'Connor's also kept up a home in the city near many other prosperous houses. While Seamus loved life in the country, Bonnie was more acclimated to city life. She wanted friends nearby and the luxuries that living in town brought. Even though she wasn't much of a socialite she insisted on having a place to invite ladies for tea and dessert. So the O'Connor's divided their time between the two homes. Half of the year was spent on the plantation, and the other half in the city.

Bonnie O'Connor ate silently while she, Margaret and her husband, Seamus, sat down to lunch. After raising four stubborn, Irish sons, and living with a talkative, braggart of a husband, she had learned to enjoy the quiet of home. Their two oldest boys had died of malaria in their teens and the youngest had been ambushed and killed by Indians while exploring the wilderness of Virginia. Each death had hit Bonnie hard and made her only draw into herself more. Their only living son, Michael, had a good head for business and lived in New York where he attended school.

"Margaret, are you ready to see the country yet?" Seamus asked loudly from across the table. "I'm thinkin' on headin' back in a couple o' weeks. The city is getting to be too much for me, and I'm thinkin' maybe we should head out early." Seamus stuffed a piece of roast in his mouth, looking in the direction of his wife to see her reaction. She merely shrugged. "You can stay here for a few more weeks if you please dear, but I think the fresh, country air would do Margaret some good. She's not used to all this hustle and bustle." He gave his niece a wink.

"I would love to see the farm, uncle," Margaret answered. "It would be nice to get away for a bit."

Chuckling, Seamus took a large swig from his wine glass. "It's a little more than a farm, sweet, but it is beautiful."

He motioned for a small black woman to clear the table. "I do believe that you will learn to love it here in the colonies. As long as you can stay clear of the Tories who think the King should run our lives, you'll do well." He sat back like a mighty Lord surveying his subjects. "Watch your aunt," he said, motioning to his wife. "Learn from her. We'll make sure you marry a good lad. In time, you'll have your own land to manage." Margaret nodded, but knew she did not want to be like her aunt for the entire world.

While in public her aunt was talkative and full of a social sort of energy, when she was around her husband it was as if all the life was sucked out of her. Margaret loved her uncle, but even she admitted that he was sometimes almost too much. She could see how, after years of never having a chance to speak, and the loss of her sons, that her aunt had finally given up. Margaret didn't want a marriage like that; she didn't want a life like that. She wanted a man who would listen to her, love her, and grow old with her like the older couples in Ireland she remembered. The ones who had been together so long, they almost looked alike.

"I told your father, a long time ago, that the best thing we could do for ourselves, for the Irish people, was to strike out on our own. To rid ourselves of the rocky soil, the cliffs, the antiquated ways. He wouldn't listen, though. We're a stubborn people you know. He simply couldn't leave her, refused to even consider it. She was cold in the ground, but he wouldn't budge." Bonnie shot her husband a wary look and he realized he had said too much. "I'm sorry, Maggie," he apologized quickly, motioning for his glass to be filled. "I wasn't thinking." Taking a nervous sip, he looked back to his niece. "You have to know that we loved her too, Maggie. Indeed we did, such a sweet woman." Her uncle took another bite of roast to bury his blunder.

There was an awkward pause as the subject was changed to the price of tobacco. Margaret had never learned anything about her mother, was never allowed to. All her father told her was that she had died during Margaret's birth. She'd never even been told her name. Guessing that pain and heartache had kept her father from saying more, Margaret didn't pry. She wanted to know about her mother, but knew she couldn't push him, not wanting to hurt him. The neighbors in Lachlan wouldn't have known anything if she did ask since her father had moved there after her birth. They were as ignorant on the subject as she was, and only knew her father as the lonely widower, something they had seen too often.

The arrival of the doorman forced her to push back the thoughts of her father that threatened to surface. "There's a man here to see Young Margaret, Sir," the livery attired man pronounced.

Seamus made a face. "Margaret? Who on earth would be coming to see you?"

Waiting to see what her uncle's reaction might be, Margaret's heart leapt into her throat. Would he let the young man see her, or would her uncle insist on speaking with him first. Several young men had tried to meet with her, but after Seamus insisted on speaking with them first, they were promptly run off.

Patrick, rushing in after the servant, expecting there to be some confusion about the sailor's arrival spoke up. "Not t'worry, Sir," he stammered, slightly out of breath. "I beg your pardon, but I gave the lad permission to call. He found a trinket of wee Margaret's on the pier and wanted to return it. I'll be proud to chaperone, Sir." Margaret saw a bit of hope. If Patrick ok'd it, her uncle wouldn't say no.

Seamus glanced at Bonnie for her opinion, but received another of her noncommittal shrugs. "Well, I suppose if he's come all of this way." He looked over at Margaret's shining, brown eyes and saw the tense hope in the young girl's face. "Keep an eye on him, Patrick," he said carefully. "I don't want him trying any nonsense on my sweet niece."

Pushing back her chair, Margaret stood, smiling in an attempt to mask the nervousness she felt. Composing herself, she followed Patrick who gave her a quick wink.

Edward paced back and forth in the sunroom as he waited for the young lady. A male servant offered him a drink, but he refused, adding a "no thank you" that took the man off guard. Edward had never understood the concept of slavery. How could one man possibly think he could own another? Indentures were one thing, and paying a man for his hard work entirely different as well, but he found it criminal to force work from someone who received only poor food and moderate lodgings depending on the standards of the owners. He learned very quickly after arriving in the south not to announce his beliefs too loudly. He could denounce the English taxes and trading restrictions to his heart's content, but he didn't dare question the concept of slavery.

The best he could do for now was promise himself that, if he ever owned a large amount of land, his workers would be some of the rare freedmen who would be paid a decent wage for their work. Before he knew it, his thoughts were interrupted and the door was opened. The driver he had met on the pier ushered Margaret into the room, her golden hair pulled back, a couple curls framing her face making her rich brown eyes seemed almost otherworldly. Moving to the corner, Patrick helped himself to a glass of whiskey, attempting to give the two some privacy.

Edward took a step forward and made a small bow. "I know this is a dreadful excuse," Edward confessed awkwardly, "but I found nothing of yours on the pier." He gave her a shy smile that looked comical on the large framed man. "I simply wished to meet you."

Margaret tried to calm her breathing and hoped he couldn't see her heart pounding. "Patrick told me."

Her lilting accent was music to Edward's ears and he smiled to himself thinking about the state his father would be in if he knew his son was courting an Irish girl.

Steadying her legs, Margaret walked towards him, holding out her hand unceremoniously. "I'm Margaret. Margaret O'Connor."

Edward blushed at his temporary ignorance. He had been so busy admiring every bit of her that he hadn't even introduced himself. "Edward," he paused to catch his breath noticing how closely she was standing to him, "Weathers. It's an honor, Margaret."

Margaret had to make a conscientious effort to keep her head clear as his strong hand took hers. He was exceedingly handsome. Thick brown hair tied back and well-made clothes framed his muscular body perfectly. Her skin grew flush as his warm lips pressed against her hand, sending a warm quiver through the tips of her fingers to the very center of her being. She was entranced. Neither one of them knew what to say next, and an awkward silence followed.

"May I call on you again?" Edward asked, not wanting to take his eyes off of hers.

"I would like that very much," Margaret answered with a smile.

"I'll call tomorrow," he said, kissing her hand again starting to leave, reminding himself to let go of her hand.

Edward rode back to the pier in record time and boarded the ship. He hurried into his cabin and checked to see how much cash he had left. Stopping, he told himself to breathe, and thought about what to do next. His mind was in chaos, incapable of deciding what to do first. Francis Toppin followed him, stack of papers in hand.

"I'm glad you're back," Toppin sighed. "Half of the cargo hasn't been delivered yet and there's been no word on when the new sail will be delivered."

"It doesn't matter," Edward answered, pulling his shirt off, changing quickly. "We're not going back."

Confused, Francis stood up a little straighter and laid his list of things to do on Edward's dresser. "Excuse me, but I thought I heard you say we weren't going back?"

Edward pulled on a work shirt. "I did. The sail won't be ready in time and, besides, there are other matters I have to attend to."

Francis was stunned. "The sail won't be ready?" he repeated, surprised that the young Captain wasn't demanding something to be done about it. "We are already two weeks behind schedule and you're...alright with that?"

"I am perfectly aware that in order to have a quality product it may take more time." Edward caught a quick glimpse of himself in the mirror and straightened his collar. "I'll find another ship going the same way and give them a cut of the profits if they'll take the cargo to France."

Francis was shocked. Edward Weathers was certainly not a man known for his patience, and always made sure he got what he wanted, when he wanted it. He had been known to pay outrageous prices in order to have things done quickly. The last thing Edward wanted was to be delayed by anything. The sooner he could deliver his cargo, the sooner he could be out again...at sea...where he wanted to be. That was how he ran his ship.

"Edward, you can't be serious," Francis said, concerned. "What are we supposed to do? Just sit here in port until we are able to move again?" Not knowing what to think about the sudden change in plans, he wasn't quite certain how to handle it.

"No. We'll have plenty of work. I've wanted to have another ship built for a while now. This will be the perfect opportunity." He placed his hands on Francis' shoulders, an odd grin on his face. "It's about time we worked on putting our roots down somewhere, make connections, and establish ourselves in the city." Edward untied the ribbon holding his hair back and mussed it.

It was obvious that Edward had a plan, and that's what worried Francis. There was something Edward wasn't telling him, part of the story he wasn't hearing. "Edward, I don't know what goes through your head, but if it wasn't for how well you paid me, I would resign right now."

Smiling broadly, Edward winked. "It will be fine," he reassured Francis before he left the cabin.

The candles blazed as the wax trickled down towards the table, a few drops of wax falling on the lace table cloth. Seamus' dining room was full of food and alive with the conversation of friends. Some of Seamus' closest business partners had been invited for dinner and they feasted on duck, roasted potatoes, and now finished a dessert of cinnamon apples.

Seamus and Bonnie were at the head of the table, flanked on each side by their other guests: Mrs. Simmons and her oldest daughter, Gemma; Seamus' lawyer, August Davis; Patrick; two other merchants from Charleston; and, of course, Edward and Margaret.

Seamus had been in rare jovial form all night, holding control of the conversation. As the night went on, Margaret had to stifle a chuckle every time she heard his voice. Looking across the table at her aunt, she would notice her roll her eyes and lean back in her chair, not caring whether the guests saw her reaction or not. Margaret had to admit that after much more time spent around her uncle; she too may succumb to silence. It would be easier than trying to carry on a conversation with him.

Under the table, Margaret could feel Edward's leg brush against hers, the warmth of him sending thrills up her spine. Catching her eyes with a gentle grin, Margaret glanced down at her plate, hoping no one would notice the blush spreading across her cheeks.

Coffee was delivered to the table, slowly drawing the conversation to a lull as the guests sat back in their chairs digesting and taking in the satisfaction of such a delicious meal. Boldly, Margaret brushed her hand against Edward's, catching his eye again. This time is was Edward who had to hide the blush that spread over his own cheeks.

Seamus, sitting at the end of the table, sighed. "Mr. Weathers, did you know the English burned my father's lands?"

The table filled with an uncomfortable silence and all eyes turned to Edward, waiting to see what his response would be. It was no secret that Edward was English, but it was also no secret that he was often seen at local meetings touting the abuses of the English government in the colonies. Everyone there knew it was an awkward situation for an Irishman to have an Englishman for dinner, but no one would have dared spoken it out loud. The room closed in around Edward, everyone waiting with baited breath for his response.

Not surprised by the question, Edward had actually been expecting something like this, and he was thankful for Margaret's reassuring presence next to him. Seamus wouldn't be doing his job if he didn't put a few stumbling blocks in front of the Englishman with a suit for his niece.

Edward, in the middle of stirring his coffee, took his spoon out of his cup and set it aside. "I am very sorry to hear that," he finally answered, not thrown by the uncomfortable situation. "The English repression of your country is uncalled for." He leaned forward. "If the English would put money into the country and establish trade with the merchants, it would be a much better situation for both countries." The guests relaxed at Edward's response.

"Look at the colonies," he continued. "Instead of letting us prosper through trade which would then extend to the crown, they have put so many restrictions on us that it seems they are begging for rebellion."

Seamus nodded and all heads turned to see what his next move would be. He gave Edward a pointed look. "And what would your family in England say about that response?"

Edward's face darkened as he took a sip of his coffee, measuring his words carefully. "I don't think they would agree with me," he answered honestly. "I haven't spoken with them in some time."

The air was heavy while everyone took in what Edward had said, noticing the change in his demeanor. Not caring whether others were watching or not, Margaret took his hand in hers. August Davis was the first to break the silence. "So you truly are a son of liberty." His words hung in the air a second before Edward smiled broadly and laughed out loud.

"Yes, indeed," he answered happily. "Yes, I am."

The O'Connor plantation sat on five hundred acres of land west of the city. The place was not only immense, but extremely ostentatious as well. Seamus had been saving whatever money he could since the age of ten to build his dream, hoping that one day he would be able to leave the poverty of Ireland and move to a place where he could thrive, and that he did.

He bought one hundred acres of land when he first arrived in South Carolina and through numerous shrewd business deals had not only tripled, but had increased his land to five times what he originally started with. Now that his fortune was made, he spent his money wherever he could. He built onto his home, dressed like a king, drank to excess, fed his slaves and servants well, and lived life to the fullest, insisting on the best of everything.

Seamus moved his rook across the checkerboard. "So tell me," he asked cautiously. "Being that you are an Englishman, why on God's green earth should I let you marry my innocent Margaret?"

Letting out a nervous chuckle, Edward moved a pawn ahead a space; one that he knew would cost him a knight. "I know I'm English, Mr. O'Connor Sir, but only by birth. When my father died, I left everything and brought his business and my inheritance here to start a new life. To be honest, I've done quite well. I have two ships that make continuous trips across the Atlantic and have just signed the papers to have a third vessel commissioned. It should be ready to sail by summer."

"And is that what you intend to do with the rest of your life? Marry my dear Maggie, leaving her alone in a cold bed every night, tending to the children while you make your way over the sea having all sorts of amusements? Don't think I don't know what kind of life you sailors lead." As expected, Seamus' knight took Edward's captive.

Edward looked at the chess board, unsure what move to make. Did he let the man win, or show that he could play the game just as well? He moved his left rook one. "No, Sir," he answered. "I have a working crew of twenty and fill in, where needed, with temporary help. I hired another captain last year and would like to hire two more so that I won't have to go to sea at all. That being said, I will be able to oversee the cargos here and stay home as much as possible."

Seamus nodded, keeping his attention on the board. "And where is home?"

"For the past year at a hotel in Charleston, but I would like to be able to buy a large farm, nothing near this size, but a place that would grow good crops, good children."

Seamus nodded, inching his queen forward. "Let me tell you, my boy," the affectionate address did not escape Edward's notice and he began to see a glimmer of hope. "I have a son so my property is spoken for. Recently, though, I did purchase two hundred acres south of town, hoping that one day it would be Maggie's. When her father died what little he had was given to me to do with as I felt best, and what would be better for her than a good piece of land. It seemed the least I could do for my dead brother's girl. You seem to be a good fellow, and God knows Patrick likes you," Seamus looked up at Edward. "I respect his opinion. If you can swear that you'll take good care of her, not let her go wanting for anything, and keep her bed warm, I would be proud to give her to you."

Beside himself, Edward stood awkwardly, accidentally knocking over the chess pieces, and grasping Seamus' hand enthusiastically. "I swear on my very life, Sir."

"That's all I needed, Son," Seamus laughed. "Now, sit down," Seamus motioned, calming him and picking up the pieces that had fallen. "We have a game to finish."

Edward stepped out onto the porch, taking a deep breath of the night air, his stomach full. Leaning against the porch railing, he let his mind wander. Seamus' sudden death had been tough on Margaret after all she'd lost, but she was handling it. He didn't know any woman stronger.

He'd never been satisfied with the answers he'd given his mother and William when he'd left England. They'd kept pushing him, "Why? Why? Why?" Edward had given them plenty of reasons, but the truth was that he honestly hadn't known himself. There was just one thing he had known. He'd had to go; there was something waiting for him.

He wished he could see them now, because now he would have the answer that had eluded him then. He'd had to leave England because God had had a plan, because Margaret needed him, because he needed her. It was all as simple as that. Taking a deep breath, Edward closed his eyes and thanked God, feeling quite unworthy, but abundantly blessed.

Chapter Six: Timothy

After three weeks in Boston William was finally beginning to become accustomed to life there. He learned to ignore the insults yelled at him when he walked the streets, and he learned the places he needed to be extra cautious about entering. Winter had finally begun to settle in and the soldiers had to bundle up on their routine rounds around the city.

He had also established a strange kind of trust with the young man named Timothy who worked in the tavern. It had happened one day when the tavern was especially busy. Going down for lunch, Pearson was terribly hung over and didn't have an ounce of patience in him. When Timothy saw to the lunch of table of colonists before theirs, Pearson started to make a scene. Knowing that things would not progress well if left unchecked William did his best to quell Pearson's anger.

Timothy had approached him later and thanked him, knowing that he had not made the wisest of choices. William chuckled his agreement, and from that moment on, a tentative friendship had been formed.

Coming back late one night to the Welch house, William wasn't surprised to find the front door was already locked. Tired and cold from a long day, he sighed, simply wanting something to fill his stomach, a warm drink, and his bed. He was about to pound on the door when he heard a voice from the dark.

"The tavern door is open, Major."

Walking towards the voice, William saw someone sitting on a barrel in the shadows beside the tavern. Recognizing the voice, he asked, "Timothy, is that you?"

Timothy nodded, but kept his eyes on the dark stables across the street where wagons, horses, and carriages were housed. Timothy, a skinny boy of sixteen, had been apprenticed to Mr. Welch before he died. The boy had desperately wanted to join the army, but knew that he was needed more at the tavern. He knew the Welch's didn't have anyone else now that Mr. Welch was gone. Besides, there was a certain somebody he didn't want to leave.

William sat down next to the young man with a groan, his body tired and aching. "What are you doing out here so late?" His breath came out in a frost in the cold air.

"She's in there with him," Timothy answered quietly, shivering under his coat. "I saw them leave together an hour ago."

William didn't need to bother asking whom Tim was referring to. He knew it was Ginny and Pearson. Had guessed as much after their first meeting by the way Ginny glowed around Pearson, and by the way Pearson intentionally avoided her gaze.

"What does she see in him?" Timothy asked, shivering, the frustration and anger obvious amidst the hurt and pain in his voice. "He's arrogant, English, no offense Major, and rude."

William shook his head. "None taken," he grinned, finding the fact he apologized endearing. "There's no telling what goes on in women's heads. I think sometimes people just want to do something rebellious because it makes them feel powerful." William thought about Edward for a moment, but dismissed the thoughts as quickly as they came. "Women are attracted to power. I think it's as simple as that." He leaned back against a barrel, making himself a bit more comfortable.

"He won't stay," Timothy said, knowing this was a battle he could never win, yet still trying to fight it. "He wouldn't take care of her like I would."

"Does she know how you feel?" William asked.

Timothy shook his head. "No, it doesn't matter anyway."

William had to admit he liked the young man. Timothy reminded him a lot of himself at sixteen. Now, listening to the hurt and pain the boy was going through, he seemed to understand him. He knew how it felt to be betrayed. Standing to go inside, William patted the young man on the shoulder.

"Ginny will see you one day, Timothy, don't worry."

"You're a good man, Major. It's just too bad you're English," Timothy said, smiling in the dark at his ribbing.

William laughed quietly. "I'll take that as a compliment. Don't stay too long; it's cold out here and you'll only make yourself feel worse." William left to go to bed, leaving Timothy staring ahead at the stable.

Waking early, Timothy heard chatter in the kitchen next to his small room that had, at one time, been extra storage space. He faded in and out of sleep slowly until the sound of Ginny's voice woke him. He couldn't make out what she said at first, but he knew she was upset. He heard her high-pitched, anxious voice followed by a sharp answer from the harsh-tones of Mrs. Welch.

Timothy wrapped himself in his thin blanket and stood a couple of steps away from his bed so he could hear. Carefully, he pushed the door open a crack and the muffled voices came to life.

"Are you sure he's gone, Mother?" Ginny asked, panic in her voice.

"For the last time, yes, I'm sure," Mrs. Welch said. Timothy heard her poking at the fire to get it started.

"Well, where has he gone?" Ginny asked again.

"To hell I hope, but other than that I don't know, and I don't care. You shouldn't either."

"Did he say anything to you when he left?"

"No," Mrs. Welch answered, tired and exhausted. "It's all the better for us. English soldiers are bad for business, and I'm just glad you're father didn't live to see it. We can only hope the Major will leave soon as well."

Timothy heard Ginny's light footsteps leave quickly as Mrs. Welch continued preparing the kitchen for breakfast. He was lost in thought when Mrs. Welch's footsteps approached his door and a loud pounding shocked him back to the present.

"Timothy! I need firewood!"

Jumping back to his bed, Timothy pulled on his clothes. "I'm coming!" he called, trying to sound sleepy and not like he had just been eavesdropping.

He hurried out of his room, past the impatient woman, and walked around to the small alleyway where they kept the firewood. As he turned the corner he heard the unmistakable sound of crying in the cool morning air. He walked around the large pile of wood to see Ginny sitting with her legs pulled tight to her chest on the cold ground, sobs racking her body. Timothy stared down at her.

"Ginny," he asked, "are you all right?" He stood over her carefully and then tentatively sat down next to her.

Wiping her eyes on her sleeve, Ginny shook her head. "I was so stupid," she said, wiping away another tear. "I thought he loved me, and he just left."

Timothy gently moved his hand to her arm trying to comfort her. "He's not worth it Ginny. He's an English Soldier. There was nothing good about it." Ginny began to cry again. "I'm sorry, Ginny. I shouldn't have said that, please don't cry, please." He handed her the old kerchief in his pocket. "You'll forget about him," he assured her. 'You'll see. It'll be easy." Timothy offered her a smile, trying to cheer her up.

Growing pale, Ginny turned to him. Her eyes were the saddest he had ever seen, making her look fragile, almost ghostlike. "I'll never be able to forget him, Timothy. You've no idea what I've done."

William had been lying in the warm attic bed awake for hours unable to sleep because of the ruckus downstairs. The tavern, which was quiet during the day, occasionally came alive at night only giving him a few hours of good sleep. It happened when Boston's patriots, riled up from having spent all day at meetings somewhere or other, made their way to the Welch place and decided to give the English some trouble. They knew officers were quartered there and made the most of it. Now, with April here, they were using the warm weather to their advantage.

It had been another restless night with only a couple hours sleep when there was a knock on the attic door. William assumed it had to be for Pearson who rarely spent nights in his bed, and, as usual, was not there tonight. Aggravated, he got up and opened the door, wishing he could take his anger out on someone, but knowing it wouldn't do any good. It had to be early morning, the sun barely leaking in through the window, but what the exact time was, he couldn't be certain.

Mrs. Welch, tired herself, stood there. "There's someone for you downstairs," she informed him and left.

Throwing on his jacket and boots, William went down to the front door. Waiting for him in the early morning light was the Lieutenant who had first shown him to the Welch house.

"Lieutenant Kelley," William said, forcing himself to banish fatigue. "How can I help you?"

The official looking Kelley spoke quietly as he looked around making sure no one else was listening. "You need to get your weapons," he said quietly. "You're being sent to Concord." Kelley was on edge. "Things are becoming tense there, and we need to make more of our presence known." William, more than anxious for some action was ready, sleep no longer on his mind. "Meet us at the barracks. Your men will be waiting." With that the Lieutenant left.

Everyone was silent as the band of British Regulars made their way towards the North Bridge. The men marched in lines and William became more and more nervous with each step. They were too exposed, he could feel it. There was no cover of any kind and if militia showed up now, the English would be sitting ducks. The plan for the raid had been simple. The commanding officers hoped that by destroying their munitions the colonists would be unable to fight and the rebellion would be ended once and for all. It was a shot at least, and one they were willing to take.

Unfortunately, as William found out, the colonists had known about the plan. Shots had rung out in the early morning and everything fell apart. William knew that this was only the beginning. There would be no turning back now for either the colonists, or the British. The lines had been drawn and neither was willing to lose.

Something in the air caught William's attention and he motioned for his men to stop. "Try not to fire unless you must," he whispered to his men. He knew things could turn bad quickly, and he had no desire to add fuel to the fire.

A sudden series of sharp cracks filled the air and William yelled for his men to get down, but it was too late. They were under attack. On his stomach, William saw the militia men rushing towards him. He aimed his musket and shouted, "Fire!"

As the weeks went by after that first battle, William was in Boston on only rare occasions since most of his time was spent in the field. On one of his trips into the city he found himself back at the familiar Welch Tavern. He couldn't resist the temptation to see how the place was running. He had no love for the tavern, but it was the only place he knew in town. He felt comfortable there. Even the sour Mrs. Welch had started to grow on him.

Major Weathers and his men were enjoying their meal when another group of English soldiers walked in. A small group of colonials who had been keeping to themselves in a corner got up to leave. "Too many lobsters for my taste," one gentleman said loudly on his way out, filling the room with tension and silence.

The English soldiers sat down at a table and William recognized Pearson and his men. Things had not been good for soldiers in the city. There had been sleepless nights and clashes that left both sides hurting. While the battlefield was certainly no picnic, the city was even worse. For once, William was actually glad he'd been deployed so that he and his men didn't have to deal with the whole mess in town.

"Major Weathers!" Pearson's voice boomed through the now quiet tavern. "It's good to see you."

William stood, reluctant to greet the man he certainly had not missed while being away. "Colonel," he said tensely, "I trust things are well with you."

"As long as I'm alive and standing, things couldn't be better." Pearson made a seat for himself across from William, pushing one of his men aside without a thought. William gave his men a subtle nod, calming them.

Pearson reeked of alcohol and the dark circles under his eyes told a different story of how 'well' things were going for him. Timothy came out of the kitchen to serve William and his men their meals. He thanked him and Timothy nodded, doing his best to ignore Pearson.

"A round for my men, Tim," Pearson said cheerfully. "I want them to know how much I appreciate their sacrifices." Pearson made an elaborate bow from his seat to the table next to him where his men agreed with a hearty 'here, here'.

Lowering his head, Timothy muttered something as he turned. Something insulting that William could barely make out. Unfortunately, Pearson must have heard, his jovial mood turning suddenly. He charged out of his seat before anyone else could move.

"Do you have something to say to me?" Pearson asked, pushing the young man against the wall. "Do you?" He cocked his pistol and put it to Tim's jaw.

Standing, William caught Tim's eye, shaking his head, warning the young man not to say another word, not now when Pearson was drunk and unpredictable. Pearson's gun lowered as the door to the kitchen swung open amidst the tension.

"Hugh!" Ginny's desperate voice called out. She looked different than she had the last time William had seen her. The pretty, young woman had grown pale and older. She looked sickly, and a small bulge at her waist showed the reason why.

"What are you doing here?" she asked. "I thought you had been sent away?" Oblivious to others in the room, Ginny hugged him.

Pearson, paying no attention to her, kept his eye on Timothy standing against the wall, each one challenging the other to strike.

"Just a visit, Miss Welch," Pearson replied absently.

William watched her face as Pearson spoke. He knew with the combination of emotions in the room, along with the alcohol in Pearson's system that this was a volatile situation. He motioned subtly to a couple of his men who stood and took position behind their Major.

Ginny tried to lead Pearson to his seat, but he remained standing. "What can I get you?" she asked. "I'll make whatever you want." She stood on her tiptoes and kissed his cheek. "I've missed you so much." She prattled along as if she didn't see what was going on around her. Smiling at him, she hurried to the kitchen.

Keeping an eye on Timothy, William hoped and prayed that he would just stay quiet until Pearson was gone, but his hope was in vain. Timothy took a brave step forward and began to speak.

"How could you?" Timothy began, his voice seething with hate.

Bleary-eyed and angry, Pearson looked at Timothy, a Goliath staring down the tiny David.

Gaining more courage, Timothy raised his voice. "How could you use her like that? You've destroyed her. You've trampled her honor and…"

William saw what was going to happen, but couldn't react quickly enough to stop it. Grabbing his gun, Pearson shot the young man in the chest then tossed him aside on the floor.

Immediately, the tavern exploded, and all the men were on their feet. The sound of twenty pistols being cocked echoed in the silence of the room as each of the officer's men stood against the other. William's men had complete loyalty for him and he knew he could count on them for anything. After the botched seizure at Concord three months earlier, each and every one trusted their commander with his life. While many English had been wounded, William's men had come out of the incident unscathed.

Ginny ran in at the sound of the gunshot. She saw Timothy's body on the floor and stumbled towards Colonel Pearson. William stood in the middle, keeping the men back.

"What happened?" she cried breathlessly, looking to Pearson for some sort of explanation.

Pearson turned and gave her the sincerest look of apology he could muster. "He questioned my honor, Miss Ginny. It had to be done." Ginny stared at Tim's body and stiffly turned her head towards Pearson, quick, panicked, breath-like sobs coming from her.

Reaching into his pocket, Pearson tossed some coins to her. They landed with a loud clang on the table. "I know you two were close, so I suppose it's better that I'm leaving town for good then." Pearson turned around to survey the standoff in front of him, stumbling slightly.

He stopped and turned as if remembering something, his eyes meeting William's. "I know you can never trust a colonial," he stuttered, "but who would have thought you would have to guard against your own countrymen." He leveled his gaze at William whose pistol was still aimed at Pearson, ready to fire if need be.

"What about us?" Ginny spoke up again, her eyes full of tears. "What about me and the baby? You can't just leave us."

Pearson turned and rolled his eyes. "I'm sure you'll be able to find someone to marry you." The girl sobbed again. Pearson sighed. "Very well." He handed her a few more coins and looked around the tavern. "Pathetic," he muttered. "Let's go, men."

William took a step forward, blocking the exit. "Since when has shooting innocent civilians become a practice of his Majesty's officers?"

Colonel Pearson moved in front of him. "Since when has it become fashion to insult his Majesty's soldiers?"

William lowered his pistol, but his men kept theirs aimed. "You're drunk."

"You're insubordinate," Pearson countered. "All of you," he said, growling at William's men.

"You will answer for this, Sir," William threatened, stepping an inch closer.

A smile crossed Pearson's lips. "Really? And what do you intend on doing…Major?"

"Tell me," William asked angrily, "hanging officers for ungentlemanly conduct was practiced in England when I left; is it here?"

Laughing, Pearson motioned for his men to lower their weapons and leave. He stepped closer to William. "I'd like to see you try." Arrogant and unstoppable, Pearson and his men left, leaving William and his men alone with the dead boy's body.

Chapter Seven: A Soldier's Call
The Weathers' farm

The Weathers family passed the summer with ease and comfort enjoying each other's company. Two of Edward's ships had been dry-docked for most of it, much to his and Sam's chagrin, but The Legacy was being used as a temporary navy vessel for the young Continental navy. The amount of goods in and out of the ports had been drastically reduced while the English patrol of the waters along the coast had been dramatically increased. Everyday ships were being boarded and cargos seized. Needless to say, Edward had plenty of time to spend at home and concentrate on the farm.

With the extra time on his hands, Edward had been able to plant a fourth cotton field, even letting Patrick convince him to try a small field of indigo. The blue dye, made from the plant, had been all the rage in Europe and Patrick was certain that it would also sell well in the colonies. While Edward was officially a Captain in the army now, his regiment had not yet been called up, although Edward knew it was only a matter of time. Until then, he wanted to get as much done on the farm as possible.

After Seamus' death two years earlier, Edward had hired Patrick on as an overseer, of sorts. Since Edward refused to own slaves, those who worked the land were mainly hired hands or tenant farmers. There were only twelve and they lived in three lodges about a quarter of a mile from the house.

Abigail was truly the only slaves on the property. She had been gifts from Seamus after Edward and Margaret had married. Edward had offered Abigail her freedom numerous times, but the woman refused. Her loyalty was to Margaret, and the way Abigail explained it, she didn't want anyone to ever question that whether it be man, God, or a British soldier. She had been there the day Margaret had gotten off that ship and would be with her till the day she died.

Patrick thrived in his new occupation, and was one of the hardest workers Edward had seen. He had an instinct about the crops that he claimed came from his great druid ancestry. He always seemed to know when the best time to plant would be, or if they needed to wait a week to harvest. He got along splendidly with the workers, even if he and Edward didn't always see eye on the subject of slavery.

For all of his help around the farm, he did, of course, have some faults. The main one being that he drank too much, although he was good enough to wait till evening, and since he never became rude or belligerent when he was drunk, it rarely caused any problems. So, Edward mostly looked the other way.

Patrick found Edward in the north field examining an ox's leg with Thomas, one of the field hands. While in the north, winter was beginning to show its full force, in South Carolina, the only hint of the season was a slight nip in the air and the smell of fall.

"What's happened with the ox?" Patrick asked as the remains of last season's crops crunched under his feet.

Standing, Edward ran a hand down the beast's back, patting its rump. "I think it's a pulled tendon. You'd better walk him back to the stable, Thomas. We won't be able to work him till it heals."

Patrick sighed. "Well, we've got a couple good weeks afore the cold sets in." Patrick stood quietly for a moment, trying to gather his thoughts and put what he wanted to say into the right words. Edward took off his hat, smoothed his hair back and started to walk back to the house, Patrick following behind. "Mr. Weathers, I wanted to talk to you about somethin'."

"Certainly," Edward answered, walking along.

"Well, Sir, I've been thinkin'. Winter's comin' and there ain't much for me to do around here 'til spring. I've heard you and Mr. Wallace talk about the trouble the troops are having in the North and I know things are goin' poorly for us. I read in town that the South Carolina militia is lookin' for men willin' to fight."

Edward stopped, carefully listened to Patrick's speech. It was obvious he had been thinking about what he wanted to say for a while and had been waiting for an opportunity to bring it up. Edward wanted to give him his full attention.

"I'm good with a rifle, Mr. Weathers, and I would give anythin' to put a hole in an Englishman." Patrick blushed deep scarlet. "No offense, Mr. Weathers. I don't even consider you one of 'em, never have."

Edward smiled, finding Patrick's honesty amusing. "When would you leave?"

It took a moment for Edward's words to register. Patrick was ready to give three more good reasons for him to go if need be. "Saturday, if I may, Sir."

"Good. That will give us a couple days to get things settled around here. Do you have a decent musket, Patrick?"

The Irishman nodded. "She's old, Sir, but she's good."

"Old won't cut it against the English." Edward gave it a moment's thought. "Come with me." He started walking towards the house again. "I have an extra musket and powder horn you can have."

Patrick grinned from ear to ear like a child. "Thank ye, Sir."

Edward smiled, proud to be able to help. "If I can help someone 'put a hole in an English soldier,'" he said, quoting Patrick. "I'd give him the shirt off my back."

"I won't let you down, Mr. Weathers." Patrick stopped. "I guess I should say, Captain." He gave Edward a grand salute. "I only hope we can share the field together someday, Sir."

Edward smiled. "I would like that very much," he said, knowing that his own time in uniform would be coming sooner than he expected.

Margaret sat on the edge of the bed while Edward suited up in his Continental uniform. He had been assigned the title of cavalry Captain a year before, but had not yet had an opportunity to wear it officially. The Continental navy had wanted him first, but tired of the sea, Edward wanted to try his hand in the army.

Standing, Margaret went to him, straightening his jacket. "Do you really have to go tonight?" she asked, sliding her arms around his waist.

He kissed her on the head and went about tying his dark hair back. "We have no other choice. The English already have ships in the harbor. If we don't go tonight, tomorrow may be too late."

It was already half-past nine in the evening and the children were tucked in bed having said their good byes to their father earlier. Edward planned on riding to Charleston at night in order to avoid too much notice. Straightening to his full height, he buttoned his waist coat and straightened his navy jacket one more time, flashing Margaret a proud grin.

Margaret smiled. She looked him over from the leather stock around his neck, to his white shirt, his navy jacket with red facing, to his white gaitered trousers. "You look very handsome, Captain."

"Why thank you, Madame." Grabbing her around the waist, he pulled her close and tight, remembering her scent, the way she felt in his arms, everything. He pushed her back slightly, knowing if he held her any longer, he wouldn't be able to leave. "I'm going to miss you," he said, looking down into her dark brown eyes. Running a hand over her hair, he laid a soft lock over her shoulder.

"Remember what I told you," he said, his face serious. "If things get bad, and I'm not here, sit tight unless you hear from me. If the English come through, let them. Give them whatever they need, cattle, food, crops, blankets, just let them go. Don't make a fuss." He wanted to make sure she understood this.

"But I thought a good colonial wife was to fight back and defend her land and country," Margaret countered with a sly smile. How many times had she heard Edward say the same thing when expounding on his beliefs at dinner after he had imbibed a little too much of Patrick's Irish whiskey?

"That's my job," he said sternly. "This is not a joke. Forget about being brave. Your job is to stay safe." He leaned over and kissed her just as there was a gentle knock on the door.

"Sam must be here," he sighed. "I told Abigail to let me know when he arrives." Picking up his tri-corn hat, he shouldered his knapsack, fastened his sword around his waist, and grabbed his pistol.

Margaret followed him downstairs and out to the front porch where the warm, humid air enveloped them. Josiah, one of their freedmen tenant farmers, was finishing loading Edward's brown stallion with food and supplies. Margaret stayed back on the porch while Edward hurried down to help him finish, watching him quietly.

"Good evening Margaret!" Sam called to her with a smile, proudly uniformed atop his horse.

"Good evening Sam. How's Catherine?" Margaret asked him.

"Probably glad I'm leaving," he replied with a chuckle, a little too much truth in the statement for it to be comfortably amusing.

Edward ran back to the porch, bounding up all three steps at once, kissing Margaret one more time. "Stay safe," he told her and rushed back to his horse.

Margaret nodded, straightening her back, praying that she could stay brave and not go running after him. She watched as Edward and Sam rode off into the darkness and said a silent prayer. He had to come back to her. He had to come back to his children.

Abigail, coming out to the porch where Margaret watched the dust settling on the road after the men left, looked at her mistress. "You didn't tell him about the baby?" Abigail asked, more of a statement than a question, knowing the woman's mind was miles away following after her husband.

Margaret sighed. "I couldn't, Abby. He wouldn't have gone if I had. He needs to do this, Abigail." She looked over at her friend in the warm moonlight. "For all of us." Margaret's hand went to her stomach, hoping and praying that Edward would get to see this child.

Reading over a list of injured men in his makeshift tent, Major William Weather sighed. He laid the list, too long for his liking, on the small desk in front of him, ignoring the cold wind howling outside.

While regular soldiers bunked together in triangular tents that barely had room for two cots, let alone three, the officers faired quite a bit better. William shared his tent with Sergeant Thomas Banks and Captain Jim Carson. Each man had a cot, a trunk for their personal belongings, and a small amount of living space, the white canvas of the walls and the poles holding up the sides, making it appear larger than it really was. There was a desk the men shared, not as fancy as the one in the general's tent, but it served its purpose, as well as a small table that was normally covered with maps and letters.

"We have to notify their families," William told his paige.

"It's already done, Sir," the young soldier, more a boy than man, answered.

A gust of icy wind blew against the tent. "How can anyone live in this?" William asked, disheartened, pulling his gloves on tighter in a useless effort to make himself warmer.

An officer playing cards taking a drink from a hot cup of coffee spoke up, "I hear the Americans are faring worse. Word is that they're on the verge of mutiny." He offered William a flask. "This will warm your belly."

William shook his head. "I wish they would hurry up so we could be done with all this."

His mood was as bitter as the wind and William made no effort to hide it. He was miserable, tired, and had seen too many good men fall in the past few days for his liking. He understood that with war came death, but he hadn't anticipated the personal and emotional toll it would take on him. He could set aside the nameless faces; categorize them as part of war. It was harder when they were his men, his friends. Men he had laughed with just hours before; men he had lived with. He couldn't erase, or put aside, the images of their deaths, bloody and violent. They brought death close, and he was tired of it lurking about.

A few other officers had gathered in William's tent for a couple of reasons. Not only was his tent the warmest, being close to a large fire outside, but he also offered good company for the most part and plenty of hot coffee, and other assortments of liquor. Because he always seemed to have extra, the tent he and the other officers shared became a place for those who wanted to get away from the trials of living in camp.

The officers brought their coffee rations and any other bit of alcohol they could find and stashed them in the Major's tent where they would be put into the pool. In consequence, their tent became known as the Tavern House. Men would gather there to play cards, have a cup of coffee, or whatever else they needed to warm their belly, tell jokes, or just while away the tedious, cold, winter days in an attempt to stay occupied and warm.

A frigid breeze swept into the tent as a rider arrived, tied up his horse, and entered the tent. "Major, new orders for you, Sir," a breathless young soldier with rosy cheeks said, bowing.

William held out his hand nonchalantly to receive the papers. "Good," he said. "Maybe it's my pardon and they are finally going to get me out of this horrid place." Captain Banks chuckled from where he was resting.

"This came from General Clinton himself, Sir," the young rider, who couldn't be more than fourteen, told him. He was young, but held his head with an extreme amount of arrogance.

William stood quickly and grabbed the note. "Clinton?" he asked concerned.

"Yes, Major," the young man nodded.

Breaking the seal on the letter, William read the note. Folding it back, he laid it on his desk.

"Bad news, Will?" Sergeant Banks inquired.

"They're sending me South," he said, slamming a hand on the sturdy wood desk. "We're at a stalemate here and they decide to send me South," he laughed cynically. "Oh, but I should consider it a compliment. General Clinton feels that only an officer of my caliber could possibly help to tame the wild, uncivilized practices there. They are throwing in a commission as well." He slammed his hand on the desk again for good measure this time a little harder.

Captain Carson, a young English officer who had recently joined his regiment, brought him a cup of coffee laced with brandy. "At least I hear it's warm there...Colonel." The rest of the men saluted his new rank. Raising his glass with a sarcastic smile, William gulped down the hot, bitter liquid.

While the rest of the men returned to their card games, William sat back at his desk and brooded over his new assignment. There was one reason and one reason only that William did not want to go to South Carolina and it went by the name of Captain Edward Weathers. William had absolutely no desire to "accidentally" run into his older brother. As far as William was concerned, they were no longer brothers, or even relations. Captain Weathers was just another colonial officer who needed to be dealt with.

He had almost forgotten, for a time, about his brother and the anger he still held towards him, because it had been easy in the North. No one knew about Edward there. His name didn't come up in field meetings, or on lists, but he would hear about him in the South. Edward would be there, fighting for the colonials, a thorn in his side, a constant reminder of what he had done to his father's memory, his mother, his country, and to William himself.

Early the next morning, William tromped through the ankle deep snow to General Miller's tent, trying to take shallow breaths so the cold wind wouldn't burn his lungs. Not looking forward to his task, he knew he had put it off long enough, and before he left, he wanted to see things taken care of.

Three years had not erased the memory of what Hugh Pearson had done at the Welch tavern. William often thought about how old Ginny's child would be now. He always planned on reporting the incident, but had never found a good opportunity. In truth, William knew that it was retribution he feared from Pearson with the Colonel stationed in nearby New York. But William figured if he was ever going to say something, now was the time. If he was afraid of retribution with Pearson being so close by, he figured South Carolina would be far enough away that even Pearson's influence couldn't reach there.

"Colonel Weathers." The general stood and greeted William with a handshake, making use of William's new title. William nodded his thanks.

The General, like everyone else in camp, was suffering from the cold, wearing a heavy coat, scarf and gloves. "You wanted to see me? I was surprised when I heard you were still here. I thought you'd be headed south?" Miller motioned for him to sit, and William thanked him graciously.

"I'm on my way now, but I had one order of business I needed to take care of." William sat down cautiously, measuring his words. "This won't take long, Sir." He took a deep breath. "How would a person go about informing a commanding officer of some poor conduct by one of our men?"

"Officer or regular?" Miller asked bluntly.

"Officer," William said.

The general thought for a minute. "Is it serious?"

"I believe so, Sir," William answered.

General Miller stopped. "Tell me, and I'll pass it on along."

William took a deep breath. "It's concerning Colonel Hugh Pearson."

General Miller looked at him smugly. "Ahh, the almighty Colonel Pearson, a man with a mighty reputation and a past full of indiscretions. Readjusting his gloves, he readied himself for what was to come.

"I can assume, then, that this won't come as a shock," William relaxed. "We were quartered together when I first arrived in Boston. While there, he had an affair with the young lady of the house. As it happens, she became with child. When he was reproached by a young man who is…pardon me... who was, the family's apprentice, Pearson shot him without any kind of provocation. He was drunk, and has abandoned the girl." William paused. The accusation was out, and there was no taking it back now.

"It's not the first time something like this has happened," Miller said, taking a can of snuff from his pocket. "I actually heard about this before. An investigation was made, but the story couldn't be verified. It appears the girl and child both died during the birth." The General looked up at William, shaking his head.

"Unfortunately, the girl's mother wouldn't say anything. No doubt she had been bribed. Pearson's family has great influence at court and our hands are tied. All we can do is move him from one assignment to the next and clean up the mess he leaves behind. I will pass this on, trust me. It's about time he learned a lesson of some sort. His family would certainly not want to hear about this.

"Pearson's uncle owns a very prosperous law firm in London and is on personal terms with the King. He has used his influence to buy his miscreant nephew a hefty commission and have him sent to the colonies under the title of an officer." The General picked up a few of the papers lying across his desk as he spoke. "I guess he hoped that under good English command, his nephew would finally learn some honor. Obviously, he was wrong."

William nodded. He knew that most of Pearson's men had similar backgrounds. They were young, arrogant, and ready to take on the world. Most had come from well-off families and joined the military because it was either expected, or they were bored with a life of hunting and trying to handle the pressure their ancestry placed on them. They hoped that, by joining the English forces, they would find adventure, power and the chance to hunt something bigger than game fowl…colonials.

"Thank you for listening, Sir." William said with a curt bow. "They were good people, and the young man didn't deserve to die like that."

"I understand," the General said, standing and seeing William out. "Good luck to you, Colonel. You'll do well."

"Thank you, Sir," William answered abruptly, leaving without another word.

Colonel Pearson stormed into his field tent. Unlike William and the other officers, he had a spacious, nicely furnished tent all to himself, a large wooden desk, bookshelves, anything he might need. Pulling off his jacket, he threw it across the tent, ignoring the cold, and slamming his pistol onto a desk. Unstrapping his sword, he tossed it onto his cot. Three of his men, who had been waiting for him, watched curiously. One man stepped forward, brave enough to ask what everyone else wanted to know.

"Are we going to the battle, Sir?"

"No, we are not," Pearson answered angrily. "We are going to stay here and support our fellow soldiers in camp."

A young officer lounging in the corner stood. "We're the best fighting men they have," he said, his personality mirroring the conceit and ruthlessness of his commander.

The amount of arrogance in Pearson's men made them a dangerous company. Often taking matters into their own hands, they did so with little or no regard for morals or their higher commanders.

"I'm well aware that we are the best they have, and so are they," Pearson barked angrily, trying to decide whether he was going to tell them the truth or not. It might actually work in his favor if they knew. "It appears that the incident in Boston, at the Welch tavern, did not go unnoticed. Someone reported it and, in response, we are being punished."

"That was years ago, who would…" Silence fell over the tent as they all realized at once the only person it could have been.

Pearson gave his men a knowing look, showing them that their assumption was correct.

"That traitor!" Balis, a dark eyed blacksmith's son shouted. "How dare he?"

Not all of Pearson's men were well-bred lads. His two right hand men were a couple thugs he had found in a seedy New York whorehouse. Balis and Jass had been 'business partners' for years. They had robbed, murdered, raped, swindled, and Pearson found them perfect for his purposes. He needed two men without any kind of conscience that he could trust to do jobs that even his own men might find distasteful. Through plenty of liquor and a handsome payroll he insured their loyalty.

Stepping forward, hiding his pleasure for turning their anger to Weathers instead of himself, Pearson spoke. "Don't worry," He assured them. "Weathers will get what's coming to him."

"Just tell us where he is and we'll take care of it," Jass said angrily.

"In time," said Pearson calmly. "We'll take care of the colonials first. Then we'll deal with William Weathers."

Chapter Eight: A Letter From Home

The field hospital was really very little more than a barn that had been converted as a place for the wounded to gather. Edward rushed through the only open doors, only having heard the news an hour earlier.

It had been a small skirmish, if one could even classify it as that. Sam had been charged with delivering some munitions to another camp, when a bullet was shot from a row of hedge trees. By the time he knew what had hit him, the sniper had already run off. It was an embarrassment really, and Sam would be embellishing the story, Edward had no doubt.

The smell of rot and death hit Edward as soon as he entered the makeshift hospital. Covering his nose and mouth with a handkerchief, he found a surgeon, grabbing him by the arm.

"Samuel Wallace," he demanded, using his size and bearing to intimidate and not feeling one-bit sorry about it.

The surgeon pointed a blood-stained hand to a row of cots along the back of the barn.

Nodding his thanks, Edward moved his way through the gruesome site before him to the calmer area where patients were recovering. He located Sam without much trouble, taking a seat next to where he slept, his leg wrapped in a bandage that would need changing soon.

Sensing someone next to him, Sam opened his eyes, groaning when he saw Edward sitting there. "It's not what you think," Sam said, trying to sit himself up a little bit, grimacing at the pain it caused him.

"Oh, I think it's exactly what I think it is," Edward laughed. "Did you at least fire back?" he asked, trying to make light of the situation.

Sam rolled his eyes. "Of course," he countered. "I tried," he finally said honestly, "but you have no idea how badly a metal ball to the leg feels." Looking down at his bandages, Sam groaned. "How absolutely ridiculous."

"You know," Edward taunted. "If you wanted to go home, you could have just said so."

"Oh, don't even start," Sam said, his round face going red. "Believe me, that's the last place I want to be. Catherine will have a hey-day with 'I told you so's' when I arrive home like this." He paused. "Maybe God will be merciful and an infection will set in and take me."

Chuckling, Edward shook his head. "Come now that's a bit extreme don't you think?"

"Have you met my wife?" Sam asked.

Edward nodded, "Yes, indeed, and more's the pity. So what did the doctor's say?"

Leaning back, Sam sighed. "Barring any infection, I will be able to keep my leg."

"Good," Edward nodded, "because I have a favor to ask of you."

"What? Would you like me to dance for you?" Sam asked, a bit of his humor returning to him.

"Please, no," Edward answered, pulling a letter out from the inside pocket of his coat. "I got this yesterday." He handed the letter to Sam.

Unfolding the letter curiously, Sam read. "Well congratulations," he said with a smile, "expecting another baby." A wistful look crossed his face. "You are a lucky man, my friend. That is a jewel you found in Margaret."

Edward grinned like a schoolboy. "I know," he said, "but I'm not there, and you will be soon. I need someone to look after her, especially now. At least until I can get some leave and get home for a bit." Edward paused, taking the letter back and looking at the carefully made slants and curves of Margaret's penmanship before putting the letter back in his pocket. "Will you do this for me?" he asked, looking to his friend, his face serious and sober.

Nodding, Sam took his friend's hand in his. "I will protect them as if they were my own."

"Very good," Margaret said, looking over Matthew's arithmetic lesson. "Now, I want you to finish your reading and you will be done." Standing, she stretched her back. Her belly, nearly nine months with child, extended out. Moving to where Megan sat scribbling on her own paper, she gave the girl a kiss. "Well done," she smiled.

"Mrs. Margaret," Abigail said, entering the kitchen. "Mr. Wallace is here ma'am. I showed him into Mr. Weather's study."

"Perfect," Margaret answered. "Would you watch the children?"

"Of course, Mrs. Margaret," Abigail said, drying her hands and coming over to the table, taking a seat next to Matthew.

Entering the study, Margaret smiled seeing that Sam had already made himself comfortable behind Edward's desk. With his spectacles on, he was now pouring over the ledger books. Ever since his return from the battlefield, Sam had taken his commission to watch over her and the children quite seriously. He came by every week to make certain there was nothing they were in need of. He helped with the accounts, organized any extra work that needed to be taken care of, and would even sit down and play a game of jackstraws with the children.

Reaching for his cane next to him, Sam stood when Margaret entered. Hurrying, as best he could with a bad leg and a cane around the desk, he helped her sit.

"How are you feeling?" he asked, watching her carefully. He had never seen a woman so pregnant and was, if he had to admit it, a bit intimidated by it.

"I'm fine," Margaret answered, a bit breathless. "How are we looking?" she asked, nodding toward the ledger.

"Plugging along nicely," he answered, closing the book, satisfied. "I talked to a couple of the farmers and made certain they would have the north field planted by next week."

Margaret smiled. "Thank you," she said, trying to hide her amusement, but not doing a very good job of it.

"What's funny?" Sam asked, looking up at her. Shaking her head, Margaret adjusted herself in the chair, trying to get comfortable.

"You," she answered. "You are so serious."

"Should I not be?" Sam asked, confused.

"Of course you should," Margaret answered, "but you've checked those ledger books every week, and every week they say the same thing." She flashed him a small grin. "I don't think things are going to suddenly disappear."

Sam nodded bashfully, his round cheeks blushing a bit. "I just want to make sure you're taken care of," he answered, giving her a sheepish shrug.

"Well, you will make me feel better if you come and have a cup of tea with me," Margaret smiled, standing. Immediately, Sam was on his feet, grabbing his cane and moving to help her. "I can even tell you that I helped Abigail make some strawberry tarts."

"Oh, by all means then," Sam said, walking beside her.

They reached the door to the study when Margaret stopped suddenly. Sam watched as her hands went to her rounded stomach and she held her breath, a look of seriousness on her face that he had never seen before.

"Margaret?" he asked. "Are you alright?"

Taking a deep breath, Margaret let it out slowly, nodding as she did so.

"Sam, would you mind getting Abigail for me?" she asked, her voice extremely calm.

"Of course, he answered, watching her carefully. "Are you…" and then it hit him. First he looked at her stomach, then her face where her dark eyes confirmed exactly what he suspected. "The baby?" he asked. "Now?"

Nodding, Margaret too another deep breath, "Yes," was all she needed to say.

"Is mother going to die?" Matthew asked, not having touched his breakfast yet. It was a simple breakfast of toast and a bit of cold ham since Abigail had been with Margaret since yesterday afternoon.

Sam, who had sent a rider back to his estate letting them know where he was, had not had much sleep, concern and worry weighing on him through the night. As soon as he knew what was happening, he also sent a rider to where he knew Edward was camped with instructions to kill his horse getting there quickly if he had to.

"Your mother is certainly not going to die," Sam assured the boy, taking a sip of coffee and praying he was right.

Next to him, three year old Megan, tired and not very hungry, had laid her head down on the table and was currently tearing her bread into crumbs. "I want my mama," she said pouting, her lower lip in a deep frown.

"You will get to see her soon," Sam said, amazed that such a small creature could make such a large mess.

"Mr. Matthew, Miss Megan," came Abigail's cheerful voice entering the kitchen. "You have a baby sister."

Standing, Sam nearly knocked his chair over. "Is Margaret alright?" he asked.

Abigail smiled, pouring herself a cup of coffee. "She is doing very well. You can go see her if you would like."

Instantly the table was abandoned with shouts and both children ran out of the kitchen and up the stairs.

"You can go to," Abigail said to Sam, urging him on.

He got as far as the parlor when the front door opened. The children, having reached the top of the stairs turned. "Papa!" they shouted, running back down the steps at top speeds, jumping into Edward's arms.

"Oh, my darlings," Edward cried, a huge smile on his face, kissing both children till they giggled with delight.

"Papa, you smell like horsey," Megan said, holding her nose.

"Well," Edward answered, standing and setting her on his shoulder, "that's probably because I've been riding one for two days." Picking up Matthew, the boy cried out, laughing.

"How did you get here?" Sam asked, amused by the familial scene playing out in front of him. "I just sent Barnabus with word."

"I finally got some leave time," Edward explained, setting the boy upright again. "I was heading this way when I saw him."

"Momma had a baby!" Megan screamed putting her arms out big with excitement.

"How is she?" Edward asked, concern and fear both on his face.

"She is fine," Sam assured him. "The children were just on their way to see them."

"You should be very proud of her, Mr. Weathers," Abigail said, coming in through the kitchen after hearing the commotion.

"She did well?" he asked, looking for assurance that his wife was safe and well.

"Very," Abigail said with a nod, "she will be overwhelmed to see you."

Turning to Sam, Edward gave him a nod. "Thank you," he said. "Thank you for keeping my family safe."

Edward let the children go in first, making them swear not to say a word about him being there. He made Megan promise twice. Standing outside the door he listened, waiting with his breath held to hear his wife's voice.

All during his two day journey home, he kept imagining the worst. He knew her time was coming and he was so afraid of receiving word that she had died during the delivery, or that she had contracted a fever, or lost too much blood. He had gone through every horrid possibility in his head.

"My dear babies," he heard her soft voice say, bringing tears to his eyes.

"Come here and see your baby sister," she said. He could see her smile as she said the words, and he wiped away tears, so grateful.

"She's so tiny," he heard Matthew say. "I can't believe I was ever that small."

He heard Margaret laugh. "Oh you were, my handsome boy."

"What's her name?" Megan whispered loudly, trying not to wake the sleeping newborn.

"Her name is Sarah," Margaret whispered back. Seeing the door open, she looked up, instantly freezing when she saw Edward standing there.

He made it to the bed in two strides, no longer caring that tears were falling down his cheeks. Leaning down, he grabbed Margaret, holding her close, being careful not to crush the infant. Margaret looked up at him, tears in her own eyes. Holding the sleeping baby up to him, she finally found the only words she could think of to say. "Her name is Sarah," she said in a quiet sob.

Edward stayed at home for a week, enjoying each and every moment. He was up early with the baby, played with the children so Margaret could rest, and held his wife at every opportunity. The night before he had to leave, Edward refused to sleep. He wanted to take in everything. He wanted to remember every minute so he could take it with him to remember on cold lonely nights. Walking through the dark house, he took in everything. He wanted to remember the way Matthew snored while he slept, how Megan slept with her thumb in her mouth.

He watched Margaret, sleeping soundly while he held the baby, amazed at how small she was. He examined her feet, her skinny legs, her round belly, her tiny fingers, her large dark eyes that looked just like her mother's. Looking next to him, he saw another pair of dark eyes watching him.

"What are you doing?" Margaret asked. "Shouldn't you be getting some sleep? You have a long ride tomorrow, and I doubt you'll have a bed as comfortable as this for some time." Her mouth curved up in a sleep smile, seeing that her husband never took his eyes off the baby.

"I will sleep later," he said, "and drink a lot of strong coffee tomorrow." He gave her a dashing grin. "I don't want to miss a moment of any of this."

Sitting up, Margaret moved closer to him, so that little Megan was in between then. Taking his hand in hers she leaned over and kissed him. "Then we'll remember it together."

Chapter Nine: The Cruel Hand of Fate

As the English moved south and conquered Charleston in May of 1780, many plantations and large estates were brought into England's service. From these new acquirements Officers lived and gave orders. Troops camped on the grounds of the estates and used them as headquarters. Horses were housed in the stables and the Royalist elite were invited to celebrate English victories.

At one such evening, Catherine Wallace, holding a drink and chatting, surveyed the room, partially listening to the endless babble of the woman next to her. She had one eye on the door where she could see any new arrivals, needing to make sure there was no one there who might give her away. She had told Samuel that she was going to the theater with a friend. Instead, she had found her way to this loyalist party. The fact that her husband was a well-known "son of liberty" only added to her resentment.

Both Catherine and Sam were from well-off English families. He was a lawyer in Charleston, promising her when they married that one day they would return to England. That never happened. Instead, he became interested in farming and not only did they move from the busy city to a large farm miles from anything resembling culture, but she saw the prospects of returning to London dwindle.

Soon after, much to her dismay, Samuel was caught up in the Revolutionary spirit that was moving across the country. He became involved with his friend Edward Weathers' shipping company and the two attended political meetings with other men. Before she knew it, he was refusing to buy English goods and Catherine became a miserable victim of the revolution. When war broke out and Samuel joined the Continentals, she'd wished that he wouldn't return. She'd even prayed for it in her own way, but he did. He was injured, but alive and more patriotic than ever. Most of the time she was forced to play the part of a good colonial wife, but whenever she could, she let her true political feelings be known. Tonight was one of those rare occasions.

No longer did Catherine have any feelings or respect for her husband. He was a traitor like everyone else, and she wanted nothing to do with him. Unfortunately, she had no fortune of her own and without her husband's wealth she was nothing. Her father had died when she was fifteen and creditors took most of her inheritance. There was only enough left over for Catherine and her mother to leave London, sail to Charleston, and live off the generosity of her mother's well-off, widowed sister.

Smiling and nodding politely, she feigned interest in Lady Dougherty's conversation. Normally, she would listen to every word, desperate to hear about society in London, but tonight she was waiting for someone else. Someone she had seen for just an instant, but was desperate to see again.

She had first seen Colonel Hugh Pearson two weeks ago when she was in Charleston for the day. Samuel had some business to attend to and they were visiting the city when she saw the Colonel riding down the street in front of his men. She was so entranced, she didn't even hear the rude comments being made by her husband.

Hugh Pearson, she discovered soon after through some idle chit-chat, was only a couple of years her junior, newly transferred to Charleston at the request of General Cornwallis himself. She had watched as he rode down the street and disappeared into the crowd as if he were some kind of returning king, home from a far off land. She had to admit that he was the real reason she was at the party tonight. She had learned that he would be there and she planned to see him again.

Lady Dougherty grabbed Catherine's arm, nearly causing her to spill her wine, and bringing her abruptly back to the present. "Mrs. Wallace, it appears that our guest of honor has arrived," her voice as excited and giddy as a woman two decades her junior. "I hear he's quite a man on the battlefield. Lord Dougherty says that he is one of the most respectable Englishmen in the country. He's been in New York working with the natives in the North and creating confusion for the colonists there, but after hearing of the troubles we've been having with militia here in Carolina he personally petitioned to come to our aid."

Catherine could tell the moment the Colonel entered the room because the buzz of conversation grew decidedly louder. He was mingling with the other officers, smiling and joking, bowing deeply to each person he met, the perfect English gentlemen. Straining to look over the heads of others in order to see him, Catherine finally found a good vantage point.

Lady Dougherty took Catherine's arm in hers. "Lord Dougherty's talking with him," she whispered loudly. "Let's have him introduce us."

The two women made their way through the party-goers to where the men stood in conversation and politely waited for their introductions. "Colonel, you must meet my better half." Lord Dougherty said, bringing his wife into the circle. "This is my wife, Lady Jane Dougherty." She made a grand curtsy as Lord Dougherty looked on proudly. "And this is our dear friend Mrs.," he paused looking somewhat befuddled.

Lady Dougherty quickly stepped in and saved Catherine embarrassment. "Our dear friend Mrs. Catherine Wallace," she finished for him.

Lord Dougherty nodded, grateful for his wife and bobbing his head in agreement. "She's a good English woman, but her husband is one of those blasted patriots. Even fought in the war," Lord Dougherty mumbled.

Stepping forward, Catherine made a low curtsy and Colonel Pearson bowed. "Your country thanks you for your loyalty."

Pearson found the woman very attractive. Her dark brown hair was almost black and while she didn't have the pink cheeks and youthful energy of most women whose company he enjoyed, she had an elegant sophistication he found intriguing. Pearson knew he could break down that wall of self-control she held in front of her. Letting his eyes linger on hers for an instant longer than necessary he brazenly winked. Unlike most women who would turn their eyes away, her gaze met his. Pearson smiled, curious about her motives.

"Duncan!" Lord Dougherty yelled, spotting his next victim. He and his wife were off, leaving Catherine and the Colonel alone.

"It's too bad your husband could not join you tonight," he said with a coy smile.

Standing tall and straight, Catherine's face showed no emotion. "It is a pity, but he was injured in a battle and doesn't travel well anymore. Not to mention the fact that Lord Dougherty was correct. He still holds loyalty to those silly farmers."

General Pearson frowned. "I find it strange that a man with such an upstanding English wife would choose to fight with this colonial rabble."

Catherine laughed. "I wish I could say it was merely for show, but he is a simple minded man. It was my ill-luck to be enticed by his prospects years ago. Fate has a cruel way of playing tricks on us."

General Pearson raised a brow. "I am certain that there are those who would have come to your aid. A woman like you should not be forced to be dealt a bad hand from fate."

Catherine smiled demurely. "And what kind of woman am I, Colonel?"

Bowing slightly, he kissed her hand. "You are intelligent and know where your loyalties lay."

"Is that all I am?" she asked, enjoying the game.

"Not nearly, I have a feeling" he countered, intrigued, "but for those reasons I think you are the perfect person to come to with a proposition." Reaching out, he gingerly touched a piece of lace on her gown.

"Really," Catherine asked, looking at him as she tilted her head. "What kind of proposition?"

"I suppose you are close to your fellow … Americans?"

"I am the very picture of society and gentleness." Catherine said, her nose in the air, a smile playing on her lips.

"Are they all militia, or are there some officers as well?"

Catherine thought for a moment. "Most of the locals are militia, except for Edward Weathers. He is a Captain with the Continentals."

"Really? Weathers. With the Continentals?" Taken aback, Pearson was confused, hoping it didn't show. Surely there was no connection, simply odd coincidence, he thought. Without missing a beat he asked, "Is he still in the field?"

"Yes," Catherine said with disgust. She didn't want to talk about the Weathers; she wanted to talk about Pearson...and herself.

He had seen her kind before, power hungry, unhappy at home, and willing to do anything to be noticed. He had come to Charleston to destroy morale in the colonists, but this was an interesting turn of events. He knew William Weathers, now a Colonel himself, was creeping around somewhere in the south and Pearson had hopes of dealing with him eventually...if he could find him, which really shouldn't be difficult.

It was because of his accusations, true though they were, that Pearson had earned embarrassment, stern lectures, and had kept him from advancing to a higher rank. When he learned that Weathers had been made a Colonel, it had been a slap in the face, and Pearson had made sure that his next assignment would take him closer to where he could find him.

Curious, Pearson couldn't help but ask, "How is the wife of this officer Weathers handling his absence?" He knew it would be too coincidental for there to be a connection with *his* Weathers, but he asked anyway. At least he would have an in with the colonial morale.

"Very well considering he's been gone four years and she's had to raise three children."

"Does she trust you?" he asked delicately.

"Implicitly," she responded. "Mr. Wallace has taken care of their finances since her husband's been away. She listens to our advice extensively." What he was wanting dawned on her as the words escaped. The thought of helping the Colonel made her pulse quicken. To have a cause, and to be of service to him, it was just what she needed.

"If you ever have the occasion to find any sort of information for us about her husband's orders, commands, or position, even if it may seem trivial, bring it to me. I promise it will be worth your trouble."

Catherine's eyes gleamed with the prospect of reward and power. "I'll be in touch," she said as she squeezed his hand and left.

Samuel Wallace had fought for a year beside Edward when a stray bullet tore through his leg and he was sent home. He now had a severe limp, but that was his only battle scar. With the help of his cane, Samuel stood slowly and made his way as swiftly as he could out of his study to the foyer where Catherine was putting on her hat and gloves. If he had known, years ago, the bitter woman she would become he never would have married her.

Catherine had been a beautiful young woman of Charleston. While her family didn't have the fortune to match her status in society, she had a wit that Sam found intriguing. She was bold and spoke her mind, little knowing how unyielding those opinions would become. When talk of revolution had begun, he and Catherine had had many a disagreement about his involvement. He had tried to make her see and understand his position, but she refused. Finally, they stopped talking altogether, distant friendship replaced by disdain. Now, when they did speak, they were terse and cruel towards each other.

"And where are you going?" he asked curiously, making sure she knew he was not pleased.

"Out," she responded in her normal, cold manner. "Mrs. Preston is having some close friends over for dinner."

"You have to go now? I don't think it's a good idea for you to go too far from home with the many English soldiers nearby now that Charleston is under their control. I think it would be best if you stayed here for awhile." Sam would never tell her so, but he did still care about her.

Catherine gave him an annoyed look with her sharp, light, blue eyes, and laughed, making him feel foolish. "Don't be ridiculous Sam. Do I look like a Continental soldier? I'll be perfectly fine." Holding her head high, she left, shutting the door behind her with a bang.

Samuel did not know what to do with her and he was afraid things were too far gone now. Since his return from the war, they spoke only in passing. Keeping to their separate parts of the house, they had almost no knowledge of the other's doings. He shook his head, giving up, and limped back to his study.

Sam's driver, Joseph, stopped him in the hallway. "Mr. Wallace."

"Yes, Joseph," Sam said cheerfully, his face changing when he heard the fear and concern in Joseph's voice.

"A couple of men were coming in from the southern field and said they saw smoke coming from the East."

"The East?" Sam was puzzled for a moment, his mind playing through a list of possibilities for the cause. "Good Lord, Joseph. Margaret and the children."

"That's what I was afraid of, Sir," Joseph said, worry etched in his face.

"Quickly, Joseph, get the horses ready," Sam ordered, letting his cane carry the brunt of his weight as he walked as quickly as he could to the door.

"Already done, Sir," Joseph answered, holding the door open for his master.

Chapter Ten: Unwelcome Visitors

The five-mile drive to the Weathers farm was uncomfortably quiet. Although it was spring the humidity was already heavy in the air and each breath had to be won. It seemed to Sam that suddenly there was no wind, no air, nothing that could help hold him in reality. His heart was beating so fast he could feel it ready to leap from his chest. He couldn't think of anything other than what he might have to tell Edward. Just a month before, Edward had been home for a week on leave and Sam had promised him again that he would make sure Margaret and the children were safe. If anything happened to them, Samuel would never forgive himself.

As they came to the Weathers' property the smoke became dense and Sam had to cover his mouth with a handkerchief. Patrick's indigo field was still burning as they rode by, flaming patches of dying crops. The other fields simply burnt embers and smoking patches of ash at this point. When they pulled up to the house, no one came to greet them, the place eerily quiet. There were no sounds of animals, children, workers, nothing. The entire farm seemed abandoned; Sam didn't like that. He stepped out of the carriage carefully.

"Stay here, Joseph. I'll look around," he said cautiously.

"Do you want me to check out the worker's lodges, Sir?" Joseph asked.

"That's a good idea," Sam said with a tense nod. "Thank you."

Walking onto the porch, the sound of his cane and boots echoed on the wood. Finding the door unlocked, he entered. The house had been ransacked, a mirror knocked over and broken while everything else had been thrown about. Unarmed, he kept a careful eye on everything to his right and left so as to avoid any sudden surprises. He'd assumed the intruders were gone, but at the moment he didn't want to bet his life on that. The house was hot and stuffy and he noticed some muddy boot prints outside of Edward's office.

"Good God," Samuel muttered, growing more concerned with each step.

Carefully, he pushed open the heavy wood door. The office was in shambles. Priceless paintings were on the floor and the matchlock musket and sword that hung on the wall were gone. Besides that, the drawers to Edward's desk were pulled out and had obviously been rifled through. Sam turned away, angry, and continued his slow survey.

He came to the kitchen and his blood went cold. Laying half way in the kitchen, his body keeping the back door open, was an English soldier lying on the floor, a bloody, gaping wound in his stomach. The kitchen itself had also been torn apart, the cabinets bare and hanging open, all kitchen goods taken. Surveying the room carefully, Sam spotted something across from him. A chair from the table had been pushed against the pantry door holding the knob in place. Taking a deep breath, fear coursing through his veins, he moved the chair and opened the door.

Jammed into the seven by five-foot pantry, sleeping soundly, was Margaret, holding tightly onto little Sarah and a pistol. Abigail was next to her, while Megan and Matthew leaned against their mother.

"Margaret," Samuel sighed with relief.

Startled, Margaret woke and aimed the pistol at him.

"Margaret, it's me," Sam quickly stated.

"Sam!" Margaret gasped, dropping the pistol as if it weighed a ton.

Everyone else woke and Sam helped them out, their legs stiff from hours of sitting. Picking up little Sarah, while Megan clung to his other arm, he led them out of the kitchen and tried to comfort them. Eight year old Matthew was the only child not in tears.

"There were soldiers everywhere," the boy explained with great enthusiasm. "We thought it was father at first," he said, before remembering something and quickly changing the subject. "Mama shot one!" he shouted, remembering the best part of his story. He was excited about the whole affair, and quickly filled Sam in on the events of the day. "They took our animals and food." His little face frowned. "We might all starve now."

Letting Sarah down, Sam knelt down in front of him and held the little boy by the shoulders. "Are you hurt, Matthew? Were your sisters hurt?"

"No," the boy said bravely. "They're just scared."

"Good boy." Sam patted the boy's head and stood.

Following after Sam, Sarah held out her arms for him to hold her. He picked her up, cooing to her sweetly while walking over to Margaret who was leaning against the wall, her eyes closed. They all started when they heard footsteps.

"It's just Joseph," Sam assured them. "He went to check on your workers."

Joseph entered through the kitchen, and Sam motioned to him, letting him know to take the soldier's body away. Joseph nodded in acknowledgement and quickly left again.

"What happened, Margaret?" he asked quietly.

Laying the heavy gun on the cabinet next to her with a thud, she looked up at him, her brown eyes glassy from trying not to cry. "We heard the horses and, like Matthew said, thought maybe it was Edward and his men," she drew in a deep breath. "There were about fifteen of them. They took everything that looked valuable and tore through Edward's things. They knew he was an officer."

She thought about that for a moment and then looked sadly over to Abigail. "The hired hands ran." Her voice changed a bit, as if trying not to remember something. "They tried to take Abby..." She paused, and Sam knew there was more she wasn't saying. "That's when I shot him." She nodded towards the kitchen, trying not to remember all of the blood on the floor, the man's body as he fell backwards, the acrid smell of the gunpowder.

Abigail, who had been standing stoically in the corner of the living room, slowly began to straighten things up. Giving up, she took Sarah from Sam and led the children away to survey the rest of the damage.

Margaret continued. "Before they left, they locked us in." She rubbed her hand over her eyes and paused, a tear running down her cheek. "I was so scared they were going to burn the house, Sam," she said, barely above a whisper. "I was afraid they were going to burn it with us inside."

Sam pulled her close to him. "Margaret, I'm so sorry," he said, comforting her. "Thank God you are all safe. Edward never would have forgiven me if anything had happened to you." Margaret's arms hugged him tightly, finally giving in to the tears.

My dearest, darling Margaret and my beautiful children,

I have been trying to write to you for days, but have not had the opportunity until now. I have been assigned as a field commander under General Gates. We expect the British to arrive any day now and are ready for some excitement. The past few weeks have been spent setting up and tearing down camps, moving to new positions, going through field practices with our new French allies and waiting. I'm afraid that if my men don't get to fight some English before long they might take to fighting each other.

I hope you know that I think of you every minute. Just the other day I passed by a little girl around Megan's age and I thought how sad it was that she would never compare to my Meg. I think about how wonderful it will be to come home and finally show Matthew how to ride. He's probably grown so much he'll be able to teach me a thing or two.

I'm sure that Sarah is learning all types of things. Before long she'll be able to write me letters. She was just a baby when I saw her last and to think that she is talking and growing into a little girl breaks my heart.

To Margaret, I hope you are well. I know there's probably not much left of the farm, but keep faith. We *will win this war, I'll come back to you, and the fields will grow again. I hear the other men speak about their wives and I can't imagine that one of them could compare to you. When the nights become too lonely to bear, I close my eyes and I can see your face. It's in those times that I am ready to leave everything and come back to you.*

I promise that I will, though, and when I do we will live in a new country, a new land. God has blessed us with the will, and I know He will show us the way to form this new nation.

Until I hold you in my arms again, you are in my thoughts and prayers. I love you all.

Your father and husband,
Captain Edward Weathers

"Sentimental idiots!" Pearson wadded up the letter and threw it on the dirt floor. "Nothing but drivel." He paced the length of his tent. "It's infuriating! I don't care what he feels for his family. I want information!" He turned to Lieutenant Emler who had led the attack on the Weathers' home. "You didn't find anything else?"

Emler shook his head. "Other than the letter I gave you, the sword and musket were all. We brought back plenty of provisions, but nothing that could tell us what the colonists are planning."

"And the other matter?" Pearson asked through a frown.

"Perhaps its just coincidence that they have the same last name," Emler shrugged, receiving an angry look from Pearson, not satisfied. "Or maybe he doesn't say anything on purpose," Emler corrected himself.

Pearson continued to pace and think. "There has to be a connection. Our colonial Weathers was born in England. Did you search everywhere?"

Emler nodded. "Yes, Sir. We ransacked the entire place, even the children's rooms."

Pearson stopped. "Children?"

"Yes, Sir. There were three, a boy and two girls, along with the wife and slave woman," Emler said, recalling their faces in his mind. They had caused too many problems and Emler wished he'd just taken care of them while he was there.

"Was the wife English?" Pearson asked.

Emler shook his head, with disgust. "No, Sir, Irish. She's the one who shot Sergeant Berry. I swear, Sir, we should have burned the place down for what she did."

Pearson took a drink from a flask on his desk. "Don't worry, she'll get what's coming to her, but for right now leave it alone. If William and Edward Weathers are related, and I'm certain they are, they'll all pay for what he's done."

Sitting down in his chair, Pearson leaned back, smiling to himself. "Just think of the honor it would be if I could prove that Colonel William Weathers is collaborating with the colonials."

Emler stepped forward. "Sir, the men were wondering what we should do with Berry's things."

Pearson looked to the table where Edward's sword and antique musket lay. "What did he leave?"

"Two pistols, and a knife," Emler answered.

"Dole them out to the men as you see fit." Pearson said, lost in thought again. Nodding, Emler left, leaving Pearson alone in his tent.

Pearson studied the weapons, hoping that somehow they would give up their owner's secrets. He lifted the sword, glaring at the blade and the care with which it had been kept. Setting it down, he picked up the musket, checking the barrel to see if it had been loaded recently. It hadn't. Agitated again, he tossed it back on the table with a thud and grabbed the letter off the floor, opened the crumpled paper, and read over it again.

"What are you hiding?" he asked with a sigh, demanding answers from the dry ink.

He knew the American captain was somehow related to William Weathers. He could feel it. They both had the same self-righteous air about them, the same quest for everything that was proper and good, the same pathetic sense of loyalty and justice. He read the letter a third time, but it disgusted him. Tearing it to pieces, he tossed it onto the dirt floor.

Chapter Eleven: Strange Visits

The afternoon sun beat down on Margaret's straw hat as she carefully picked some of the last few balls of cotton from the scorched field. She knew there wouldn't be much, but she wanted to gather whatever she could from the ruined fields. Placing a couple of the prickly balls in the bag around her shoulders, she wiped some sweat from her cheek with her gloved hand. Megan was helping her, but losing energy quickly and starting to move slower and slower.

"Mother!" Megan called out in a whine as she trampled over the dead plants. "There's a carriage coming!"

Straightening herself up, Margaret squinted in the sunlight to see who it was. She recognized the Wallace carriage as it drew closer and smiled, thankful for a visit from Sam and a respite from work.

"Are we done?" Megan asked hopefully.

"Yes, we're done," Margaret said, stretching her back and taking the bag from around her shoulders. She followed Megan, the energy suddenly returning to the five year old as she ran towards the house.

Catherine Wallace fanned herself in the heat of the carriage as she pulled up to the Weathers house. She hated these tedious visits, but now that she had a job to do it promised to be much more exciting. The Weathers house was full of too much noise with children running in circles that she only made appearances when she felt it absolutely necessary. She didn't know how Samuel could stand to spend as much time there as he did.

Now, with Edward still gone, the trips were even less exciting. At least he had been a handsome treasure to their society, much more impressive than her simpleton of a husband, even if his political beliefs did leave something to be desired.

His wife, on the other hand, was nothing more than an Irish peasant with only a moderate sense of humor who preferred to spend time with her children. Granted, she was disgustingly pretty, but nonetheless, she still had too much of the commoner about her for Catherine Wallace's taste.

The carriage stopped and Catherine's driver helped her down. Catherine was appalled when she saw Margaret coming towards her, plainly dressed, sweating, and red from the sun.

"Catherine, what brings you here?" Margaret asked with a smile, greeting her with a delicate kiss on the cheek.

Margaret tried to look fondly on Catherine. She had always been cordial to Margaret, even though their relationship had never grown into a friendship, and Margaret was more comfortable in the company of Samuel. Still, she welcomed his wife. While Sam had such a kind and open personality, Catherine was intimidating. You never knew what she thought about you. She was tall with the bearing of nobility, and Margaret had always felt small and insignificant next to her.

Taking a step back, Catherine looked over Margaret's appearance like a perturbed mother. "Margaret, dear, what are you doing?"

Smiling like a child caught causing mischief, Margaret untied her large straw hat. "There was a little bit of cotton left in the fields so I thought we would pick what we could. Every little bit helps," she added.

"Margaret, this is not a job for a lady. What if the English were to see you? They already think we're backwards as it is and you're doing nothing to help our reputation." Taking her by the arm,

Catherine led her to the house. "If you need someone to pick cotton, I'll loan you a couple of my women." They made their way into the kitchen where Abigail set down two cups of tea.

"Samuel told me about the English coming through your place," Catherine confided. "I'm just glad Edward wasn't here. You know how men are with their pride, there's no telling what he would have done. But," she sighed, "I suppose it's always a risk for one's family if you're an officer in wartime."

Margaret kept silent as they sipped their tea, not exactly sure what Catherine meant by her statements.

Making a face, Catherine set down her cup, blasted embargoes, they really did need sugar. "It's so quiet," she noticed. "Where are the other two children?"

"The Newman's had some new puppies so Matthew took Sarah to play there for the day," Margaret answered.

"Well, how sweet for them." There was a moment of silence before Catherine spoke again. "It appears you've been surviving quite well, considering. Have you heard anything from Edward?" she asked conversationally. "What was he again? I know he was a Captain, but was it in the army?"

"Cavalry," Margaret replied, taking another long sip of tea. Things like this had been a luxury lately, and it felt good to have a bit of normalcy back.

They had finally been able to get some food and staples thanks to Edward's connections in Charleston. When his investors had heard about the raid, they sent a wagon full of grain, meal, vegetables, tea, and coffee with instructions to Margaret that when they needed more to let them know. Margaret had nearly cried when she'd opened the containers.

"Oh how I missed Edward the other night," Catherine said with a smile. "Some old friends and I had a small party in Charleston and I remember thinking how much enjoyment Edward brought to parties." She shook her head. "He was so charming. Does he have many under his command? I'm sure he makes even the drudgery of war tolerable. It's no wonder he's so well respected by the Continentals."

"He is a wonderful commander," Margaret said quietly, suddenly uncomfortable with the line of conversation, not knowing where it was leading or why it was taking place.

"Well, Edward was always a good man," Catherine smiled and took a sip of her tea, again making a bitter face. There was another awkward silence. "Do you receive many letters? I know Sam wrote to me almost every day when he was in the field," she said dramatically, trying her best to sound like a loving wife.

"He writes as much as he possibly can," Margaret answered carefully.

Catherine gave her what could be considered a small smile. "I'm sure you treasure them dearly. Is he far away?"

Margaret shook her head. "I haven't heard from him in awhile," she confessed. "The post is running so slow right now, but I believe they're still in the Carolinas somewhere."

Margaret could hold back no longer. While Samuel visited every week or so, it had been at least six months since Catherine herself had made an appearance. She spent most of her time in Charleston and Margaret only saw her on very rare occasions so her sudden visit just seemed odd.

"Catherine," she began, "if you don't mind my asking. Is there something you needed? It's nice to see you of course, but…"

"I just mean to watch out for you dear," Catherine said maternally, reaching out and patting her hand. "It's difficult with such a large family and no husband around. Let Samuel and I help you however we can." Standing stiffly, she smiled politely at

Margaret. "Thank you for the tea. I'll send Samuel around in a couple of days to check on you."

Standing, still confused, Margaret walked Catherine to the door and they said their farewells, leaving Margaret uneasy and curious about the strange visit.

When Catherine returned home she found Joseph speaking with another of their housemen. Both men quieted as she came towards them and Catherine motioned for the men to come forward.

"You may be dismissed, Joseph," she said coldly.

"Yes, ma'am," he said, leaving to go about his chores.

"Reginald, is it?" she asked coldly, addressing the middle-aged man.

"Yes, Ma'am, but they call me Reggie."

"How long have you been with us, Reggie?" Catherine's voice was cold, demanding.

"Five years, ma'am," he answered, his nerves showing.

"Have you been treated well?"

"Yes indeed, ma'am. I consider myself very lucky."

"Do you have a family?" Catherine's tone began to change to something that bordered on kindness.

Reggie nodded nervously. "I have a wife and two sons, ma'am. They work here in the fields."

Catherine looked the man over, deciding that he seemed trustworthy enough. "I have a very special job for you, Reginald. I'm going to send you, for a short time, to Mrs. Edward Weathers' farm. The English attacked and left her with only one woman. They need a man around to do some of the harder chores. Do you think you would be capable?"

"Yes, ma'am," he assured her.

"There's a more important task I want you to undertake while you're there," Catherine said, lowering her voice. "I'm concerned for Mrs. Weathers." Trying her best to sound sympathetic, she continued. "She is alone with three young children and in a desperate state. I need you to watch after her for me. If she gets any news about her husband, or if she says anything as to his whereabouts, please let me know," Catherine sighed. "As an Irish woman, she is very stubborn and doesn't easily let her close friends help her when she needs it. I want to do everything I can for her because she's in a very delicate position right now." Catherine leveled her gaze at Reggie. "Do you understand what I'm asking?"

Reggie knew her requests were more than those of a concerned friend. "Yes, ma'am," he answered uncomfortably. "You would like to know everything that happens in the house."

"You will be compensated," Catherine said, her voice now sounding like that of a slick businessman. "If you do this, I can promise you, and your family, freedom." She held the prize up for him, knowing that he wouldn't refuse.

A thin line of sweat had collected on Reggie's brow. He swallowed slowly, his mouth having gone dry. "I promise that you won't be disappointed, ma'am."

Catherine smiled. "Good. Then we're clear." She started to leave, but turned back to him. "And Reggie," she said kindly. "If you fail me, well, I would hate to say it, but things have been rather tight lately with the war and all, and Mr. Wallace has spoken of the need to sell some of our people. I would hate for you to lose your family." Smiling at him again, she walked inside.

Less than twenty-four hours later, Reggie was standing at the front door of the Weathers' home. Tentatively, he raised his hand and knocked, unsure exactly himself what he was supposed to say. He stood there nervously for a few minutes before he heard the pounding of footsteps behind the door. Suddenly, the door was flung open and three little faces were staring up at him, three little stair steps looking at him curiously.

"Abigail!" the oldest, a young boy called. "Someone's here!"

Coming into the family parlor and to the door was a motherly looking black woman. "May I help you?" she asked.

"Um," Reggie muttered, suddenly feeling even more anxious than before. "Mr. and Mrs. Wallace sent me to help out?" he said as a question more than a statement.

The woman looked at him curiously, and then smiled. "Of course." Moving to the side, she allowed him to enter. "I'll just go get Mrs. Weathers," she said, the children following after her.

From the moment he stepped into the Weathers' home, he could feel the warmth and comforting atmosphere. After being in the Wallace house, which was more like a museum, the Weather house was a nice welcome. While everything was neat and orderly, there were a few toys scattered about, which made him smile.

A lovely woman soon entered, smiling. "You must be Reggie," she said, reaching out and shaking his hand, completely taking him off guard.

He nodded. "Yes, ma'am."

"Please, it's Margaret. Sam told me you would be a great help."

"Yes," Reggie said, "Mr. Wallace is a very good man."

"Well, we are glad to have you here. I'm certain we will be able to keep you quite busy. Would you like me to show you around?"

Reggie nodded again, not sure how to respond. He had never been treated in such an equal way by someone above his station before. He knew Captain Weathers and his wife worked differently than most plantation owners. He had heard the rumors, but found himself surprised at the reality of it.

"Matthew," she called to the boy standing and watching from the staircase. "Would you take Reggie's stuff to the back room?" Jumping down the last two steps, the boy took Reggie's bag and disappeared into the kitchen.

Margaret showed him around the farm, even explaining what the fields used to look like before the English had burned them. Once they had finished, Margaret showed him back to the house.

"I didn't want you to have to stay out in the worker's houses by yourself, so we've converted an extra storage cupboard into a room for you." Margaret looked at him apologetically. "It's small, but close. Abigail's room is right off the kitchen. I just thought you would be more comfortable closer to the house."

Reggie looked at the empty storage room containing a cot with sheets, a pillow, a blanket, and a lantern, his bag laying invitingly on the cot. "Of course, Mrs. Weathers, this is more than adequate."

"I'll let you get yourself settled," Margaret said, giving him another charming smile. "Abigail will let you know when lunch is ready."

"Thank you," Reggie said, for the first time in his life feeling as if someone cared and not knowing what he was going to do.

Chapter Twelve: Piece by Piece

The black carriage hurried towards Charleston under a bright, full moon. It rocked down the dirt road and pulled up to a tall brick townhouse. Stepping out carefully from the carriage, dressed completely in black, from her bonnet to her delicate boots, Catherin Wallace climbed the stairs to the front door, keeping her head down. Steadying herself, she knocked lightly.

An older looking Englishman answered the door. Not amused at the late hour of Catherine's visit.

"I'm here to see Colonel Pearson," she informed him.

"Colonel Pearson has retired for the evening," the man told her unceremoniously.

"I assure you, he will want to see me," she insisted.

Sighing, the man put on a very annoyed look. "Your name... Miss?"

Catherine raised her chin, annoyed by his insolence. "Just tell him it's regarding Captain Weathers," Catherine said sternly, showing the man that she meant business.

The door closed and was opened a couple of minutes later. This time the man's attitude had improved considerably and he invited her inside. "Wait here please. Colonel Pearson will be down in a moment."

Catherine paid no attention to the decoration surrounding her in the landing of the house. Dark oak paneling lined the walls and decorative candelabras held up candles that were burning dimly.

Before the butler left, he lit five more candles in the hall and the landing grew brighter, lending it a soft glow. A plush red carpet ran up the stairs and the butler held onto an ornately carved railing as he went after Pearson. All she could think about was what he would say about her information.

Catherine checked her appearance in a mirror on the wall and, satisfied with what she saw, waited for the Colonel. He came down the stairs quickly, taking them two at a time. She could tell his clothes had been thrown on in a hurry and there was a difference in his appearance from the other night at the party. There was none of the social politeness about him, his look determined and slightly frightening. It was no wonder he made a formidable enemy on the battlefield.

"You have some information?" he demanded, leading her to a sitting room. She shivered as she past by him, smelling brandy and tobacco. He motioned for her to sit down while he poured them each a drink.

"I had an interesting conversation with Margaret Weathers this afternoon," she said, thanking him as he handed her a glass and allowed her hand to accidentally touch his. "It appears that the Captain is a very devoted husband who enjoys writing to his wife. Apparently, he and his men are stationed, for the time being, somewhere in the Carolinas. I'm assuming under Gates' command."

Pearson sat down across from her and took a sip. "Of course," he said to himself, annoyed he hadn't figured that out for himself. He smiled and looked up at Catherine again. "Do you know if he has any other family in the colonies?"

"I don't believe so," she answered. "He and my husband are thick as thieves and, as far as I know, the rest of his family is in England. His father died before he came to the colonies and his mother passed away years ago, I believe." She took a long drink of her claret. "I believe he has a brother though." She tried to recall his name being mentioned in past conversations.

114

Pearson interrupted her thoughts. "Did she say anything else?"

"No. Other than that it was simply friendly chitchat. Nothing important." She took another drink. "I do believe I have enlisted the help of one of my slaves. The Weathers' home was ransacked by English troops and their 'workers' taken into the king's service," she said sarcastically, sounding very pleased with herself. "The least I could do as a friend was loan her one of my men."

"Can he be trusted?" he asked.

She laughed. "Oh no, but I made it clear that I am simply wanting to watch out for her," she said raising her glass, smiling.

"Very clever," Pearson nodded. "I'm impressed. You work faster than I expected."

Standing, Catherine set her empty glass down. "I should get back. I just wanted to bring you what I found."

Pearson walked her to the door. "If she says anything else let me know right away." He turned to her, taking hold of one of her hands. "Don't hesitate…ever."

"William," she said suddenly, stopping Pearson in his tracks. "William is his brother's name."

Smiling at her gently, he brought her hands to his lips, and then leaned over, kissing her lightly on the lips. "You've done your country a great service," he whispered.

Catherine tried to stay strong as her head spun, and not just from the brandy. Letting her hands stay in his a moment longer, she slowly moved them to her side. She stepped close to him. "Serving England is my only priority," she said softly and left, making sure to keep her head down as she went and quickly climbed back into the dark carriage.

115

Pearson's commanding officer was not amused by Pearson's sudden presence in his office. "Why should I send you to North Carolina? You just requested this assignment in South Carolina, and now you wish for another? The army is not at your personal beck and call."

Pearson stood at attention and tried to make his case. "No, my Lord, I have every intention of returning back to my position here. I simply thought that my men and I would be able to add to our forces north of us. The colonials are expecting us at Camden, and I know my men would be more than willing to be of service."

"Your men are extremely good soldiers, but that's beside the point." The General thought for a moment. As much as he disliked Pearson and his ability to get away with whatever he pleased, they could use his men. He didn't want Pearson to know that, though.

"I want to be part of this battle, Sir." Pearson was not above begging as unbecoming as it looked and felt. He knew Gates' forces would be there, and he wanted to see them. He wanted to get a look at Edward Weathers. "It will be a momentous victory for us," he said, summoning as much humility as he could.

"Very well, but I want you back here as soon as the battle is over," the General said, dismissing him, his warning clear.

"We will return that very day," Pearson replied with a bow. "Thank you, my Lord."

The smell of burning wood from nearby campfires was in the air. Birds chirped back and forth to each other, no idea of the horror the day was about to bring forth. It was a warm morning that, on any other day, would be full of promise. Today, though, there was only expectation as muskets were cleaned, gunpowder loaded, and cannons put into place.

Edward stood in his tent, brushing off his uniform, making sure it was in sparkling condition. He'd been up since before dawn, making certain is saber was sharp, his horses shod, and his men prepared. Now, standing in his crisp white shirt, breeches and boots, there was only one thing left to do before he donned his jacket and weapons and faced what the day would bring.

Kneeling next to his cot, he folded his hands in prayer, closing his eyes, and letting out a long, deep sigh.

"Oh, Father," he began, his hands clasped. "Dear God, deliver us from this day. I pray for the souls of the men here today. I pray that they find peace and joy in you. God, I ask that you protect my family, keep them safe. Keep me safe, Lord. I want to see them again. I want to hold my wife again. I want..." he stopped, the emotions too deep to speak out loud. "Protect William. Keep him close to you."

"Captain?" called a voice from outside the tent. "I'm sorry, Sir, but it's time."

Standing, Edward nodded, pulling on his jacket, fastening his sword, and holstering his pistol. He took a letter from his desk that he had been writing and stuffed it in his pocket. "Are the men ready?"

The young man nodded. "We have about a third of the men we should, but they are ready for a fight," the young man said, eagerly walking behind Edward as they strode out of his tent.

Edward stopped before mounting his horse, straightening his jacket and checking his weapons. "You say they want a fight?" he asked. The soldier nodded. "Good," Edward added, looking out over the camp, "because they're going to get one."

Edward shook his head as he and his men rode to their positions. The men were skinny, ragged, pathetic looking. He didn't see how they could possibly have the strength to fight. Cannons from both sides began to volley in the distance and

117

Edward's heart pounded with excitement as the sound echoed in the air.

"Captain Weathers!" a voice from one of the militia lines called out. "Captain Weathers! Over here!"

Hearing the unmistakable voice, Edward turned his horse down the line. He found Patrick half way down the line and in the front, one smiling face amidst hundreds of gloomy ones.

"I knew we would share the field one day, Captain, Sir."

"How goes it with you, Patrick?" Edward asked, smiling, It had been years, but the Irishman hadn't changed.

Patrick ran a hand down the musket Edward had given him. "I've sent fifty Tories to hell, Sir, and I hope to make it fifty more today."

"You look well, Patrick. What's your secret?" Edward was amazed at how markedly better he looked compared to his fellow militiamen.

"It's me family's recipe for the whiskey, Sir. A man can live on it for years and be better off for it."

Edward laughed. "You haven't changed a bit." He turned his horse back around. "You take care of yourself, Patrick. When this is over we'll share some of that famous whiskey. Maybe give the General the recipe for the rest of the men."

Patrick grinned. "Sounds like a fine idea to me, Sir."

The morning fog hung heavy in the air as the two sides convened. They positioned themselves on a piece of solid land bordered by swamps on either side. The heat of the morning, along with the anticipation of finally killing some English, temporarily took away a bit of the hunger and weariness from the Colonial troops. The men, poorly armed and mostly militia were taken aback by the size of the English army. When some movement confused the British and caused them to attack with loud cheers and bayonets shining, most of the militia fled.

   Battle plans fell apart as hundreds fled the field. Swearing, Edward ordered his men to charge. His horse pounded forward; the cavalry rushing onto the field. This was the part of battle he loved. It was chaos, but if a man kept a clear head on his shoulders he could survive. Colors meant nothing at this point; it was about survival. Occasionally you would see a glimpse of blue or red, but other than that they all ran together. You couldn't worry about who your enemy was. All you could think about was who was aiming a sword or pistol at you.

   Hugh Pearson held back as he surveyed the Continentals formation. "We wait for the cavalry. He's a Captain. If you see him, take him down." Balis and Jass nodded and readied their weapons.

   "Why go after him, Sir? Why not go straight to Colonel Weathers?" Connor, the youngest of his men asked.

   Pearson grinned devilishly. "I want to see how deep his love for England truly is, not to mention the look on his face when he finds out his brother is dead. He's ruined my career and I plan to do the same to his…piece by piece."

   Edward heard a canon in the distance and when the ball landed nearby he lost his concentration for a moment. That was all it took for his horse to rear up after a bullet grazed its flank and fall. Tossed to the ground, Edward's leg caught under the horse's heavy body, but he managed to free it without much fuss.

   He had to get up. He had to stand. The longer he waited the easier a target he would become. The ground was the one place he didn't want to be. On a horse he could see over heads, he was safer there. On the ground, he was in hell. Grabbing his sword in one hand and his pistol in the other, he went in search of another horse.

Pearson rode to the field, searching for the cavalry captain. He saw a man thrown from a horse. When the man stood, Pearson knew it was Weathers. He had the same bearing and spirit as his brother, the same brown hair and rugged features.

Firing one shot, Edward caught a redcoat coming for him. He cut through two others, asking for forgiveness for the lives he was taking. The English cavalry arrived, firing their weapons at the nearest enemy. Edward loaded his gun in record time and caught the eye of an English colonel on top of a horse. The man pulled his pistol when he saw Edward's aimed at him.

Edward cocked the gun, but couldn't fire. He felt something burning in his back and a warm liquid spilling down his shirt. The English Colonel smiled, watching the color drain from the colonial captain's face. Edward felt another burning sensation, this time in his stomach. The world stopped and froze around him, and he dropped his sword and gun to the ground, his strength giving out.

The battle moved forward, but Pearson remained where he was, a grim smile spreading over his face as he dismounted his horse and walked over to where the colonial captain lay on the blood stained grass. He wasn't dead yet and Pearson stood over him, blocking the morning sun with his shadow.

Edward's face was growing ashen by the minute. He had to fight for every breath. Looking up, he saw the dark outline of a figure standing over him. He wanted to tell the figure something, but thoughts were hard to put together. Trying to reach the letter in his pocket, Edward failed, unable to feel anything other than a dark coldness creeping though his body, gasping as images painfully slammed to the surface of his consciousness.

Pearson watched him struggling for breath as the blood slowly drained from his wounds. The captain turned his eyes from Pearson and looked up into the sky as if he was listening to something, causing a chill to run down Pearson's spine.

"Please," Edward whispered, the words coming out slowly. "I don't want Margaret to be alone. You can't do this to her." He was talking to someone only he was aware of. "I'm all she has." A tear ran down the side of his face, and he pulled in a ragged breath. "Too many people have left her already." Edward's eyes searched the sky above him. "What about the children? Don't they need me?"

As if receiving an answer from somewhere, Edward's pale face lightened and he let out a sigh that almost sounded like a laugh. "William," he said breathlessly. "William."

Edward's eyes closed, but Pearson watched him for another moment to make certain that he was dead. Mounting his horse, he went to rejoin the battle, smiling to himself as he rode forward, satisfied.

The battlefield was littered with bodies. After the wounded had all been removed it was time for the cleanup to begin. They were ready at sunrise, hoping they could finish before the summer sun heated the ground, and the bodies, making the job unbearable. The order of the morning was to remove the officer's body's first, then the enlisted men, the militia, and finally the horses. They tried to salvage whatever they could, coats, boots, bullets, anything reusable. Keeping a list of names and ranks was difficult, but they did a fairly good job. They tried their best to keep any letters and forward them to the families.

Harlan Kalp was wrapping up what was left of a man who had been hit by a cannonball and then trampled by a horse when his assistant came to him with a question.

"I found this." The man handed him a dirty, blood stained letter. "It was on an officer, a Continental. I found it in his pocket when I was going through his jacket."

"Is there a name?" Harlan asked.

"I don't know, I can't read," the assistant replied, annoyed.

Harlan looked at the man, telling himself to hold his tongue and not inform him what he really thought. Opening the letter and squinting, he held the letter close and then farther away trying to make a couple of the words come into focus.

"My eyesight is certainly not what is used to be," he mumbled. Finally, he recognized a couple of words on the front of the letter: 'English' and 'Colonel'.

"It's for an Officer. Put it with the others and they'll send it to him." He dismissed the man as two other men brought in another body to be wrapped.

Chapter Thirteen: Decisions

The sun was setting and the front room of the house was growing dark, all of the rich colors of the room temporarily washed with gray from the dim light. Margaret Weathers sat on a chair, gingerly sipping on a cup of tea.

"Are you sure you'll be able to manage my dear?" Mrs. Cummings, a middle-aged woman whose husband had died years ago, sat across from her asking her the same question for the fifteenth time. She had a small farm, one son who was still fighting in the war, and two daughters. One lived in Boston, the other in Raleigh. Both girls had married men too old to fight and so, without having heard word from her son, Margaret was the closest person she had to share her concern and grief with.

"We will be fine Mrs. Cummings," Margaret said coldly.

"But, Margaret, what about your land? Will you have a crop?" Reverend Bates was there as well. Margaret had been doubly blessed that he decided to pay them a visit on today of all days.

Margaret let out a laugh, even though it was inappropriate. "There is no crop, Reverend. What the English left when they came through is barely enough for us to live on. They were kind enough to leave us a cow for milk and we've received a few chickens from some of Edward's business partners. Other than that, we have nothing."

"Do you have any family nearby?" he asked.

Margaret wasn't used to this kindness from him, she being Irish and all. Since Edward was Anglican, the Reverend felt it was his job to comfort her, or at least offer her a couple words of wisdom.

He tried to do his best, but this was only one of many stops like this he had made that day and he was too tired to display his normal distrust of Papists.

"Is there anyone around who might take you in or help you in any way?" he said as he tried to stifle a yawn.

"We are getting plenty of help from Edward's friends. Thank you though, but this is my home. My family is in Ireland and Edward's died in England long ago." Margaret stood up, hoping that this might bring an end to their visit.

"I hate to bring this up dear, but could you sell one of your slaves? It might just get you enough to get by on till next spring." Mrs. Cummings set her tea down and stood to leave.

"Our workers were freedmen, but what few we had were taken by the English. Thankfully Abigail was spared. The Wallace's were kind enough to send one of their men over to help." Margaret knew she sounded rude, but could care less at this point.

Standing, the reverend put on his hat, not knowing what else he could say. Mrs. Cummings took hold of her hand. "If you need anything, let us know."

"God will take care of us as He always has." Margaret tried to smile, but simply couldn't.

She led them to the door and watched them leave, both of them talking and shaking their heads over her pitiful state. Margaret slammed the door once they were in their carriage. Opening it, she slammed it again, feeling a release of some of her anger, and taking a lesson from something she had seen Edward do hundreds of times. Turning, she leaned against the wooden frame, the black satin and lace of her gown suddenly too tight. She took as deep a breath as she could and let it out slowly, forcing herself to remain calm, to keep the anger at bay.

It had been a week now since Edward's name had appeared on the roster of dead soldiers, but things weren't any easier. She just wanted people to leave her alone. Surely there was another poor widow around that they could offer their sympathies to. She closed her eyes, but all she could hear were canons, all she could see were the different ways that Edward could have been killed. It haunted her dreams every time she closed her eyes. She'd seen Edward shot, stabbed, bayoneted, blown apart.

"Are you all right Mrs. Margaret?"

Opening her eyes, she saw Abigail bringing some candles in the room. Warm light filled the darkness and Margaret was glad to see a glimpse of regularity back in her life.

She nodded. "Thank you Abigail."

Abigail sat down the last candle. "The children have already had their dinner and yours is waiting. I tried to make a lot of clatter in the kitchen to show that old biddy that it was time to leave, but I guess she didn't hear."

Margaret smiled. "No, I don't think she did." Margaret moved away from the door and went to help Abigail with the cups. "I know they are trying to help, and I guess maybe they are, but right now it's the last thing I need. There are people all over whose sons and husbands have died. Why don't they go help them?" she said, not meaning to sound as bitter as she did.

Nodding, Abigail agreed, even though she knew Margaret was hurting more then she let on. "Let them make a fuss over you for a day or two. It will be somebody else next week."

Abigail stopped Margaret, taking the empty cups out of her hands. "I got these. Mrs. Margaret, you need to go get yourself something to eat. I haven't seen you do that in days. You have to take care of yourself because those children are counting on you."

Margaret moved past Abigail, ignoring her. "What I need to do, Abigail, is put this house back in order."

Her feet were heavy as she walked into the kitchen and sat down at the table to her dinner. The two oldest children, Megan and Matthew were upstairs, but Sarah was slowly picking at some green beans. With the entrance of her mother, Sarah saw a glimmer of hope.

"Mother, I have had ten. Don't you think that's enough for a small person like me?" she asked logically.

Margaret smiled in spite of herself. Even at three, Sarah was a clever girl and always tried to talk her way out of punishment. Kissing the top of her head, she gave her an answer. "You may be excused, but I want you to go upstairs and work on tracing your letters. Ask Megan if you need help."

Getting up from the table, Sarah reluctantly made her way upstairs to a punishment far worse than eating green beans. Margaret looked at her dinner, but all she could do was move some of the food around. She tried to eat a bit of bread, but it felt like chalk in her mouth, spitting it out in her napkin, she pushed her chair back.

"I'm going to get cleaned up," she said tiredly as Abigail came back into the kitchen. Standing to go upstairs, Margaret left her plate of food uneaten.

News of the colonial defeat at Camden spread through the South to each regiment. While some celebrated, others greeted the news with skepticism, knowing that there were many more battles to be won. In one camp the news was greeted with little cheer. They had been fighting the militia for months now and while some were ill-prepared for the field of war, others were more than willing to fight with conviction and deadly ability.

Now a Colonel, William Weathers and his close friend Sergeant Phillip Mitchell were overseeing the unloading of supplies for their camp a day after the news of the battle came. Some regulars unloaded the boxes off of the wagon while William and Phillip labeled and counted them, the heat stifling. Both William and Phillip tried their best to ignore the complaints coming from the men about the heat, but numerous suggestions had been made that they wait until evening to unload the carts. William listened patiently, but told the men to keep working; it had to be done. In the couple of years William had been in the South, his time had been spent in small skirmishes, helping plan battles, and making life as difficult as possible for the colonists who got in the way.

The men had finished unloading the supplies, and one handed Phillip a leather bag containing letters for the men. Phillip, a young Englishman of eighteen with a newly bought commission, rifled through the letters until the name on one caught his eye.

He and William had become fast friends ever since Phillip had been transferred under his command. Despite the differences in age, the two came from similar worlds, although Phillip's actually came with a title. While William's family's wealth came from business, Phillip's had been handed down to him. William was a born soldier, while Phillip was a born clerk. He simply didn't have the makings of a soldier and probably never would. Nevertheless, William found him indispensable.

"Colonel, this came for you." Phillip said, holding out the weathered envelope.

Looking confused for a moment, William went back to work. "It's probably just some new orders. It can wait until we're finished here."

"Do you think we'll be moving again?" Phillip asked curiously.

"There's no telling. Hold onto it for me, will you?" William asked, concentrating on opening a crate full of musket balls to inventory.

Wiping his reddish, blond hair from his eyes, Phillip sat down on a crate. He examined the letter, but stopped short before pocketing it. "William, there's blood on this letter."

Annoyed at the interruption, but curious, William walked over where Phillip sat and took the letter from his hand. The worn letter had a dark, red stain on the corner. Phillip was right; there was only one thing it could be. William recognized the handwriting on the envelope, broad and heavy like his father's, but different in spirit, a lot like the man William now realized had written it. He stared at his name on the envelope, his face pale.

"Is it from your brother?" Phillip asked, knowing only a little about William's past. Phillip had always wanted to ask more about what had happened between the two, but every time the subject was approached William grew angry and would say nothing. Phillip knew when he was ready, William would tell him.

William nodded, not wanting to read the letter, not wanting to touch it, but knowing he had to. Strangely, William felt numb looking at the piece of paper in his hand, as if he was a part of some different reality. Slowly, he opened the letter, afraid it might crumble under his fingers.

William,

I know it's been too long since we've spoken and I know that both political and emotional binds may be too strong to overcome the years of silence, but I'm praying that they are not.

I have a family and I am worried about what would become of them if I am killed. Margaret is strong, but not as strong as she believes herself to be. If anything should happen to me, I want to make sure that someone will watch over them. The only family either of us has anymore is you.

If anything should happen to me, I know that you will find out, please look after them. Make sure they are safe and cared for. I ask this, not as a fellow soldier, but as your brother.

Captain Edward Weathers

The men were all in their bunks, stomachs full from the shipment of rations. William, hot and sticky, sat in his tent with his sleeves rolled up. Both ends of the tent were open, in the hopes that some sort of a breeze would come through. He had been brooding over Edward's letter all evening and wished that it had never come into his hands, that he had never read it. He should have thrown it away the moment he received it. How on earth had it even found its way to him? Of all the letters that could have gotten lost...

"Colonel?" Phillip entered his tent carefully, pulling up a chair and having a seat. "Thought maybe you would want to talk. You've been awfully quiet."

William stared ahead for a minute, sighed, and handed the letter to Phillip. He looked into the distance as Phillip read.

"Do you think he's still alive?" Phillip asked.

William shook his head. "From the looks of the letter I doubt it, but I haven't seen any lists of recent casualties yet."

"What are you going to do?" Phillip asked, folding up the letter and handing it back, knowing he was treading on dangerous ground.

"Nothing." William's voice was pained, but his face remained cold and obstinate. He tossed the letter on his desk, dismissing it.

"Nothing?" Phillip repeated, trying hard not to judge, but simply asking a question.

"Why should I?" William burst out angrily, the guilt becoming too heavy a burden, one he didn't want. "He ruined our father's good name. He turned his back on *everything* my father had worked for, on his country, his life's work. He abandoned our mother. All she wanted while she was dying was to see him, but he wasn't there. She called me by his name, Phillip. She didn't even see me there!" William paused. "He's a traitor, and no longer has any claim on me."

"Don't you think that's a little harsh?" Phillip asked.

"No," William shot back. "*He was the oldest son. He* was supposed to follow the order and do his duty, not leave it for others to clean up his mess."

Phillip sat back, suddenly understanding where William's anger came from. "You know," Phillip said cautiously, with wisdom older than his eighteen years. "I followed the rules. My father expected me to join the British army and that's what I did, even though I desperately wanted to go on to the University. Without even consulting me, he bought me a commission and here I am.

"I'm no soldier, William, and my father knows that as well as I do. I'm a laughing stock in camp. I can't even aim a musket, let alone fire one. I hate that, just because of my father's position, while brave men are dying every day in the field they have to tolerate me here in camp and find something for me to do. They can't send me home because no one wants to defy my father, even the generals.

"I may have a small title on a piece of paper, but it means nothing to me. If I wasn't such a coward, I would defy my father and leave, but I can't. I pray every day for courage like your brother had." Phillip sat forward. "He did what he had to do, William. I wouldn't wish my fate on anyone, and neither should you." With that, Phillip left, leaving William to himself and his thoughts.

Standing, William walked over to his desk. Picking up the letter, he held it over the candle flame, sorrowfully watching as a corner began to burn. He closed his eyes, not wanting to watch, but his conscience got the better of him. He blew out the flame and stuffed the letter into an inside pocket of his jacket hanging on the chair. Letting out a deep sigh, he left to get some fresh air.

Samuel Wallace frowned as he went over the numbers in front of him. Margaret's stomach dropping each time she saw a new furrow on his brow. The air in the room seemed to stand still as she waited for him to finish reading.

Finally, taking off his bifocals he sighed, not knowing where to start. He had been helping Margaret with the farm since he came back from the war, but he was afraid things were beyond his help now.

"It's worse than I first thought," he began.

His pale eyes met Margaret's dark ones. How could he tell her this? He knew it was going to break her heart, especially after Edward's death. Looking back down at his papers, he sighed. "There's nothing. As you know, Edward lost a large amount of money smuggling, and without the crops you have no income. Edward's inheritance is substantial, but not enough to sustain you without a crop every year. It will be at least three before you see a decent yield if you planted again now, but with the war there's no telling when that will be able to happen."

Margaret sat quietly, not moving a muscle, her eyes fixed on a corner of the desk. "So what do we do now?" she asked, not moving her gaze.

Samuel looked again at his papers, not wanting to tell her the rest. "I think it's time to think about selling, either the land, or the ships, preferably both."

Margaret sat back and sighed, giving him an imploring look. Up until now she had still hoped that maybe there had been a mistake. Maybe Edward was alive and would come riding home as brilliant and confident as he always had been. Now, as she went over these affairs, she felt the truth finally wash over her.

Samuel spoke again very carefully. "The problem is that with the war, nobody is going to be very interested in buying a ransacked plantation. I'm sure we could find a wealthy privateer who would be willing to buy the ships at a good price, or perhaps the navy would be interested in purchasing them." He took a deep breath. "We could easily sell to the English for cheap. They've bought quite a few farms in the same condition."

Margaret's eyes flashed angrily. "You can't be serious, Sam. Do you hear what you're saying? Those ships were his dream. This farm was everything he ever wanted." Standing, she went to the window, checking on the children playing in the yard. "We'll simply have to make it work until we have a crop."

"Margaret, be reasonable." Sam said, standing and coming up behind her. "What fields you had have been destroyed by the English. After the war, if they're still intact, you'll have three of the best ships ever made sitting in the harbor making no profits. Your husband is dead, and you certainly can't afford to pay anyone to farm the land. There is no possible way you can manage by yourself." His tone changed and he spoke softly, knowing the truth was ugly.

"The idea of selling is as repulsive to me as it is to you, but it might be the only way. Think about it, you could buy a house in Charleston. It would be comfortable for you and the children. You'd be safe, and one day, maybe you'll marry again. If not, you would have enough to live nicely off of for a long time."

Margaret turned her head to the side, not wanting to listen. "I realize it's not the best option, but for now it's the only one you have," Sam said softly.

Margaret closed her eyes for a moment. "It's not an option Sam. What if the English lose?"

"Then we'll find a colonial buyer. This war's not over yet, but it wouldn't hurt to begin looking."

"I suppose not." She turned to him. "But nothing is definite," she said strongly. "We're simply weighing our options."

Samuel smiled and, using his cane, limped back over to the desk, picking up his books. "If I were you, I would pray for a..."

"Don't, Sam." Margaret cut him off. "I will take care of us."

Sam frowned. This was not the Margaret he knew speaking. Limping back to where Margaret sat, he took her hand. "Darling," he started softly. "God did not..."

"Sam, please," Margaret stopped, her voice choked. "Allow me this little bit of anger." Her eyes looked up at him, pleading. "Right now it's the only thing I can hold onto."

Sam nodded, placing a hand over hers. "I understand completely." He picked up his ledger books and Margaret walked him to the door. "If you need anything…" He stopped and turned to her.

"I'll come," she said, finishing the sentence for him.

"You're a smart girl," he said fondly, sighing deeply. "I suppose I should go home. Trust me, I don't want to."

Margaret couldn't help but smile. "Is it that bad? Surely you exaggerate."

"Worse. Catherine's like an ill-tempered cat. One wrong look and she'll scratch your eyes out. I'm surprised I could even find my way here with the mauling I've been receiving lately."

Margaret laughed, it felt good to do. "Why don't you have dinner with us? The children would love it," Margaret tried to convince him to stay, laying a hand on his arm.

"I can't. I have plenty of business to bury myself in at home," he said with regret.

Margaret held his arm as they walked to the door. He told her goodbye with a kiss on the hand and limped to his carriage. Joseph helped him in, climbed to the driver's seat and they were gone.

Chapter Fourteen: A Parable Rewritten
Somewhere outside of Charleston

William woke with a groan when the sound of movement and daily camp life outside his tent woke him. He had not slept well the night before, his dreams strange and odd, leaving him feeling out of sorts.

He had been in a house, one he didn't recognize. There had been children's laughter coming from somewhere, but try as he might, he couldn't find it. He remembered feeling alone, as if he couldn't find the laughter because he wasn't trying hard enough.

He turned a corner and his mother was there with Pearson. Both of them were shaking their heads in disappointment when they saw him. Frustrated, he left them, continuing his search.

Outside the house, the wind was blowing, making it difficult to keep his bearings. To his relief, he saw Edward walking up the drive. Smiling at him, Edward clapped him on the shoulder. He began to speak, saying something obviously important from the look on his face. William tried to hear what he was saying, but the wind was too strong and carried his words away so that William couldn't understand a word. William tried to explain that he couldn't hear, but Edward paid no attention. He just continued speaking. When he was finished, Edward gave him a huge smile, pulling him into a hug. Reluctantly, William's arms went around his brother, enjoying the strength and power in the embrace, tears coming to his eyes. Pushing him back at arm's length, Edward gave him a grin. "It's all in the letter," he said, as if it were as simple as that.

William woke up angry. He didn't want to think about the letter. He didn't want to think about Edward. Stepping outside his tent for a breath of fresh air, the silence of the night overwhelmed him, and brought the dream back again into his reality. He couldn't do it. He didn't want to think about it.

Back in his tent, William dug through his trunk, finding a half bottle of whiskey and did his best to forget. Now, with morning arriving too soon, he was seriously regretting his decision the night before.

"Good morning!" Phillip called, entering the tent far too cheerfully. "Oh," he said, seeing William sitting on the bed, his head between his hands. "Late night?" he asked, not hiding the smirk on his face. "That's certainly not like you."

"Don't ask," William moaned, feeling extremely foolish, and hoping to change the subject. "Are the men ready?" he asked.

He had been given the orders the day before. There had been reports of a stash of weapons in a broken down cabin hidden in the hills. William's orders were to take his men, find the cabin and bring the weapons back to camp.

William was not happy about the assignment knowing how the colonials fought. Too often, British soldiers had been ambushed in circumstances just like this one. The colonials may not have the resources of the English, but they knew the land, and that was an advantage. He'd heard too many stories of ambushes, had seen the scars on too many men, brought on not only by colonials, but also by natives. It was a dangerous task, and not one he was looking forward to.

"Almost," Phillip answered. "Do you need me to get you some coffee?"

Standing, William shook his head. "No, I'll be fine." Moving to his clothes, he pulled on his boots and jacket, tying his hair back with a piece of dark, felt ribbon.

"How long do you think it will take you?" Phillip asked. "There haven't been any reports of trouble in that area, but you never know."

William frowned, putting on his sword belt and checking the gunpowder for his pistol. "I plan to be back by sundown tomorrow." He gave Phillip a grin, a bit of his normal self returning. "If not, send out a search party."

William didn't have a good feeling about this place. Since his instincts had served him well in the past, he trusted them. Motioning for his men to be careful, the company slowed, trying to be quiet and surprise whatever might be waiting for them along the dirt road.

They rode forward through the dense brush, listening carefully for any sound of trouble, stopping in their tracks when the report of a rifle echoed in the air. The Lieutenant on the horse next to William fell to the ground.

"To arms!" he yelled.

He and his men jumped from their horses and shielded themselves as they waited to fire. There were more shots from the woods, and they could see the flash of fire and smoke from the guns hidden in the trees.

William raised his pistol. "Fire!" he shouted again, but before his men had a chance, the colonials ran out from behind the trees, spooking two of the horses, as well as one of his soldiers who was quickly shot in the back.

"Steady!" Weathers yelled, trying to calm his men, but a hand fight was on.

William decided to save his powder and grabbed his sword. The woods that had been quiet, peaceful, and still just a few minutes before were now full of blinding smoke and men shouting. Bullets were flying everywhere, the scene becoming confusing even for a seasoned soldier like William. A man in scruffy trousers and a dirty shirt ran towards him. William thrust his sword out in front of him to stop the man who froze as he was impaled on the sharp blade. The colonist fell to the ground and William pulled his sword out of him.

Turning, William ducked as a hatchet came towards his head, but he wasn't quick enough to avoid getting the butt of a musket in his stomach. The wind was knocked out of him and doubled him over. While he was down, he grabbed the pistol from his waist, and shot the man at point blank range, splattering blood everywhere. Gritting his teeth, William moved forward.

Another man, dressed in rags, fired at him. William felt the bullet hit his leg, but kept fighting. Furious, he loaded his gun again and shot the man squarely between the eyes. Bodies began to litter the ground, but William kept on fighting till only a few men remained standing. A man with a month's worth of a shaggy beard ran towards him and thrust a hunting knife into and out of William's side. Shocked, William pushed the man backwards onto the ground and ran him through with his sword. Straightening back up, William pulled his sword from the man's belly.

The ground in front of him began to spin. His head feeling light while his body was as heavy as lead. Trying to regain his senses he shook it off, taking a step forward before everything went dark.

William woke slowly and made it up to his hands and knees. His head pounded, pictures of what had taken place beginning to surface. The horses were gone, taken by the colonials no doubt, and bodies from both sides were strewn across the road. As he stood, pain shot down his leg, but he gritted his teeth and ignored it. The rebels would not get the best of him. He found his gun amongst the bodies, and held it in his hand, sheathing his sword. With his gun loaded he took off as quickly as he possibly could.

The evening came, a cool breeze filling the house taking the weight of humidity out of the heavy air. The small family was gathered in the front room of the house, finally easing back into routine. Megan was reading in the corner, while Matthew was busy showing Sarah the fine art of playing war with two of her dolls as she sat beside him pouting.

Abigail came into the room carrying another lantern. "Do you need anything else, Mrs. Margaret?" she asked.

"No Abigail," Margaret said with a smile. "We are fine."

William's leg was on fire, and there was a sharp pain in his side. Walking forward, he stumbled over a branch. He put some weight on his leg, but fell back down as a wave of nausea and blinding pain came over him. Fighting against it, he forced himself to his feet, honestly not knowing if he would be able to stand or not. His leg was heavy as lead and he could feel warm blood gush down his thigh each time he took a step. Holding his hand to the wound on his side, he moved forward, hoping to somehow keep from losing more blood.

The sun had set, but William's mind was too fuzzy to care which direction he was headed. He trampled through the tall grass and leaned against a tree to catch his breath. Feeling the darkness coming on again, he recognized it, and he fought against it as best he could. Hearing cannon fire in the distance, he quickened his pace through the field and moved towards where he thought he remembered the sun had disappeared.

After an hour William had lost all sense of time and direction. Loss of blood and fever had set in and he was beginning to have bouts of delirium. Phantom images passed in front of his eyes. He saw a group of rebel soldiers running through the trees, heard bullets whizzing past his head, the sound of marching drums and fifes nearby. As he came into a clearing he saw a large house ahead of him. Fumbling for his pistol, he headed towards the house, focusing on the light inside.

Margaret picked up some embroidery and began to sew while Megan read aloud from the family Bible. "And He said a certain man had two sons: and the younger of them said to his father. 'Father give me the portion of goods that falleth to me.' And he divided unto them his living. And not many days after the younger son gathered all together, and took his journey into a far country, and there wasted his substance with ri…rio.."

Matthew and Sarah giggled as she stumbled over a difficult word. Margaret gave them a stern look which quieted them.

"Riotous," she told her.

"Riotous living." Megan put the bible down. "Why did he leave his home?"

Laying down her sewing, Margaret thought for a moment. "Sometimes people need to set off on their own and have an adventure for themselves before they can really appreciate what life has given them already."

"Do all adventures end up that badly?" she asked.

Margaret shook her head. "No, your father set off on an adventure when he was young and look how it turned out. If he had never left England he wouldn't have come to the colonies."

"No, but he would be alive," Matthew said with knowledge much too old for him, frowning.

Margaret wasn't sure how to respond to that. Matthew was right, but how could she possibly explain it to him. "Your father was meant to leave England, come here and be your father, even if it was for just a short time. We don't know why he had to go, and maybe we'll never understand, but we have to trust that there was a reason," her voice was dry, knowing those were the words she was supposed to say, though, at the moment, she didn't want to hear them. "Even if it was just so you could be born." She gave her son a wink.

"Mama, Matthew won't give me my dolls," Sarah interrupted with a cry of frustration.

Margaret turned to Matthew ready to play mediator, but the boy was sitting completely still, holding one of Sarah's dolls by the neck, his frightened eyes focused on the door.

"Matthew, what's the matter?" Margaret stood to go to him, but her son's frightened voice stopped her.

"Someone's at the door," he whispered.

Looking at the door, Margaret saw the handle turning. Fear ran down her spine and coursed through her veins, pounding in her ears. The girls and Matthew stood while Margaret motioned for them to back up against the wall. Placing herself in front of them, she couldn't decide what to do. There was the pistol, but it was in the kitchen and she wouldn't have time to get to it without leaving the children alone.

The door opened in slow motion. There was a bloody hand, a red sleeve, and then the dark, blood soaked coat of the man. For a second Margaret thought it was the ghost of the Englishman she had killed. She tried to ground herself in reality and not panic, but it wasn't working as well as she hoped with her hands trembling.

The English soldier limped forward a couple of steps towards Margaret, a ghost seeming to come from the grave. She could smell the blood, dirt, and sweat on him as he came closer. His hair was falling out of the ribbon that held most of it back at the nape of his neck. Shaking, he aimed the gun at Margaret, the sound of the hammer being pulled back echoing in the silent room. He was so weak he could barely hold up his arm.

Margaret was careful not to make any sudden moves. She knew he was sick, could see the fever in his eyes, the sweat on his skin. Their eyes met and he brought the gun up level to her face, but Margaret stood firm, finally taking hold of the situation when the soldier swayed backwards a bit and dropped the gun. Megan and Sarah screamed as it fired, but Margaret reacted quickly and caught the soldier as he fell forward, nearly falling under his weight.

"Children, upstairs, quickly!" she shouted. They ran up the stairs as fast as they could.

"Abigail! Reggie!" she called the weight of the unconscious man dragging her to the floor.

Abigail and Reggie rushed in. "Goodness!" Abigail shouted, staring at the sight before her. "Was that a gunshot? What happened?"

"He's injured," Margaret informed them quickly. "Help me lay him down."

Reggie and Abigail hurried to where Margaret was, helping her lay the man on the floor. His red coat had a large tear in it and was crusted over with blood. Undoing his buttons, she opened the coat. All she could see was flesh and more blood.

"Good God," she said, seeing the huge gash in his side.

She carefully covered his side back up and moved down to look at his thigh. The wound was deep and from the shape of it she could only assume it came from a bullet. Picking up his leg she looked for an exit wound, but didn't see one, only dark blood that had soaked the cloth. The bullet must still be in his leg, she thought.

Abigail held a lantern down close so her mistress could see. Margaret looked up at their concerned faces. "We have to get him upstairs."

"Mrs. Margaret, you can't have an Englishman in this house," Reggie argued. "I think I should ride for Mr. Wallace, he'll know what to do." Fear and concern were evident in his voice. Reggie did not need to decide what he thought should be done with the wounded man.

Margaret stood. "No, Reggie," she answered speaking calmly. "We are going to take him upstairs and then decide what to do. You get his feet, Abigail and I will get his arms."

Setting down her lantern, Abigail shook her head. "I have to agree with Reggie, Mrs. Margaret. I don't think this is a good idea. I know what you're planning, and it's nothing a decent woman should be involved in."

Margaret picked up the man's shoulders. "What would you have me do?" she asked impatiently, a lock of hair falling across her face. "Throw him outside to die? I won't do it. Now help me," she commanded.

Struggling, they managed to get the man up the stairs and into a spare bedroom. When they got him to the bed, they laid him down with an ungraceful thud. Margaret winced at the indelicacy of it.

Taking off his jacket and waistcoat, Margaret carefully laid them on the floor next to the bed. "I'll need a knife, a bottle of whisky, tweezers, and boiling water." She gave the orders without thought, knowing what needed to be done, the tone in her voice not allowing any questions or other options.

Giving her a cautious look, Abigail left quickly, knowing there was nothing to be done about changing the woman's mind.

Margaret went to work taking off the man's boots. Boots that had been well polished at one time, but were now covered with mud and dust. She removed the stock collar around his neck and the officer's sash at his waist in feverish haste.

Standing, she called to Reggie who was standing just inside the bedroom door. "Reggie, I need you to go down and get his gun," she handed him the muddy boots, bloody jacket, and sash. "Take these and hide them and his gun in the attic…in Edward's trunk," she said quickly. Reggie came forward reluctantly, holding them away from himself not wanting to touch them.

"Reggie," she ordered calmly, catching his eye. "I need you to help me with this."

"Yes Ma'am," he said, still unsure.

Turning back, Margaret stared at the man on the bed wondering what in God's name she was going to do. Abigail returned with the supplies and sat them next to the bed. "I brought some scraps of cloth and some rags as well." Knowing there was nothing she could do to change Margaret's mind, she figured she should be prepared for whatever her mistress was planning.

"Thank you Abigail." Taking the scissors, Margaret began to cut his shirt off.

"What should I tell the children?" Abigail asked cautiously.

Margaret thought for a moment, brushing a piece of blond hair from her face, leaving a streak of blood on her forehead. "Tell them that everything is fine and to go to sleep. I'll be in later."

"Yes, Ma'am." Abigail left to attend to the children.

Margaret had no idea what she was doing, but knew that she had to help him, English or not. She had all of his clothes off, leaving his undergarments on for modesty's sake and stuffed them under the bed. Pulling back his hair, she re-tied it back with the dirty ribbon to keep it out of his face. She wet a cloth and wiped off the dried blood around his stomach and thigh, amazed at the amount and shocked that he was still alive.

First, she decided to address the gash in his side. Watching his shallow breathing for a moment, she wondered exactly how unconscious he was, partly because she didn't want him to wake up, and partly because she didn't want to cause him more injury. Tentatively, she poured a drop of whiskey on the gash. When he didn't move, she decided it was safe and poured in enough to clean the wound. Keeping her eyes on him the entire time, she tried to anticipate any sudden movements, praying that he would just stay unconscious. She could see a thin layer of sweat on his face and knew he was burning up with fever. Taking two cold rags, she laid one on his forehead and one behind his neck.

Bandaging his side, she prepared herself to move on to his leg. She sat silent for a moment trying to decide the best way to go about it. "I hope this doesn't hurt," she apologized, knowing he couldn't hear her, "but if it does I'm sorry. The bullet has to come out and this is the only way."

She took the glass off one lantern and held the tweezers to the fire for a minute. Taking a deep breath, she bit her lip, and put the tweezers in the wound. She felt around for anything hard, her entire body tense. The tweezers brushed against something foreign, and she held onto it tightly.

The soldier jerked his head to the side and Margaret froze, waiting to see what he would do next. When he didn't move again, she pulled the bullet out quickly, setting the round metal ball on the nightstand, and poured some whiskey in the wound. Bright red blood began to pour out again. Bandaging the leg tightly, she replaced the cool rags on his head and behind his neck. Reaching under the bed, she grabbed his torn clothes and left the room.

The hall was cool and refreshing. She hadn't realized how hot she had been until she leaned against the door in the hallway taking in slow, deep breaths, trying her hardest to calm her pounding heart. Abigail was waiting for her.

"All we can do is wait," Margaret told her.

"And then?" Abigail asked cautiously.

"And then, I don't know," Margaret answered with a frown. She handed Abigail the bloodstained clothes. "Burn these. Are the children all right?"

"Yes, Ma'am," Abigail answered with the pile of clothes in her hand. "Matthew's awake, but the girls are asleep." Nodding, Margaret walked slowly down the hall.

Margaret opened the door to Matthew's room quietly. Pale moonlight filled the room and she could see Matthew's eyes shining in the dark as he lay in bed staring up at the ceiling. Walking to his bed, she sat down next to him, his room a complete contrast to the one she had come from. A cool breeze came from the window and the cicadas sang their nightly song of the summer. It was as if the other room had been a dream. Matthew's room smelled of powder and fresh air, unlike the smell of dirt and blood. She was glad it was dark and Matthew couldn't see the officer's blood that stained her dress.

"Matthew, you need to go to sleep," Margaret said running a hand through his soft hair as if none of the commotion earlier had happened.

"Why did he come here?" he asked quietly.

"He was hurt and lost," Margaret replied. "He didn't know where he was."

Matthew was silent. "Did he kill father?" he finally asked.

Margaret's stomach dropped. "No," she answered him and put her hands on his soft cheeks. "I am certain that he did not kill your father. Many people are injured and killed during war." She kissed him on the head. "Now, I want you to close your eyes and go to sleep." Reluctantly, Matthew turned over in bed and closed his eyes.

Ten minutes later, Margaret was back in the soldier's bedroom to check on him. He was still breathing, but not yet awake. She changed his bandages, already soaked with blood again, pulled a chair up next to the bed, and sat down to wait for whatever was going to happen next. Margaret listened to the now steady rhythm of his breathing, her eyes growing heavy because of how late it was. Laying her head back in the chair, she waited out the night.

Chapter Fifteen: Jealousy and Faith

Catherine sat across from Lady Dougherty in the grand parlor of the Dougherty estate. The afternoon sun pouring in from the tall windows made the room bright and airy. Catherine stared at her cards, unable to find any good suits in her hand. The women had been playing for an hour and both were growing bored.

Lady Dougherty laid her cards down with a sigh. "I simply cannot continue. I am having deplorable luck today."

Catherine did the same with her poor hand. "I'm glad I'm not the only one," she added.

Lady Dougherty stood and went to pull the servant's bell. "I say we have some lemonade. It's so warm in here, perhaps we should take a walk," she said, turning back to Catherine with enthusiasm.

"After our lemonade, of course," Catherine said. "Besides, you haven't given me any new gossip yet?"

An older black woman brought in a tray of drinks and served the women who paused their conversation as they waited for the slave to leave. As soon as the door closed, Lady Dougherty's face turned instantly from stoic to the animated face of a town gossip.

"I can't believe I haven't said anything, my dear. What on earth is wrong with me? Well, I'm sure you heard of our victory at Camden. I tell you the best thing King George did was place Lord Cornwallis in charge of the South. Colonel Pearson was there you know." Lady Dougherty's eyes grew wide and she leaned forward. "He told Lord Dougherty that the militiamen fled like a frightened flock of birds."

Catherine sat back. "Colonel Pearson was at Camden?" A strange thought ran through her head, but she dismissed it as quickly as it came. Camden was where Edward Weathers had fallen, how curious.

Lady Dougherty sat back and took a long drink of lemonade and then appeared startled. "Oh my word, you don't know," she replied with a giggle. "Colonel Pearson is staying here. He was slightly injured in the battle so Lord Dougherty invited him here to recuperate for a couple of months.

"It appears that the whole scene was quite heroic. He took on a whole pack of bloodthirsty militia. Can you believe that some of them didn't even wear uniforms? Anyway," she continued. "One of our enemies stuck him in the arm with a bayonet, probably a stolen one," she added, "but our dear Colonel Pearson didn't let that stop him, though. He kept on fighting, and at the end of the day, when someone suggested he have his arm looked at? He said that there was no need. It was only a scratch. Only a scratch! Have you ever seen such bravery?" Catherine's hand began to tremble as she listened.

"He and Lord Dougherty went hunting for the day. They should be back before sundown," Lady Dougherty added at the end of her story.

Catherine looked towards the window. Indeed, it was growing dimmer outside and the room was beginning to take on an orange color from the setting sun. She couldn't believe what she had heard. Colonel Pearson was there, and he would be back anytime. Her head was in such a fuss she didn't hear a word of what Lady Dougherty said next. Her mind immediately went to her state of dress and why she hadn't worn her navy gown instead?

"Anyway, I received a letter from my sister in London, of course she wrote it months ago, but because of this ridiculous war everything is in shambles. It appears that Mrs. Butler was horrifically scandalized. She was caught with a man fifteen years younger. Her husband has all but thrown her out of the house and cut off her funds."

She began to say something else, but stopped when they heard dogs barking and the stomping of boots in the hallway. Before Catherine could gather her thoughts the doors to the parlor were flung open and an exhausted Lord Dougherty, a powerful Colonel Pearson, and three hunting dogs barged into the room.

"My dear, did you have a good day?" Lady Dougherty asked as she approached her husband with a quick kiss on the cheek.

Flopping himself down in a chair, Lord Dougherty stretched out his legs. One of the hunting dogs took a seat next to him, panting from the hard day's work, and waiting for a well-deserved pet from his master.

"We did well, Lady Dougherty. Three turkeys and almost one doe, but the creature was startled by a confounded sneeze."

Pearson chuckled as he sat down. "I don't think Lord Dougherty is quite accustomed to the Southern vegetation."

Dougherty frowned. "I swear, it is a shame when a man ruins his own hunt because of a blasted sneeze."

Lady Dougherty gave him a pouty smile and handed him a glass of lemonade. "We were just going to go for a small walk. Would you like to join us, dearest?"

"My dear, I am too exhausted to move. Forgive me, but you will have to go without me." He gave her a slight bow from his seat.

Colonel Pearson stood. "I would be more than willing to escort Lady Dougherty and her guest," Pearson said, giving Catherine a sly smile. "Mrs. Wallace, isn't it?" Catherine nodded, forcing herself to appear nonchalant.

Lady Dougherty turned to Pearson. "How very marvelous of you, Colonel Pearson, thank you." She turned to Catherine and gave her hand a quick squeeze.

Pearson led the women to the doors looking out on the lawn and held one open for them. The dogs, seeing the open door, ran out to chase some birds, not quite finished with their hunt. The three walked slowly around the grounds discussing the difference of the weather in Boston compared to that of the South and other idle chit-chat.

Finally, Lady Dougherty asked a question Catherine herself had been about to ask. "How is your shoulder healing, Colonel?"

"It's doing better. There is a little pain, but nothing too troublesome," he said as they strolled.

Catherine glanced inconspicuously at the imposing man next to her. "How were you injured, Colonel Pearson? I hope it wasn't anything serious." Catherine did her best to play the frightened woman. "Lady Dougherty told me a bit about it. It sounds just absolutely frightful."

"Oh no," Pearson said humbly, brushing off the concern. "I caught a bayonet in the shoulder, but it was only a very minor injury."

A butler came outside looking for Lady Dougherty and the group came to a stop. "Pardon me, I should go see what's needed," Lady Dougherty excused herself, leaving Catherine and the Colonel alone.

They continued their stroll through the garden in silence. After a few moments, and the promise that Lady Dougherty wouldn't be returning immediately, Catherine spoke. "Did you hear that Captain Weathers was killed?" she asked, taking the Colonel's arm.

"I believe I did read his name on one of the lists of fallen officers," he answered nonchalantly. "I was injured early in the battle so I didn't see much of what happened."

There was another pause in the conversation. "How is his wife?" Pearson asked cynically, allowing a bit more of his true nature to come out now that he and Catherine were alone.

Catherine caught the sarcasm in his voice and was able to match it with her own bitterness. "The woman needs to be taken down a peg or two. No matter what happens, she ends up being the picture of a dutiful wife. It's absolutely revolting. Samuel thinks she is the epitome of the colonial woman."

Pearson smiled. "Is that a bit of jealousy I hear?"

Catherine laughed. "No. He can certainly have her. It's just that she annoys me so. Margaret Weathers should be planting potatoes outside a hovel in Ireland. She has no right to the life she was brought into." She shook her head disgustedly. "*Bought* her way into is more like it. Her uncle, another Irish slob, owned a large plantation."

"Has your man found out anything more about the family? Perhaps there is something we can use to reduce the size of her… spirit, shall we say?" Pearson could feel his plans to ruin William Weathers become easier. Through the petty jealousy of Catherine Wallace he had found a willing partner.

"You mentioned that Captain Weathers had a…brother, I believe…in England." He chose his words carefully. "If you could find out more about him, and his whereabouts, or what ties his brother may have, perhaps we would have something you could use."

Catherine stopped and looked at him coolly. "Why the concern for them?" she asked. "Surely there must be reason for your curiosity."

Pearson's face betrayed no hint of his true purpose. "I admit that, at first, my goal was to give my commanding officers some information on the enemy's plans and whereabouts. When I met you, Captain Weathers was the first name you mentioned. I could have cared less, but now I want to do you a favor in return for the one you did for me. I think, if we work together, we will be able to bring an abundance of pleasure into your life."

The two were hidden from view of the main house by a line of shrubbery and Pearson used this to his advantage, bending down to kiss her neck as he finished his speech. Catherine felt lightheaded as Pearson's arm went around her waist and she gave into the powerful grasp that drew her close. Closing her eyes, enjoying the pleasure of his powerful body so close to hers, she whispered close to his ear. "Can we really destroy her?" she asked, her voice husky and soft.

Pearson's sharp, gray eyes gleamed with delight. "Completely."

Margaret woke to a loud crash of thunder that rattled the windows of the house. Sitting up, she realized that the English soldier was stirring, mumbling something that she couldn't understand. Turning up the lantern, she went to him quickly. He was burning hot to the touch and drenched with sweat. Infection was setting in and Margaret knew that she had to cool him. Throwing the covers and sheets off of him, she ran to the window. Opening it as high as it would go, a wave of panic came over her. The wind whipped into the room bringing in cool rain with it. Calming herself, Margaret walked steadily back to the bed.

His face was paler than he had been before, even the night before when he had stumbled in. He was mumbling incoherently, tossing his head from side to side. Margaret held his head still, placing a wet cloth on his forehead, wiping his cheeks, arms and wrists with another.

Taking a deep breath, Margaret tried to steady her nerves. She had never seen anyone as sick as he was. When her father died it was drawn out and he had slowly wasted away. This was different. In front of her was a healthy man in the prime of his life torn down by violence. Tears welled up in her eyes as she tried to cool him. She had to be strong. She tried not to think about Edward's last moments, but when she looked at the man in front of her she couldn't keep the questions back any longer. If Edward had come to her injured, could she have saved him? Had someone held his hand and comforted him? Were his last moments peaceful, or was he wracked with pain?

"Shhh," she whispered with a stifled sob. "You'll be just fine." She held his face still and talked to him. "You have to fight," she ordered, tears falling, mingling with his sweat.

Rain blew in and thunder shook the house as Margaret cried and fought to save the man in front of her, hoping to make up for the one she couldn't. It was up to her to save him, no one else. She couldn't burden Abigail and Sam wouldn't understand. This was an undertaking she had to do herself. She could save this man, and that's what she intended to do.

Margaret woke with a start, her head dizzy from raising it so quickly. Familiarity returned to her when she saw the unconscious man in front of her. Steadying herself for a moment, she stood, stretching her muscles, sore from sleeping awkwardly with her head on her arms. The lantern had gone out, but morning light was coming through window. Taking a deep breath, and enjoying the cool, wet morning air coming in the window, Margaret looked around the room. A moment of strange recognition passed by and was gone just as quickly, but she knew where the memories came from because they had haunted her all night.

She remembered the same breeze coming in the door of a small cottage as visitors came and went. Margaret had sat next to her father's body in the same place she had been for days. He lay on the bed, dead, but looking as if he might wake at any second. For the first time in a year he was at peace, no longer tortured by illness, but Margaret felt as numb and dead as her father's body. The number of people who came to pay her father their respects with a couple of tears and a couple of drinks had dwindled. Now all she heard were the hushed voices of her aunt and uncles discussing what to do with her.

"She certainly can't live with me. Her mother's relatives still live there and there's bound to be talk." Margaret's aunt's snobbish voice always made her angry, and when she spoke, the conversation inevitably turned to Margaret's mother, the ever-elusive woman she had never known, and no one ever discussed unless it was in passing.

"The girl simply wouldn't be suited for life with me. It is bad enough Michael raised her here. I wouldn't want to subject a pretty girl like her to life up North. It would ruin her." Her Uncle Sean had always been kind to her, yet she was still a burden in his eyes.

She heard the heavy footsteps of her Uncle Seamus ready to make another rash decision. "It's settled then. Maggie will come to South Carolina with me. We have more than enough room and I'm sure Bonnie would enjoy having a young lady around the house." There was silence for a moment. No one disagreed. "A young woman like her will blossom in the colonies."

Margaret was brought out of her memories by the sound of small footsteps on the wood floor. Standing in the doorway was Sarah, her long blond hair in braids, her sleepy eyes staring at the man in the bed.

"Sarah, you should go downstairs for some breakfast?" Margaret said, trying to keep the girl from looking towards the bed, but Sarah's eyes were fixed.

"Is he sick, Mama?" she asked in a quiet whisper, trying not to wake him.

"Yes, sweetheart, he's very sick." Margaret ran a hand over the child's hair.

Sarah walked over to the side of the bed and studied the soldier. "He looks like papa," she said matter of factly.

Curious, Margaret studied him. "I suppose he does a little." Pain hit Margaret, trying not to think about what Edward had looked like on the battlefield littered among the bodies of other fallen soldiers. She didn't want those memories to return; they had been bad enough last night.

Pulling the little girl away from the bed, Margaret picked her up and walked her towards the door. "You, young lady, need to go down for breakfast. I'll be there in a minute."

Sarah got as far as the doorway before she turned back around. "Will he be all right?"

Margaret smiled at her concern. "I certainly hope so."

Chapter Sixteen: Resurrection

That evening the English soldier still showed no sign of waking. He had stopped losing blood, but the fever was still raging. Margaret cleaned his wounds with warm water every few hours and rewrapped them, hoping to wash out the infection. The children went back to the Newman's to play for the day, but when they returned for dinner things were as noisy as usual. While Margaret ate with the children, Abigail sat with the soldier in case he woke. After putting the children to bed early, Margaret went to relieve Abigail.

Reggie's voice followed her down the hallway. "Mrs. Weathers, I still don't think this is a good idea. What if he wakes? There's no telling what he might do. Have you forgotten that he's an English soldier? Wounded or not, he is the enemy, and any Englishman I've ever met has had little mercy for colonials."

Ignoring him, Margaret entered the room carrying a pillow, followed by Reggie, holding a blanket still protesting loudly. Abigail stood and smiled to herself, knowing how headstrong Margaret could be and how useless his argument was.

"Reggie," Margaret said, turning to him. "If he wakes up, I need to be here. Can you imagine what it would be like to wake up injured in a strange house with no one in sight?" She laid her pillow on a small settee that sat in the corner.

"I will stay here, Mrs. Weathers, and if anything happens I'll come get you," Reggie tried to plead with her. He had grown very fond of Margaret and didn't want any bad falling on her. She was kind, sweet, a good Christian. She was a strong woman, who would do anything for whoever needed it, and he admired that.

Secretly, he wished that he had found his way into the service of the Weathers a long time ago.

"Reggie," Margaret smiled. "I appreciate the offer, and I understand the concern, but I have to be here. I know you don't understand, but I have to stay." Margaret felt the soldier's warm forehead and placed a cool rag on it.

Reggie began to protest again, but Abigail put a hand on his arm as she left, letting him know his argument was useless.

Reggie paused for a second longer. "I still think it would be best to speak with Mr. Wallace, he would know exactly what to do."

Margaret's head snapped up at the words and Reggie knew he had gone too far, her eyes dark looked firmly into his. "You cannot say a word about this to Mr. Wallace, do you understand me?" Her voice was serious. "He is a wonderful man, but he wouldn't have the same ideas about what should happen to the soldier." Reggie looked down at the floor. "Do you understand me, Reggie? *No one* can know about this."

Nodding, Reggie laid the blanket on the settee for her, but he wasn't ready to let it go. "Promise that you'll get me if you have any trouble. I'll stay downstairs tonight."

Margaret smiled at him. "Trust me, I won't do anything foolish, but if need be, I can defend myself." Reluctantly, Reggie nodded and left, closing the door behind him.

  Margaret was awake early the next morning, tired, but rested after having been half-awake all night. She, like most mothers, had perfected the art of being able to sleep, while still being aware of the slightest noise. The first thing she noticed on waking was that the soldier's head was turned to the side. Rising quickly, she felt his forehead. For the first time he was cool to the touch. Margaret sat down on the bed and sighed. The fever was gone.

The door creaked open slowly behind her and Margaret turned to see Sarah's little head peeking through the door again.

"Mama? Can I come in?" she asked in a whisper.

Figuring it wouldn't hurt anything, Margaret nodded. Sarah smiled and ran in, taking a seat in the chair next to his bed while Margaret went about changing his bandages.

"Is anyone else awake?" she asked.

Sarah sighed. "No. Megan is sleeping and I tried to wake Matthew up, but he told me to go away." She pouted for a moment as she watched her mother cut his old bandages off, wash his wounds and redress them.

Margaret gathered the dirty bandages and laid them on the nightstand. She went to open the window, but stopped when Sarah spoke happily. "Mama, his eyes are open."

Pearson was halfway through his dinner when Balis and Jass entered the dining room of Pearson's newly acquired town home in Charleston. Pearson knew right away by the sour look on Jass' face and the look of disgust on Balis' that something had gone wrong. He motioned for them to have a seat and join him, one of the nearby servants, setting them a place.

"What happened?" was all he asked, pouring them each a drink.

Jass grabbed a fork and stabbed at a piece of meat angrily while Balis spoke. "It's Colonel Weathers, Sir. He's gone missing. A number of his men were found dead on a trail down south. They were ambushed by militia, but there was no sign of their officer."

Pearson cleared his throat. "Did you check the prison lists?"

"Yes, Sir. He's nowhere to be found," Jass growled.

Standing, Pearson walked to the window, throwing his glass on the floor with a crash, trying to decide what to do next. "He has to be somewhere," Pearson argued. "I'll give you leave for a week. Someone has to know something. Sniff around taverns, medical tents, farms, anywhere he might turn up."

Pearson turned back to them, crushing the shards of glass under his boots. "Weathers is a stickler for rules. If he's been injured, he'll get himself to a camp. Just find him."

For what seemed like years, William had been sleeping and had dreamed of strange things. He kept seeing faces of people he had known, Timothy's death played constantly in his mind, and he heard his mother's voice asking over and over for Edward. Pearson drunk, and stumbling into the tavern attic just before dawn, played a large part, but the worse dreams were the ones when his men were under attack. There would be screaming, and he would hear himself commanding them to fire, but the onslaught would continue until they were each dead over and over again.

He felt coolness and heat, heard voices around him, but was unable to understand them or respond. His body felt heavy and his muscles were stiff, his head in a fog, unaware of where he was or what day or time it was. With no more memory of where, or who he was, he felt suspended in time.

William tried once to open his eyes; hearing voices nearby, but gave up and fell again into peaceful darkness. Slowly, he didn't know how much later, he finally managed it, his eyelids heavy, fuzzy images taking a moment to come into view.

The first thing he saw were two small, blue eyes staring back at him. Something registered in his mind, but vanished just as quickly and there was no way of getting it back. Striking pain shot through his body when he tried to move, taking his breath away.

Margaret rushed back to the bed. "Sarah, fetch Abigail."

The little girl ran off quickly, while the sudden commotion brought memories back.

"My men," William said with a raspy voice. "Where are my men?"

Margaret held him down as he attempted to sit up, clenching his teeth and trying to bear the pain in his side. She laid him back down carefully when he finally gave up the effort to sit.

"Your men are fine," she reassured him. "You need to calm yourself down and relax. You were injured very badly."

William lay back carefully, confused by the woman's accent and, for a moment, thinking he was back in England, but he knew that couldn't be. Taking a deep breath, he filled his lungs, trying to hold back the pain, closing his eyes again, desperate to put things in order.

He remembered the ambush and killing the man that had stabbed him, but after that there was nothing. When he opened his eyes again two more people had entered the room. One, a middle-aged black woman wearing an apron, her hair pulled back in a cap, the other, a skinny black man who stood in the doorway keeping his distance. The Irish woman immediately took control of the situation and he decided that he was definitely not in England.

"Abigail, would you bring some broth?" Margaret asked, watching the soldier carefully as he tried to get his bearings.

"Yes, Ma'am," the woman said, leaving as suddenly as she had appeared.

Margaret gave Reggie the handful of old bandages. "Reggie, there is a small bottle of laudanum in the study, the high cabinet behind his desk. We're going to need it."

The man left to do her bidding and the woman approached him. She was extremely pretty. He may have been injured, but he was still aware enough to notice that. Slowly she helped him up a bit and she placed another pillow behind him so that he could lean back comfortably.

"Is that better?" she asked. William nodded, mesmerized by the woman's eyes, dark brown, haunting.

"Drink this." She held a cup of water to his lips. "We'll get you something stronger for the pain in a minute." William swallowed the water in a matter of seconds, coughing at the sudden intake. He couldn't remember the last time he had had clean water.

"Where am I?" William finally asked, groping for breath.

Margaret responded as Reggie came back with a small, dark bottle. "You're in South Carolina, about ten miles from Charleston. You stumbled into the house bleeding to death three days ago." Margaret gave him a spoonful of something thick and syrupy with a bitter aftertaste. "It's for the pain and will help you sleep," she explained. He took it gratefully, hoping it would take away the ache in his side and leg.

Closing his eyes, William waited for the medicine to take effect. "We were ambushed by militia," he said slowly. "That's all I can remember." He stopped there, not wanting to share too much information.

Abigail came back into the room with a bowl of warm chicken broth and a small loaf of bread. Margaret took it from her and set it on the tray next to him. "There was a bullet in your leg, and a deep cut in your side," she informed him. "It's a miracle you didn't die before you found us." She handed him the broth. "You need to eat."

William waited a moment and asked a tentative question. "Does anyone know I'm here?" Margaret looked at him seriously, and William didn't know what to make of it.

"Only us," she answered quietly. "The children know better than to say anything and Abigail and Reggie are very trustworthy."

"Are they the only ones here?" William asked, taking a spoonful of broth carefully.

The woman's face changed with a distant sadness. "Yes. It's just us." She straightened up the room a bit while William took a few more spoonfuls of broth. It was about all he could handle to get these down. He handed the bowl back to Margaret with an apology.

"You don't want to rush it," she said, pulling his covers up around him, checking his forehead again for fever as if he were a child. It left William feeling a tad foolish, but he knew he didn't have any room to argue about it. Besides, his body was certainly in no condition to put up a fight.

"Your appetite will return," the woman said flatly.

Margaret began to leave, but William had more questions. Unfortunately, he was growing tired quickly. She must have sensed it because she drew the curtains. "You still need rest. I'll be back in a few hours with something more for you to eat."

William watched as she went to the door and then turned back to him. There was a look of concern on her face. "Is there anything else you need?" William shook his head, already fading off into the comfort of darkness.

When Margaret finally made it downstairs the children were finishing their breakfast. She greeted each of them with a kiss on the head and a smile.

"Is the soldier really awake, Mother?" Megan asked.

163

"Yes, but he's still weak so I don't want any of you bothering him." Margaret sat down and looked at her children very firmly. "Now, it's very important that none of you tell anyone about him being here. Do you understand?" They all nodded.

"Do you think he killed anyone?" Matthew asked, a spoonful of oatmeal in his mouth.

Sarah laughed. "That's bad." Then, like a miniature young lady, she added, "I think he's very handsome because he looks like Father."

Megan gave her sister a stern look. "You don't know anything, Sarah. Father was an American, he's an English."

Quickly ending the argument, Margaret suggested they go and play outside. They left, kindly waiting until they were outside to shout. Finishing her breakfast, Margaret headed upstairs to change clothes.

Hating to admit it, she had been trying her best to spend as little time as possible in her bedroom the past few weeks. Even though she had been alone in the bed for the better part of four years, there was always the hope that it was only temporary. Now that Edward was really gone the place seemed lonelier than ever. In a way, she was thankful for the diversion the injured soldier had brought.

She changed the dress she had slept in and looked at herself in the full-length mirror. There was something different about her. She could feel it. She could see it. She had crossed another of life's bridges, one that she desperately wished she could run back over.

Sitting on her bed, she found herself staring at the floor, taking in slow, deep breaths. Silently letting the anger and resentment rise, fill her, calm her. It was an emptiness of her own making. She knew it wasn't right, but for now she clung to it, let it envelope her until she found the strength to move. She knew God would understand, knew that if anyone could take it, He could. She could block him out, rant and rave at Him like an angry child, and He would forgive her. He had before, again and again.

The first time had been when her father died. For months, she blocked out any and all prayers. When the local priest and neighbors gathered to pray the rosary, Margaret had sat stoically at the kitchen table, ignoring the chanting of prayers for her father's soul. She knew he didn't need them anymore. He was happy and safe; she believed that with all her heart.

It wasn't until she was in Charleston at mass with her aunt and uncle for the first time that she finally let down her guard and prayed again. She had tried to hide the tears from her uncle, but he'd seen and placed a loving arm around her. "Sometimes it's harder to stay angry isn't it," he had whispered.

Edward had said the same thing after she'd miscarried a child between Matthew and Megan. She had taken no time to mourn, and as soon as possible, Margaret was back on her feet running the household, but she had closed herself off again. Edward could see it. When he knelt to pray before bed, she would suddenly have forgotten something Matthew needed. There would be instructions she needed to leave for Abigail. Her Bible remained unopened for weeks until Edward finally confronted her about it.

He had come into the room and shut the door, pulling her down to her knees with him. "Edward, no," she moved to get up, but he stopped her. "I can't do this, please," she begged.

Taking her face in his hands, Edward asked simply, "Why?"

Tears welled up in Margaret's eyes, the pain she'd been holding back for so long surfacing. "Because, I don't want to. I can't."

"Why?" Edward asked again softly.

"Because I'm angry!" she spat. "God has taken everything from me...my mother, my father," she sobbed, tears flowing, "and now my baby." She fell forward into Edward's arms, heavy sobs wracking her body. "I don't understand," she moaned. "What have I done wrong?"

"You've done nothing wrong," Edward answered, his voice strained to see her so desperate. "But we can't possibly understand His plan. Don't you see?" He held her tear-streaked face up to his. "If your father hadn't died, I never would have found you. We don't know why these things happen, but God does, and He's not going to let us down. We may not see it now, but He does." He kissed her salty cheeks. "You can't push Him away forever. The only person it will hurt is you." Edward looked down into her eyes.

"I've seen the emptiness and pain in people before, and I don't want to see it in you, and neither does your true father. He loves you too much." Edward leaned forward, kissed her, placing his forehead against hers. "I love you too much to see that happen," he whispered.

Closing his eyes, Edward had held her close. "Oh dear father," he prayed. "Show your daughter how much you love her. Comfort her and guide her."

Margaret sniffed, closing her eyes, letting herself pray, letting herself forgive. She clasped her hands around Edward's in agreement. Anger and despair were not what she wanted for herself.

And they are not what she wanted now. She wiped away a tear, remembering that she couldn't do it by herself then, and she couldn't do it by herself now. Falling to her knees, Margaret prayed, opening the door to her heart again, knowing it was the only way. She prayed for herself, for her children, and for the soldier upstairs.

She didn't know how, but she knew it was time. Margaret had loved her husband, always would, but she couldn't live holding onto a ghost. The children were relying on her, and she had to live for them.

    Putting up a good front had been effective for awhile. She had everyone fooled by her bravery and restraint, but, in truth, she felt like a porcelain doll, hard on the outside, but empty on the inside. Unfortunately, the porcelain doll had cracked. Margaret had nothing left and the past few weeks when she'd looked in the mirror she hadn't even recognized herself. That was going to change. She was going to live for Him, like Edward would have wanted.

    With a weight lifted, she let down her blond hair and brushed it. After pulling it back, she tied a thin black ribbon around it. Nothing fancy, but just enough to make her feel less drab in the black mourning dress she wore. She added a little color to her cheeks and looked again into the mirror. Feeling prettier, and younger, she decided to force herself to be in a brighter mood than her clothing allowed. Edward would want that for her. He would have told her so if he could. She smiled, thinking of what he would say. He would put his arms around her and tell her she could make the moon weep she was so beautiful.

    She paused for a minute before she began her next task, knowing Edward would have helped a fellow soldier no matter what side he fought on. She still felt an ache when she pulled out a pair of breeches and a shirt from his wardrobe for the Englishman upstairs. She knew they would fit fairly well because the two men were close to the same size. Edward was...she corrected herself...had been, a little taller.

    She met Abigail on the landing. "Abigail, I suppose we should put Edward's clothes up in the attic."

    Nodding kindly, Abigail knew what a difficult decision that had been. "Yes, Ma'am," she said. "I'll have Reggie bring Mr. Weathers' trunk down when he gets back."

Margaret shook her head. "There's no need for that. I'll take the clothes upstairs myself."

"Well, at least he can help you carry them," Abigail added. "It'll be a heavy load."

Margaret nodded. "Let me know when he gets back."

Chapter Seventeen: Frustration

Once a week Reggie walked the short distance to the Wallace's so that he could see his family. It was during these visits that Catherine managed to corner him and ask about what had been happening in the Weathers' house. Up until now, he'd had nothing to report, but Reggie could tell that Mrs. Wallace was growing impatient. She wanted information, and he didn't know why. Too frightened of her to not obey, and not trusting her in the least, he didn't know what to say. He liked Mrs. Weathers and knew what kind of trouble she would have if word got out that she was harboring an injured soldier.

People didn't always think with their heads when the English were involved. If people knew about the soldier, the aid from Mr. Weathers' business partners would probably cease, she would be cut off from society, and he wasn't sure whether or not they tarred and feathered women.

Perhaps it was only temporary and as soon as he was well enough she would send him on his way. Reggie decided to give her one-week. If the man wasn't gone by then, he would have to say something.

Reggie knew Mrs. Wallace would be mad this week as well, and she would threaten him with selling his family so at least he had a little bit of information. She wanted to know everything she could about the late Captain's younger brother. Reggie had asked Abigail and she told him quite a bit of his story. Apparently, William, Captain Weathers' brother, never accepted the fact that his brother left England and the two never spoke, or wrote, after he left.

Edward's mother kept him informed about the whereabouts of his younger brother, but the updates stopped when she died six years ago. William was in the English army, a major, when their mother died. That was all Abigail knew. Reggie only hoped that it was enough to suffice and keep his family safe for another week.

It has been two weeks since Pearson had sent Balis and Jass in search of information on William Weathers and there had been no word. There hadn't been a single message or hint that they had found anything substantial.

Standing in front of the full-length mirror he'd had brought into his field tent, Pearson attempted to dress in his uniform and was doing a dastardly job of it. His hands were shaking, his temper angry and hostile thanks to the dangerous combination of a lack of whiskey, and a letter from the uncle who had raised him.

Frustrated with the buttons of his vest, he turned from the mirror and tore it off, sending a couple of the gold fasteners to the ground searching the tent for anything he could drink, wine, port, rum, anything would work, but found nothing. After a series of defeats here and there, British rations were becoming tighter and it didn't help being out in the middle of nowhere. He just needed something to get that letter out of his head.

Pearson could still hear his uncle's voice reciting the letter to one of his aide's. He had only read it once, but that was enough for each word to be etched into his memory.

"*My Son,*" it began, so tender, so loving, such an absolute sham. "*I hope this finds you well and sober. I have not been pleased to know that still, after fifteen years in the military you have yet to obtain an office higher than that of a Colonel. The Pearson name has played an impressive role in the history of the English military for generations...until now. Our ancestors fought beside Henry V against the French invaders."*

There it was, the ever-constant reminder of Hugh's failure. His inability to compete with what people who lived before him had accomplished.

"Perhaps if you spent more time with your fellow officers by studying them, imitating their manner and bearing, learning from them, you would advance yourself to a more suitable position. I don't believe one learns much of warfare in taverns and brothels while guzzling liquor and consorting with women of ill repute."

His uncle always did enjoy stating exactly how he felt. Pearson knew what was coming next without even having to read the words.

"I realize that you have too much of your grandfather and mother in you, but you must fight their power. You must not allow the rebellious spirit to destroy the man in you." If it were only that simple, Hugh thought. *"I expect to be hearing better when I receive word again from the colonies."*

His uncle had spies everywhere. Thousands of miles away and he still knew each move his nephew took, how much he drank, and where he stayed the night. It had been fifteen-years since he had lived under his uncle's roof, but it might as well have been a day ago.

Two horses rode up to his tent and Pearson put his thoughts away in hopes that it was the news he had been waiting for. Balis and Jass entered, both with a week's growth of beard and smelling strongly of horses.

Without a greeting, Pearson walked to Balis, stuck his hand into his open jacket and took out his flask. Taking a deep breath, he opened it, and drank. "Well?" he asked when he was done.

Jass began, "We rode near a couple different prisoner camps, but no one had heard of him. We also managed to find a militia hangout, but no one said anything about taking prisoners, or leaving any English wounded behind. They were certain that everyone had been killed."

Balis spoke next. "We did find out that Weathers had a good friend who had different orders and didn't go out with him that day. His name is…" Balis reached into his coat pocket and pulled out a torn piece of paper. "Phillip Mitchell, a young sergeant. They say his family owns an estate somewhere outside of London." He laid the paper on the table. "We heard the two were pretty close. Supposedly this Sergeant is more of a secretary than a soldier. If Weathers was siding with the enemy, or just in hiding, maybe he would get word to him."

"Whose command was Weathers under?" Pearson asked.

"A General Trummel," Jass answered.

Cursing, Pearson shook his head. "I should have guessed."

"Is that a problem?" Balis inquired, scratching at his stubby beard.

Pearson shook his head. "No, not as long as I'm careful. Trummel and I went our separate ways before Boston. We had a difference of opinion on how to deal with some colonial spys. He wanted to hold them prisoner, but I dealt with them in a quicker, more effective manner, a little messier, but no extra baggage."

Pearson, much calmer now, took his jacket from where it was hanging, stood in front of his mirror again and put it on calmly. "It sounds to me like Sergeant Mitchell needs to be paid a visit." Bending down to pick up his vest from the floor, he flung it at Balis. "Have this fixed."

When William woke the second time he was starting to feel like himself again, one who had been beaten soundly, but a bit more human. He didn't know whether the medicine was dulling the pain, or he was beginning to recover, but either way, he was actually able to pay attention to his surroundings and make sense of what was going on around him.

He sat up slowly, careful not to do anything too quickly. He noticed some clothes folded on the nightstand. Slowly, he stood, curious how much weight he would be able to put on his leg. Gingerly taking a couple of steps, he found that, as long as he was careful, the pain wasn't too bad, but he couldn't go very far. He proceeded to dress as best he could. With more than a few grimaces and painful moments, he managed.

The day was growing warm and instead of a breeze, the open window brought in the sound of shrieks and laughing from outside. Making his way to the window, William looked out over the yard. He was on the second floor of what he assumed was a large farmhouse. Magnolia and willow trees shielded a lush lawn, while past that were two or three fields that were either dead or dying.

Below him in the yard he saw where the sounds were coming from. Three children were running around and playing, falling on top of each other, jumping up, running, and repeating the action. Feeling weak and useless, he watched them for a minute. It was almost impossible to believe he had once been young like that. At the moment, he felt elderly, pale and weak. A couple days in the grave would do that, he supposed. The door behind him opened and the woman he had spoken to earlier entered.

Shocked to see him standing, Margaret rushed to his side. "You shouldn't be up!" She said, coming to a stop when he turned to her. Hearing the children outside, Margaret apologized to him, closing the window to quiet the room, the intimacy they had gained while she had nursed him back to health replaced with shyness and social proprieties. "I am so sorry," she apologized. "I hope they didn't wake you?"

The soldier, who did bear a strange resemblance to Edward, shook his head. "No, I was just watching how much fun they were having. Are they yours?" The woman smiled as she watched them play. For the first time he noticed that she was wearing a black dress, a recent widow no doubt.

"Yes," she replied. "The oldest, the boy, is Matthew, he is eight. The girl with brown hair is Megan who is 5, and the youngest, at three, is Sarah." She looked back at him, his tired, blue eyes thinking about something, but she didn't ask what. "You should lie back down," she ordered, helping him back over to the bed. "I hope you're not bleeding again."

William shook his head, using her as crutch, his arm around her shoulder. "I don't believe so. Was it a bullet in my leg?" He asked, exhausted already.

Margaret nodded. "It was still in your leg when you came here. I'm just glad you were unconscious with fever when I took it out."

Feeling silly, Margaret was suddenly nervous being in the room with him, his strong English accent strangely disarming. It was one thing when he was lying in the bed unconscious, but another completely when he was standing next to her, strong, powerful, and very much an enemy soldier. For a moment she wondered if maybe she should have listened to Reggie. Her strong confidence was quickly fading.

William stared at the woman underneath his arm, helping him to bed and stopped. "You did this for me? I've been in field hospitals before and no one ever leaves in as good of shape as I am now. Thank you," he said sincerely. "You could have a career on the battlefield."

Blushing at the compliment and trying her best to ignore it, Margaret helped him into bed, checking his bandages. Satisfied, she pulled the covers over him. Her face was serious now, but William couldn't stop watching at her. "Rest," she ordered.

Margaret noticed the drawer of the nightstand was open and shut it. "Your gun is safe," she let him know, figuring that's what he was looking for. "I also saved what I could of your uniform. I know that you'll need to get back to your regiment as soon as you're well." She busied herself with straightening the curtains, making certain too much sun didn't get in.

"The nearest English troops are in Charleston, but that's a good half-a-days ride from here. One you can't make yet. I would have Reggie take you but…" she stopped, feeling awkward about how to explain. "The English came through a month and a half ago and took everything, so we don't have any horses left. The best thing is for you to sit tight until you're well enough and we can find a horse for you."

William nodded, thinking she would make a very good commander. Then, just as suddenly it hit him, the reality of war slapping him in the face. This woman had saved his life and not a few weeks earlier her home and land had been ravaged by his fellow soldiers. Now he understood the dying fields and the lack of slaves. It's a wonder the house and barn were still standing and not a pile of ash. He was in enemy territory, and she was risking everything for him.

"I am very sorry," William said sincerely. "Did your husband die in the war?" realizing only after he spoke how harsh it sounded.

 "Yes," she answered stiffly. "He was an officer with the Continentals."

175

"How long ago?" William couldn't stop the words. It had been years since he'd really spent any time with a woman. There were, of course, trysts in England, but since he'd set foot in the colonies, his life had consisted of soldiers, horses, and weapons.

Aside from his mother, women had never played an important part in his life. Perhaps that's why he was so intrigued by the woman in front of him. She wasn't the simpering debutant one would find in London, or the young royalist's daughter setting her cap on an officer. She was a real woman, with depth to her and a beauty that was more than skin-deep.

"Four weeks ago," she answered quickly. Taking a deep breath, she quickly changed the subject. "For now, we have to keep you out of sight." Reaching up on the dresser, she poured him a small spoonful of the syrupy medicine. Something mixed with opium, he assumed. "A number of neighbors would love to present an English officer to the South Carolina militia."

William nodded, worried that he had upset her, his mind still focused on the previous conversation. "I didn't mean to pry," he apologized.

Margaret smiled at him, sorrow hiding behind it. "It's perfectly fine," she said, shrugging off his apology. There was a knock at the door and she rose to answer it. The African woman, Abigail, if he remembered her name correctly, brought in a tray of food for him.

"Do you need anything else, Mrs. Margaret?" she asked. Margaret shook her head and thanked her.

Setting down the tray down for him, Margaret gave him one last look over. "I'll leave you in peace so that you can eat and rest. The laudanum will make you tired, but it will help the pain."

William stopped her, his hand taking hold of her arm. "Margaret, it is Margaret isn't it?" he asked, hoping he had heard correctly. "Would you mind staying? I feel like I've been out of touch for weeks. It's nice to have someone to talk with," he said sheepishly.

She sat back down carefully, remarking to herself how odd it was to hear him say her name. "Do you remember how you were injured?"

William frowned slightly. "We were ambushed by some of your fine militiamen. My men fought hard, but I've a feeling most died." Pausing, William tried to search back through the broken pieces of what had happened. "I remember being stabbed, and I remember killing the man, but the next thing I knew I woke up here." He stopped himself. "I suppose I shouldn't speak of such things in front of a lady."

Margaret laughed. "Don't worry, I've heard far worse. If my uncle had enough whisky in him he would tell stories that would make Cuchalain blush. One evening, by the night's end, he had taken an entire English division down outside of Dublin, beheaded the officers, and ate their hearts with his tea."

"Cuchalain?" William asked, the name was foreign to him.

Margaret explained. "An old Irish myth. Ireland's version of King Arthur and Hercules put together."

Taking a bite of muffin, William laughed gently. "My brother married an Irish girl, and I have to admit it's a good thing he waited till our father died." He shook his head, not knowing why he shared that. Perhaps it was too many years of loneliness. Maybe it was because, for some reason he didn't understand, he trusted her.

He appreciated her confident shyness and the motherly way she cared for him. "It's sad to say, but I don't think you would have wanted your uncle and my father in the same room together. Their discussions might not have ended well." Margaret smiled.

There was a soft knock on the door and Abigail entered. "Reggie's back, Mrs. Margaret."

Margaret nodded. "Thank you, Abigail. I'll be right there." Margaret stood. "Sleep," she ordered him this time. "I'll check in on you later."

William tried to sit up a little more, but couldn't quite accomplish it. "Thank you," he said, the drowsiness overcoming him again.

Chapter Eighteen: Old Trunks and Muddy Camps

Carefully, Margaret folded a few more of Edward's shirts and laid them in his trunk. This was where Edward had kept all of his important documents. There were valuable account statements from smuggling, and piles of fake manifests for his different trade routes and expeditions that he couldn't risk leaving in his study. The chest also contained letters he had written to Margaret while he was away as well as a stack of letters from his mother.

Rifling through the letters from Edward's mother, she picked up one written with expert penmanship, not unlike that of Edward's mother. An aunt had written after his mother's death to let Edward know that his younger brother had been sent to the colonies. Edward never saw that letter because it arrived after he had left. When he was home for a two-week leave, Margaret told him that she had saved it, but Edward didn't want to hear anything about it. She often wondered what had happened to William. Having never met him, she regretted that the two brothers had never reconciled.

Putting the letters aside, she picked up the bloodstained coat of the English soldier. She looked inside to see if a name had been stitched inside, but there was none. It had only just dawned on her that, foolishly, she hadn't even asked his name. She'd been too concerned about keeping him alive.

As she folded the jacket, laying it aside, a piece of paper fell out. One corner was burned and the other stained red, the handwriting on the front catching her eye. Recognizing it immediately, she quickly dismissed the idea. There was no way it could have been written by Edward. It must have gotten confused with the other things she was handling. Curious, she opened it and sat on the wood floor to read the familiar broad hand.

Margaret sat, stunned for what seemed like hours. She couldn't breathe. She couldn't think. Finally, realizing what she was holding, unable to put down the last words her husband had written, she picked up the soldier's gun that had been lying under the coat.

Knowing what she was going to find, she picked it up slowly, almost afraid to look. Her pulse quickened feeling the heavy wood and metal in her hand. Turning the gun over, from a thin ray of light coming through the small attic window, she saw the inscription carved in the handle…Col. W. Weathers.

Phillip Mitchell found himself at an encampment near King's Mountain. While the other men rested in their tents, trying to avoid the muddy paths throughout camp, Phillip attempted to cook a meal. His task was being made doubly difficult by the damp wood he was trying to light. Mud was everywhere and he had given up trying to keep clean long ago. He could taste mud in his mouth; it was caked into his hands.

Frustrated and discouraged at not being able to light the wet wood, he stood and wiped a dirty hand on his pant leg. The six eggs he had would be wasted unless he could somehow build a fire to cook them. Phillip swore that if he had to eat one more piece of dry cornbread, or jerky, he would wretch.

Looking up from his task, he watched as an officer rode into camp. Which officer it was he didn't know, and Phillip let himself hope that maybe the man brought word of William.

While William took his men out, Phillip had stayed behind to help the commanders in camp. When no one returned, scouts were sent to look for Colonel Weathers and his men, but all they found was the bloody carnage of soldiers and militiamen. Without William's body being recovered, Phillip thought that maybe the enemy held him as a prisoner, but he couldn't imagine William Weathers letting them take him alive. Since then, Phillip had been patiently waiting for word from the enemy, or for William to come walking back into camp, the latter being preferable.

Phillips had protested moving the camp, but those higher in command had told him it was a must. "There are enough British troops scattered around South Carolina. If Weathers shows up, they can point him in the right direction," General Trummel had told him. Having no choice, Phillip packed his things, and followed, hating himself for it.

The unknown officer stopped his horse, the beast's hooves sinking into the deep mud. "You're not going to have much luck building a fire with that wood, Sergeant."

Phillip eyed the man, trying to sum up his character and his purpose in a single glance, not amused at his stating the obvious.

"At this point, I'd do anything for some decent food," Phillip answered, running a hand through his grubby, reddish blond hair. The officer's gray eyes hid something that Phillip didn't like.

"Your name, Sergeant?" the officer asked.

"Phillip Mitchell," he replied, standing and reaching up to shake the man's hand.

Atop his horse the officer towered above Phillip and the friendliness of his voice didn't answer for the overbearing way he positioned himself. Phillip didn't have much respect for officers who lorded their power over others, and he had a feeling this man had mastered that practice.

"I'm looking for a good friend of mine," the officer continued, addressing Phillip, but looking elsewhere. "We were childhood friends and I heard that he was in this company. I have some news to deliver to him."

Phillip's brow furrowed. This arrogant officer was wasting his time, and his stomach was growling in annoyance. "Perhaps I can help, Sir," Phillip answered, trying to sound kinder than he felt. "Who's your friend?"

The officer smiled. "William Weathers. I believe he's a Colonel now if I'm not mistaken."

"Colonel Weathers?" Phillip asked. Making a quick decision, he paused. "He was with us, but he was killed a couple of weeks ago by some Continental militia."

The officer was silent for a moment, measuring his words. "Killed?" His gray eyes flashed at Phillip. "Are you certain?"

Phillip nodded. "We received word that his body was found only yesterday."

Anger passed over the man's chiseled face. "You're absolutely certain that it was Weathers?"

"I saw the body myself, Sir," Phillip answered nonchalantly with a shrug. "I'd be happy to deliver your message to any family he has."

"That won't be necessary," the officer muttered. "I can deliver it myself." The officer turned his horse abruptly.

Phillip watched as the horse raised his hooves out of the mud. "Would you care for an egg?" Phillip called to him. "At least then your journey won't have been worthless."

With a scowl the officer slapped his whip hard on the horse's rump. The horse kicked, throwing mud everywhere, and Phillip watched with satisfaction as the officer left. He didn't know if he'd done the right thing or not by lying about William's death, but there was just something about the man that Phillip didn't trust. One of his gut feelings, William would call it.

A soldier approached Phillip once the officer was out of sight. "Excuse me, Sergeant, but what did that officer want?" he asked cautiously.

Reaching into his pocket, he tossed one of the useless eggs onto the ground watching it sink into the mud. "Directions," Phillip lied, still trying to put together what had just happened. "Why?"

"He was a Colonel in the camp I was assigned to in Boston. Forgive me, Sir, but he was not a nice man. I just thought it strange that he would be here, thought maybe you should know, Sir."

Phillip looked confused. "Who is he?"

"His name is Hugh Pearson," the soldier said without hesitation.

Phillip frowned. "Are you sure that was him?"

The man's eyes widened. "Absolutely. Once you've been in the same company as Colonel Pearson, you never forget." He went to leave, but Phillip stopped him.

"Is General Trummel is his tent?" Phillip asked, a thought forming in his head.

"Yes, Sir," the soldier called back.

There was trouble brewing, Phillip knew it. He remembered William having said he'd been quartered with a colonel named Pearson in Boston, but all he had said concerning him was that they never really got along well. Phillip decided he had made the right choice in lying to him about William's death. William was in trouble, that much he knew, and he needed to be found. If Phillip could play his cards right, he could get a few day's leave and try to find his trail. He might not find him, but he couldn't call himself a friend if he didn't try.

As he tromped through the sticky muck to the general's tent, Phillip's mind wondered where William could have ended up. He couldn't have just disappeared. If he had been captured, they would, most probably, know it by now, especially since William was an officer. Demands would have been made, ransom asked for, something.

If he were dead, his body would have been identified and since no unidentified bodies had been found in that area, Phillip could assume that he was still alive. But if he had been wounded and tried to run for safety, where would he have gone? Phillip knew where he, himself, would run: to the nearest Continental camp to surrender and switch sides, but this was William Weathers he was thinking about. William may not enjoy the war, but would do nothing to jeopardize the British cause or his family's honor.

Phillip arrived at General Trummel's tent. Ducking his head under the white canvas, he entered. While commander's tents were normally amazingly kept and had most of the fineries of home, the mud didn't care whether you were an officer or a hired gun. The richly furnished, makeshift command tent was just as dirty as the rest of camp.

The general and three other officers were pouring over a map on a large desk murmuring to each other in conversation. The General looked up when Phillip entered. "May I help you Sergeant Mitchell?"

"Yes, Sir," Phillip said nervously. "I wanted to see about taking a short leave."

"A short leave? Are the rigors of camp life too difficult for you?" The General teased, nodding to the other officers who were picking up their orders and leaving.

Phillip chuckled slightly, "Not yet, Sir," he answered, not finding the joke nearly as amusing. "I'm more concerned about Colonel Weathers than my own selfish cowardice right now."

The General began to roll up the map. "Colonel Weathers," he said with a sigh. "Is there still no word?"

"No word, Sir. I have a feeling he might have been injured and have gone for help," he measured his words carefully. "I would like to try and find where he is."

The General paused for a moment. "Do you really think you could?"

"I have to try, Sir," Phillip said adamantly.

"Colonel Weathers was one of our best men and I hated to have lost him. I admit that a search party would be ideal, but I simply can't afford the men. With the losses we've been taking, I'm strapped."

Phillip saw an opportunity and spoke. "I know I'm not much on the battlefield, Sir, but I could go alone. All I need is a horse and some provisions."

The General studied him for a moment, obviously trying to decide if Phillip would return or run off as a deserter. "If you are not back in two week's time, I'll charge you with desertion. You will be an outlaw and hung if caught."

Phillip nodded. "I'll be back, Sir."

The General took a piece of paper from his desk and began to write. "I'm giving you permission to take a horse and a week's worth of rations. If I were you, I'd wear civilian clothes. Check farmhouses, out of the way taverns, and slave quarters. Perhaps you'll be lucky and find that a good Tory family took him in." He handed the orders to Phillip, and then added, "You may not think so, but you are a very courageous young man Mitchell, and I will tell that to your father the next time I see him."

"I appreciate that, Sir," Phillip said, taking the orders and putting them in his pocket. "But right now, I just want to make sure that William is all right." With a nod Phillip was dismissed and left to gather his supplies.

Chapter Nineteen: Ninevah

After a few days, William was able to walk more than just around the spare bedroom where he was staying. Soon, with Margaret's help, he was able to manage going up and down the stairs to join the family for meals. While the girls loved having 'the Colonel' around, Matthew was a little more skeptical of the invader. For the most part, everything was peaceful, except for the strain that was becoming more and more noticeable in Reggie, so Margaret encouraged him to visit his family twice a week instead of once, hoping that would take some of his anxiety away.

Margaret tried her hardest to keep the secret of whom William was just that. She avoided asking for his name, telling Abigail, Reggie, and the children, that it was best not to know in case anyone came looking for him. Instead, everyone just referred to him as the Colonel. Knowing his identity was not easy on Margaret, though, finding herself watching him, looking for the little things he did differently, or similarly, to Edward.

She noticed that they held their forks the same way, as if they were attacking their food. She noticed that William's hair was darker and that he preferred to part it on the left, while Edward had favored the right. She noticed his eyes had flecks of gold in them while Edward's were ringed with dark gray. She noticed that he had the same habit that Edward did of brushing hair behind his right ear whether there was any there to brush out of the way or not.

She noticed, uncomfortably, that they had the same smile, broad, and contagious. It was a smile that lit up their face when they showed it. Margaret would try her best to pretend that it was nothing, but would find herself studying him again, noticing how the skin around his eyes crinkled when he was in pain, but didn't want anyone to know, how he tried to measure his words carefully, not wanting to offend her.

The strangest thing to hear in the house was his accent. Edward had tried very hard to get rid of his English accent, only having it appear when he was angry, or thinking very hard about something. To hear the strong accent spoken continuously was odd, and a bit daunting. It didn't matter to Sarah and Megan; they loved to hear the Colonel talk and would bring him stacks of books to read to them, not caring whether they understood what the books were about or not. They would simply giggle and marvel at the different way he said words that were so familiar to them

When William was able to go further, he and Margaret would walk around the yard while the children played, usually in the evenings when there was less chance of a rare visitor stopping by. On one such warm evening Margaret was helping the children catch fireflies while Abigail furnished the Colonel, who was watching while sitting on the steps of the porch, with a jar to hold them.

Matthew, having caught his fair share, decided that it was time to rest. He sat down near the Colonel, but said nothing to him.

Sarah, cupping her hands very carefully, came to where William and Matthew sat. "Look, Mr. Colonel! I caught one, and he didn't even die."

Smiling, William helped her put the little bug in the jar. "Well, let's make sure he stays that way," he said, guiding her small hands to the mouth of the jar. Pulling herself up onto his lap, Sarah was completely comfortable.

William was constantly taken by surprise at the little girl's affection for him. It humbled him, and he didn't discourage it, admitting to himself that he didn't mind. Never in a million years would he have thought it, but he had grown quite comfortable having the three year old in his lap.

"My father was a Captain," she told him cheerfully, gently playing with the fabric of his shirt.

"Was he in the army?" William asked, watching the fireflies in the jar turn their yellow tails on and off behind the glass.

"No, he was in the calvary."

Matthew shook his head. "Sarah, you are so dumb. It's not the *calvary,* it's the *cavalry*."

Sarah frowned at her brother in the moonlight. "I know just as much as you, Matthew. He was Captain Edward Weathers with the Continental's. I bet you didn't know that." Sarah sat back against William very proud, her head held high like a mighty queen.

Standing angrily, Matthew glared at her. "Great job, dummy. Now he's going to hold us for ransom because he knows father was an officer. It's a good thing father's dead or King George might hang all of us." Matthew stormed inside.

Sarah turned to William, pushing her mussed blond curls out of her face, her eyes full of tears. "Are you going to have King George hang us?"

William could barely find the words to answer her. Shaking his head, he pulled Sarah close to calm her, breathing in the scent of the evening in her hair. "No, no," he answered. "I'm not going to let anything happen to you," he choked out.

William looked out into the yellow spotted yard, knowing he should have guessed it sooner. The Irish bride his mother talked about named Margaret, the children. He watched as Megan tripped over a branch trying to catch a fly. Matthew had been the baby his mother had so desperately wanted to see. Closing his eyes, he rocked the small child in his arms.

How could this have happened? Of all the homes in South Carolina, why had he stumbled feverish and dying into this one? The sound of Margaret's playful laugh shot like an arrow through his heart. Opening his eyes, he watched her help her oldest daughter stand. She turned to where William sat, brushed the hair from her face and smiled. In that instant he knew the answer as sure as anything he had ever known...for her.

Suddenly the words Edward had spoken in his dream made sense. "It was all in the letter," he had said. William shook his head. Edward had known, had come back to tell him.

Feeling a bit like Jonah, he knew he couldn't win. No matter what he did, which direction he took, his Nineveh would find him. He was being forced to face his brother's legacy and he might as well give into it. He couldn't fight or run anymore. He would do what he had to, what he should have done a long time ago...forgive.

Pearson fumed as he rode back to Charleston, furious at his luck. After years of being patient and waiting for the right time to take his revenge, he finds out Weathers is dead. He was mad at himself and livid with Balis and Jass for not finding out about Weathers' death before he had made a complete fool of himself trying to get information from an idiot Sergeant. At least he had made it in and out of the camp easily enough without having a run in with Trummel.

Reaching his home, he handed his horse to one of the stable boys without a word. Pulling off his gloves, he barged in the front door, ignoring his serving man running after him. He stormed into the parlor, slammed the door in the servant's face, and poured himself a very large and very stiff drink. He drained the glass in four gulps, slammed it back on the desk, and turned around.

That's when he realized what the doorman had been trying to tell him. Sitting quietly on the settee was Charlotte Wallace, dangerously appealing. She stood, her smile sultry, and her eyes dark. Coming close to him, she began to say something, but he held his hand up to stop her. He didn't want words. He wanted to forget about Weathers, revenge, and the quest to prove that he was better than them all, and she would help him do that.

William had fallen asleep on a sofa in the sitting room. Waking, he felt a cool breeze touch his face and he realized it was coming from the front door. Feeling around for his gun, but remembering he didn't have it, he stood up and cringed, putting his weight on his leg. Holding onto the back of a chair for a minute, he waited for the pain to subside before he could move. He was then able to take a few tentative steps forward.

The front door was open, the chirping of crickets and the metallic hum of locusts floating into the house. The moon was full, lighting up the landscape like a soft lantern. Walking onto the spacious porch, William cautiously looked around for anything suspicious. He checked one side, found nothing, and turned to check the other. It was then that he saw Margaret sitting on the edge of the porch in front of the white railing that ran along the edge.

William caught his breath when he saw her. Her sleeveless shift was illuminated by the blue moonlight, her hair down, falling in blond waves over her shoulders. She hadn't noticed William's approach, but kept her head lowered looking at the dark grass under her feet.

He stood and watched her for a moment, seeing exactly why his brother had fallen in love with her. One didn't have to be a genius to figure that out. The real question he had was how Edward could have left her. If she was his, William thought, he never would have left her side. He would have adored her, treated her like a queen, and no amount of political feelings would have ever come between them.

William stopped himself. What was he doing? He shouldn't be thinking like this. She was his brother's widow. He shouldn't be thinking about the vanilla smell of her skin when she was close to him. He shouldn't be thinking about how her lips curved into a smile when she was trying to be strict with the children, or the way her musical laugh carried up the stairs to his room making him smile.

"You're going to catch a chill if you sit out here too long," he said tentatively, stepping forward, forcing himself to put his other thoughts aside.

Startled, Margaret looked up.

"I'm sorry," William apologized, "I didn't mean to intrude."

Margaret shook her head. "It used to be so beautiful," she said sadly, looking longingly at the fields in the distance. "All you could see was a blanket of green fields."

"Was it all cotton?" William asked, his voiced strained, walking down the steps with difficulty.

"Mostly," she replied. "There was also an indigo field, but that's gone as well. It was a very promising farm."

"How do you do it?" he asked, sitting down next to her.

"Do what?" She looked up at him with those eyes that seemed to reach to the depths of his soul. Those eyes that he knew he would never forget.

"How do you manage to get through it all? I've seen grown men collapse because the strain and anticipation of a battle was too much for them. I've seen men run into gunfire because they could no longer handle what they've seen, but here you are. You've lost everything, your husband, your farm. And yet you act as if it's nothing you can't handle. Where do you get the strength?"

Margaret said nothing for a moment and when she answered there was a distance in her voice, a pain he had never heard before.

"Sometimes I feel the fear and anger boiling up inside of me. I'm afraid that if I make just one wrong step, or let myself go for a second, that it will all fall apart, but I know I can't let that happen," she said, shaking her head. "I know that if I do, if I let myself give in to the pain, it will destroy me, and I'll never find my way back." She stopped for a moment.

"I have to stay strong," she continued, "for my children. I have no other choice. They've already lost one parent and I refuse to let them lose another to despair. Sorrow plagued my father most of my childhood. He tried to put on a cheerful face and raise me the best he knew how, but the sadness was always there, just a breath away. It was like living with a ghost sometimes, and I don't want that for my children." She looked up at William.

"Instead, I used my anger like a shield. I use to rely on that. I would block everything and everyone out so I could stay strong. I thought I could do it on my own by relying on myself, but I couldn't. Ed.." she caught herself, knowing she wasn't ready to acknowledge who William was yet. "My *husband* taught me that if I don't find my strength in God, I don't have anything."

William watched her intently as he spoke. A tear lay on her cheek, threatening to fall. "You've known loss before," he stated.

Margaret bent her head in a nod. "I never knew my mother, and my father died when I was nineteen. Seven years ago, the uncle who brought me to the colonies died as well. My husband was the only family I had."

"Have you ever thought about returning to Ireland?" he asked carefully. "Do you have any relatives there?"

Margaret laughed sadly and shook her head. "An uncle and an aunt, but they didn't want me when I was nineteen. They're certainly not going to want me now with three young children. No, we will be fine. Perhaps I'll sell the farm and move to the city." She attempted a smile. "God will provide for us somehow. I have to remind myself of that."

William nodded and started to stand.

"I killed one of the soldiers," Margaret whispered.

Frozen where he stood, William carefully sat back down.

"When the English soldiers came, they gathered Abigail, the children, and me into the kitchen. One of them tried to force himself on Abigail, but I was not going to let them do that to her, not there, not in front of the children." She looked down at her hands. "I had grabbed a gun from the study when we realized they were English and I shot."

William stared out into the night letting her speak.

"I'm not proud of what I did," she confessed, "but I don't regret it either."

"I don't know how many men I've killed, but I'm certain most of them were good men, men who were only doing their duty for their country and friends." William spoke to her as he would if she were one of his men. "You were only defending the people you loved." He laid his hand on top of hers gently. "If you hadn't have killed him, he surely would have done much worse to you." Margaret took his hand in hers and nodded.

They sat, each of them silent, both with too much to say to speak it out loud. Finally, William stood, reluctantly letting go of Margaret's hand. "Don't stay in the cold too long," he told her quietly.

Chapter Twenty: A Broken Man

Samuel was finishing his breakfast when he heard the back door open and saw a driver bringing in some of his wife's luggage. Wiping his mouth, he stood to greet the lady of the house. Catherine came in the back door without as much as a glance towards Sam. He pushed back his seat and stopped her before she could leave the room.

"Welcome home, my dear," he said in a caustic voice full of sarcasm. "Where have you been keeping yourself the past few days?"

Catherine turned coldly towards him. "I had some business to attend to, a luncheon and a dinner with friends. I decided it would be easier to stay in Charleston instead of running the horses back and forth."

Tired of the games, and the sarcasm, Sam was ready to demand respect in his house. "Catherine, there will be no more of your gallivanting around the country," he stated. "I am your husband and I demand that you respect my decisions. It is my say where my horses go, and if I want you back before sundown you will be back. Do you understand me? I've put up with this nonsense for far too long, and it is going to end today."

Catherine was silent for just a moment before she burst out laughing. "Are you serious?" She looked at him, astounded. "What exactly are you going to do, throw me out?" she challenged. "You don't have the courage."

Samuel clinched his jaw. "Come now, dear. Do you really want to test me?" he called after her, bating her for another round.

"Who are you seeing? You certainly don't favor me with any of your charms, so who's the lucky recipient?"

Catherine turned to leave, insulted. "You're ridiculous."

"Am I?" Samuel asked, following after her as best he could. "Shall I send someone to follow you, or will you come clean now?"

Catherine laughed again. "As if you don't have any secrets of your own? Trust me; I know enough about business to realize that not all of your practices are on the up and up, especially those concerning Edward Weathers. I don't think that would be news you would appreciate having thrown about. Smuggling is a dangerous business now days," she said, her voice threatening.

Sam came forward. "You will silence yourself!"

Her eyes glared at him. "Oh, I'm not finished yet. Don't let's pretend like I'm the unfaithful one in our marriage. I know how you feel about your darling Margaret." Sam's face paled as she raged with anger. "I've seen how you look at her, following her around like a pathetic schoolboy.

"Now, Samuel," she said condescendingly. "Is it really necessary to visit so often?" Pausing, she wanted her next words to hit the mark she intended. "I'm sure you were overjoyed when Edward died. Now you'll finally get your chance with her."

Samuel boiled, his face red with anger. "How dare you speak to me this way in my own house? I have never heard such filth!"

Catherine, as mad and angry as he was, fought back. "How dare I? Because you're nothing but a broken man. You're a broken man with childish ideals who will come to a miserable end."

Incensed, Samuel raised his cane. "You will not speak again!"

"Go ahead!" Catherine yelled. "Strike me, but don't pretend that you are any better than I am." Finished, she stormed out of the room, leaving Samuel stunned.

Fuming, Sam raised his cane and brought it down on the table with a slam before limping out to the stable. Throwing aside his cane, he went about with great effort, trying to saddle a horse. Joseph, who had seen his master walk towards the stable, hurried in after him.

"Mr. Wallace you must let me do that." Joseph took the bit from the wall and flung it over his shoulder while he hurried to help Sam secure the saddle.

"I can do it myself, Joseph," Sam said, taking the bit from him and placing it in the horse's mouth. He limped to the side of the horse, but knew he wouldn't be able to mount the horse without great difficulty.

Defeated, he stopped, throwing the bit aside. "I am just a crippled man, growing older everyday," he said quietly. "I'll never ride again. I'll never be able to farm my own land, be a father, or a decent husband." Sam stood for a moment and finally, resigned to his fate, turned to leave. "Let me know when the carriage is ready."

The family was in the kitchen getting ready to have lunch. William had been able to make it down by himself to join them again and the kitchen was alive with the smell of roasted chicken and vegetables. Abigail laid a small chicken, some carrots and beans on the table while the children ran in and took their places, filling the room with noise. When everything was ready, Margaret lowered her head to pray.

She hadn't been this happy in a long time and couldn't remember the last time she actually felt like a family again at dinner, even if it was a bit fragile and strange. Glancing across the table, she watched William as he bowed his head, closing his eyes and saying a silent prayer. She couldn't help but wonder what his prayers were for.

"For what we are about to receive, may the Lord make us truly grateful." Everyone responded with an 'Amen' and Margaret made the children's plates. They were just about to begin eating when a voice called from the front parlor.

"Margaret? Abigail?" called a familiar voice.

The women froze while the children jumped up to greet the caller. Matthew was the first one out the door.

"Matthew, no!" Margaret yelled, but it was too late.

"Sam!" Matthew shouted, his voice echoing in the hall. "There's an English soldier here. You have to go or you'll be in trouble too."

"What do we do, Mrs. Margaret?" Abigail whispered. "We can't let Mr. Wallace find him." Abigail's face was concerned.

Standing, William watched the panic around him. He motioned for them to stop, but no one was paying attention.

"We'll put him in your room, Abigail," Margaret ordered. Abigail nodded.

Steadying herself, Margaret went to greet Sam, but it was too late. Samuel was walking into the kitchen, Matthew hanging onto him as Margaret was coming around the table and Abigail was dragging William away. The four just stared at each other for a moment, Samuel puzzled by what was going on. Instantly Megan and Sarah burst into tears, begging him not to kill the Colonel. Holding up his hand, Sam silenced everything but the sniffles coming from the girls.

Margaret swallowed and came forward, her eyes pleading for understanding. "He was injured, Sam. There was nothing else we could do."

William stood outside the study carefully listening to every word of Margaret and Sam's fight. He desperately wanted to do something for her, but didn't know what that would be. Abigail brought a lantern in and set it on a table, listening for a moment herself.

"Abigail, is there anything I can do to help her?" William asked, thoroughly concerned.

She shook her head, obviously nervous. "No, Mr. Colonel. This is something Mrs. Margaret and Mr. Wallace have to sort through for themselves. I think you should just let them be."

Helpless, William leaned against the wall and lowered his head.

"Margaret, what in God's name were you thinking? Bringing an English soldier into your house? Are you mad?"

After dragging her to Edward's study, Sam paced in front of the desk while Margaret stood silently against the wall, waiting for the coming storm.

"I didn't bring him into the house, Sam," she tried to explain quietly. "He came in himself. He didn't know what he was doing. He was dying, what was I supposed to do?" Margaret asked calmly.

"You should have sent Reggie to me immediately and we would have sent for the proper authorities. Do you realize you could be charged with treason for harboring an enemy soldier?"

"Sam, he was hurt," she said. "I couldn't let him die." She tried to reason with him, but he was beyond reasoning at this point.

"He deserved to, or did you forget that someone, just like him, killed Edward, and put a bullet through my leg?"

Margaret shook her head, feeling her own anger rising. "Of course I didn't forget, but I was not going to stand by and let him bleed to death in front of me, nor was I going to let him be taken prisoner to live in filth and starve to death." Margaret was just as upset as Sam was now, her voice matching his. "He deserves better than that."

Samuel came towards her. "Why? Why does he deserve better? Why does he deserve your mercy, after everything they've done to you? Tell me?"

"Because he's Edward's brother!" she screamed at him. Letting out a long sigh, glad to finally be rid of what she had been hiding. "He's his brother, Sam."

Stunned, shocked, and confused, Sam leaned against the desk.

"I found this in his coat." She pulled the letter from a pocket in her gown and handed it to him. "I looked at the pistol he had with him. There was an inscription for Colonel William Weathers."

"Are you certain, Margaret?" he asked, not convinced. "He could have taken them from the real William Weathers' body."

"Who else could he be Sam?" she asked with a sigh. "You take one look at him and you can see the resemblance."

"This is madness," Sam scowled. "It's an illusion, Margaret. You miss Edward so much you're seeing things. It's not true. It can't be." Sam moved towards her, taking her by the shoulders. "Edward is gone, and he is not coming back."

Margaret shrugged off his touch, and shook her head in disagreement. "Sam, you don't understand."

Sam's voice lowered. "We need to get you out of this house. You and the children will come stay with us for awhile...until things calm down."

Margaret pulled back, stepping away. "No, Sam," she said firmly. "You don't understand."

"I do understand," Sam shot back. "You're just not listening to reason."

Margaret stopped him, placing a hand on his chest, holding Edward's letter in front of his face. "Sam, you know this is Edward's writing." She shoved the letter at him. "You probably know more than I do. How could Edward have known where to send it?" Margaret was breathing hard. "What don't I know Sam?" she demanded.

Pushing the letter away, Sam turned, not wanting to face Margaret at the moment. Making his way slowly to the other side of the room, he finally spoke, his voice quiet. "Edward had kept an eye on his brother through his connections as an officer. He knew his brother had been transferred to South Carolina under General Trummel. He told me that if," Sam stopped and sighed, shoulders slumped, "that if anything happened to him, I should find Colonel William Weathers and ask for his help." He stared up at the ceiling. "I guess he didn't trust me to do it and sent a letter himself." Margaret placed a hand over her mouth not knowing if she wanted to scream at him, or cry over the whole situation.

Sam turned to her, time stopped as he waited for her reaction. After what seemed like an eternity, Margaret moved towards him. Quietly, she spoke, her voice more of a whisper. "We lost Edward, Sam. We owe it to him to take care of his brother."

"I just wish you weren't so stubborn," Sam sighed. He thought for a moment and then turned to her. "Keep him here," he said, resigned, his voice tired. "When he's well enough, I'll bring a horse for him. In the meantime I'll find out what I can about his regiment."

Margaret took his hand and brought it to her lips. "Thank you, Sam."

Sam held his hand to her cheek. "What wouldn't I do for you?"

The door opened and Sam limped out. Putting on his hat he left without so much as a glance in William's direction. When Margaret didn't follow, William took a cautious step into his brother's study.

"So you knew," he said, his voice pained, but relieved at the same time.

Margaret turned around, surprised to see him, her eyes glistening in the light. "You knew?" she asked, the shock of it taking her by surprise.

"The children helped me figure it out," he said sheepishly.

"They were very proud of their father," Margaret said with a nod, understanding.

William lowered his head. "So was I. I can't tell you how many times I've regretted our last words to each other. For years I have been running in whatever direction would be opposite his, because I was angry and hurt. It wasn't until I realized, by watching you, that I had only been jealous. I was jealous of his prosperity, his good fortune. I even hated the faceless woman he married, but…I could never in a million years have hated you."

Moving forward, Margaret clung to William, holding onto him tightly, hoping to somehow connect with the man she desperately missed. Suddenly aware of his nearness, she pulled back. Finding herself conscious of the maleness of him and his strength, the silence that filled the room deafening.

William was the first to recover. Still very close to Margaret, he gently brushed a piece of golden hair from her eyes, leaving tingles along her skin where he touched her. "I'll leave as soon as possible. I've caused you enough trouble already." He paused for a moment, trying to force himself away from her.

"William," Margaret said. Hearing her speak his name for the first time shocked the both of them. She whispered it again just to feel it on her tongue. "William, Edward did love you." Pausing, he gave her a half-hearted smile and made his way slowly back upstairs.

Chapter Twenty-One: A Long Night

After the day's events, the last place Sam wanted to go was home. He gave Joseph orders to take him into the city. They stopped just outside of Charles Towne at a tavern named The King's Quarters. The name had been changed to The Quarters when someone had attempted to paint over King, unfortunately it was still very visible and just seemed to emphasize the word. While Joseph fetched water for the tired team, Sam silently got out of the carriage and went inside for a drink.

The dark interior of the dingy drinking place took a moment to get used to as Sam came in from outside and the glare of the sun. Limping over to a table in the corner, he paid no attention to the looks and side glances he received from The King's Quarters usual customers. They didn't get many newcomers there, especially well-dressed ones.

A buxom, middle-aged woman came to his table and asked what he wanted, bending over the table so that the wealthy patron could see her ample bosom. Sam ordered the hardest whiskey available. The woman, seeing he wasn't interested in what she had to offer, changed her demeanor and left to get his drink.

Sam wanted to forget the entire day. He wanted to forget the fight with Catherine and the hateful words she had said. He wanted to forget the trip to the Weathers' farm and what he had seen there. But most of all, he wanted to forget Margaret.

The woman brought his drink and he gulped it down. It burned his throat and stomach, but he didn't care. Handing the glass to the woman, he ordered another. By now, most of the other customers were watching him, curious about what had brought the man there. A skinny man with long, gray hair, and a wrinkled face sat down across from Sam. The man stuck a pipe between his teeth and propped a boot up on another chair.

"You get that limp in the war, Mister?" he asked through clinched teeth. Sam nodded, but continued to look down at his glass. "What side did you fight on? We don't allow no redcoats in here."

Sam sighed and looked up at the man. "I fought for a year with the continentals in '76, but I was injured." Sam finished his second drink.

"Glad to hear it. The name's Pike." He extended a dirty hand out to Sam who quickly shook it.

Another gruff looking man with a scraggly beard brought Sam a drink and sat down next to him. "My brother died his first day out," he said, spitting some tobacco juice on the floor. "He was loadin' his musket to take his first shot when a stray bullet went straight through his head. Took half of it off. Damn shame, never even got to fire his weapon."

Sam slammed back the third drink and chuckled at the man's story. The longhaired man named Pike spoke again. "Well, you look awful low for someone who came home with only a limp. Is it money troubles?" he asked, leaning forward and taking the pipe from his mouth.

A couple other men joined them bringing a bottle of whiskey and setting it in the middle of the table.

"I bet he's got woman trouble," one of the men said.

The bearded man spoke loudly, making sure the buxom woman, lighting more candles as it grew dark, heard. "Women are no good. They don't care about anything, save themselves. When they do care about you, they're usually after your pocketbook." Sam laughed again as he poured himself another.

"I think you've hit on something, Simon," Pike said while he sat back and puffed on his pipe. "Come on, Mister. Besides talk of the war we get a little bored around here. Maybe we can help."

Sam finished his drink again and thought for a moment. He poured some more, this time most of the whiskey missed the glass.

"I am married to a cold hearted, evil woman," Sam began. Pike laughed at Sam's frankness. "I give her the best of everything and she appreciates none of it. She hates me, sees me as an invalid. We hardly speak anymore, let alone share a bed." He took a drink. "I'm at the very end of my rope. This woman is beyond tolerating."

Simon poured himself a drink. "Sounds to me like you have a problem. If you ask me, your woman has too much freedom. You need to show her that you are the man of the house. *You* are the one in charge."

Pike looked Sam over. "But that's not all is it? There's someone else you're thinkin' about."

Sam nodded. "God how she moves me. The girl could spit in my face and I would still love her. I served under her husband in the war. He was a very good friend."

"Does she love you?" Pike asked.

Sam shook his head. "No, I'm just a trusting old friend. Now there have been further…complications."

"I'll tell you," Simon said. "Leave that young one alone. It'll be nothin' but heartbreak. If things go wrong, she'll end up hating you and I don't think that's what you want." Sam shook his head. "Now, your wife is a different story. You need to get that woman under control. Take a whip to her if you have to. A man shouldn't take any guff in his own home."

Pike nodded. "Now you listen to what he says. I agree with every word."

Sam nodded and took a drink, trying to hide the tears forming in his eyes from the release of finally speaking his feelings out loud.

Somewhere in the house there was a crash. Margaret woke suddenly in the darkness, unsure whether she had really heard a noise or if she had been dreaming. Sitting up in bed, she held completely still, waiting to hear if there would be anything else. A warm breeze blew through the half-open window in Margaret's room, but everything was silent. There was another crash and she knew then that it hadn't been imagined. She thought perhaps it had been Abigail, but Abigail never left her room at night unless she was needed, and Reggie had taken to staying out in the lodges a quarter mile from the house.

Slowly she got out of bed and found the pistol she kept loaded and ready under her mattress. Opening the door, she quietly stepped into the dark hallway. The house was still and she began to doubt herself again, until she saw a soft, orange, glow moving downstairs. She tiptoed down the hallway, trying to ignore the frightened, sickening feeling in her stomach. Opening the door to the guestroom, she crept inside.

William was still in bed sleeping soundly. Moving to the bed, she knelt down beside it, touching his shoulder.

"William, William please wake up," she whispered.

William woke with a start and sat up, his head foggy from sleep. "Margaret, what's wrong?" he asked instantly on guard.

"Shhh," she motioned for him to be quiet. "There's someone downstairs."

William was awake and out of bed before she could say more. "Are you sure? It's not Abigail?"

"No, ever since the English came she keeps herself locked in her room at night," Margaret answered.

"The children?" he asked putting on a pair of pants as quickly as he could manage, ignoring the discomfort in his leg. Margaret shook her head as there was a thud from downstairs.

Margaret handed him the gun. "It's primed and loaded."

William gaped at her. She never failed to amaze him. Taking the pistol from her, he motioned for her to stop. "Stay here," he demanded.

Margaret followed after him. "I don't think so."

He turned to tell her 'no', but knew that she wouldn't listen. "Stay right behind me," he whispered. Margaret nodded and they left the room.

When they got to the staircase at the end of the hall, they could see the orange glow of a candle moving towards the kitchen. Holding onto William's arm, Margaret stayed close behind him as they made their way down the stairs. They reached the landing, the light from the candle now coming from under the crack of the kitchen door. William pulled the hammer back on the gun with a loud click.

Making their way past the study and to the entrance of the kitchen, William carefully pushed open the swinging door. Standing in the kitchen was a rather short man rummaging through the cupboard. William stepped in front of Margaret so that he was in front of her in case the man was armed.

"Turn around slowly." William's voice echoed in the kitchen as he aimed the gun.

The short man raised his hands and turned. With a strong Irish accent, he spoke. "Don't shoot, Cap'n Sir."

Margaret recognized the voice immediately. "Patrick?"

"Oh, wee Maggie," he said, grasping his chest. "Ye scairt me to death," he said, smiling at her as she stepped out from behind William.

The candle illuminated a small area of the kitchen counter, but the rest was still in darkness. William stood with the pistol aimed at the frightened, and less than sober, Irishman.

"You know him?" William asked Margaret, taking hold of her arm, not letting her get too close to the stranger yet.

"Yes. He worked here, and he's a good friend," she answered.

At that moment, Abigail came from her room, carrying a lantern that finally gave the room some brighter light. "Is everything...Mr. Patrick?"

"Abigail!" Patrick said with a wide smile. "How are ye?"

Margaret led Patrick to the table. "Abigail, would you mind making some coffee?" she asked.

Nodding, Abigail set the lantern on the counter. William, the only one still a little shaken up over the whole affair, remained standing. He let down the hammer of the pistol and stuck it in his waistband.

Patrick sat down and eyed William. "Who's this lad, Maggie?"

Margaret led William to the table. "Patrick, this is Edward's brother, William. He is staying with us for a while."

Patrick reached a hand out and shook William's a little too tightly. "Anyone of the Captain's blood, is a good man in me eyes."

"Sir," William said coldly.

"Is the Captain in the field? I saw him at Camden a'fore the battle, but when the militia lines broke things were chaotic. I tell ye, there was so much dust, I couldn'a see a thing. The second coming could a ta'en place and we wouldn't a known." He paused. "Oh, I tell ye Maggie, our Captain looked mighty fine that mornin' as he rode by on his mighty steed leadin' his men. The man would'a made General Washington embarrassed at his own appearance." Abigail set a pot of coffee on the table. "You would'a been verra proud, Maggie."

Margaret's stomach dropped, not knowing how to tell him. Patrick had adored Edward and to compound the matter, it appeared, had seen him the day he died. Reaching over the table, she took his hand. "Edward fell at Camden, Patrick," was all she could say, her mind picturing how Edward must have looked that last day, strong and brave and proud.

Patrick's mouth fell open. "Oh, Maggie, I'm sorry. I'm just so sorry. Like I said, t'was chaos that morn."

The room was quiet for a few minutes and William watched the interaction of the two old friends feeling very much like he was the intruder, feeling the cold reality of his brother's death wash over him. He knew Edward was dead, but he had never heard how it happened or where.

Margaret tried to lighten the mood. "Is your service done then, Patrick?"

He nodded, still somber from the news of Edward's death. "T'is my age, I s'pose. I was gettin' too shaky t'aim the musket. I decided t'would be best to quit whils't I had ninety-eight English dead to me name."

Margaret glanced uneasily at William. She could tell he didn't care much for Patrick's abrupt manner, and tried to catch his eye to reassure him. One look from William told her that that was going to be a harder task than she thought.

Abigail brought Patrick a drink of something stronger than coffee and the man sat back with a sigh. "Ahhh, it's good to be home."

Abigail looked at Margaret; there was just too much bad news Patrick needed to know. Margaret sighed. "Patrick, a lot has changed."

She gave William a glance, warning him that what she would say might be harsh. Nodding slightly, his eyes as stubborn as hers, he let her know that he wasn't leaving. Margaret took a deep breath and began.

"The English came through and about twenty soldiers ransacked the farm. They burned the crops. All of the workers scattered." She stopped short of telling him about killing the soldier.

William looked at the floor, saying nothing.

"T'was dark when I arrived, but I knew the fields were lookin' mighty bad. God and the Saints above, what has become of the world?" Patrick turned his attention to William.

"Now, my mind may be muddled, but I don't remember the Captain sayin' anything about a brother. Where have you been all this time, lad?"

Margaret stood, almost knocking the chair out from under her. "He's been up north," she said quickly. "I'm sure you're exhausted, Patrick. Do you want to stay in the house tonight?"

"Mercy, no. My old place is still in order. I'll gladly make me way home. I was just a wee bit famished, so I came lookin' for a bite to eat. I didna mean to wake anyone." Standing, Patrick walked forward, stumbling a bit. Margaret caught him before he fell. "I found a bit of me old sauce in the cabin, better than the day t'was made."

Margaret smiled. "You haven't changed, Patrick."

He patted her hand. "I'm sorry to see the state o'things."

"Do you need help to your cabin, Patrick?" she asked, letting go of his arm.

"I walked all the way from Richmond," He answered in a louder voice than need be. "A little more fresh air will do me good." Addressing everyone in the kitchen, he continued, "Goodnight to you all and may the good Lord keep you safe." With a nod, he shut the door behind him.

War certainly hasn't changed Mr. Patrick," Abigail said, shaking her head. "I'm going back to bed, Mrs. Margaret."

"That's fine, Abigail," Margaret said with a smile. Turning to look at William, her smile disappeared.

William stood silently, his face stern, and Margaret knew he was upset. She approached him carefully. "William?"

He glared at the door. "I don't trust him, Margaret," he said, swinging the kitchen door open with force and limping to the staircase.

Margaret followed closely behind him. "He's harmless, William. He's worked with my family for years so he's really more like an uncle to me then an employee."

William turned to her angrily. "He was drunk."

Margaret couldn't help but smile. "He's always drunk."

"Well, I don't like him," he said gruffly.

William was furious; even so, Margaret couldn't help but find it amusing. Whenever Edward was angry, he would get very quiet and pensive, finally let out a few good English swear words, slam

212

something, and that would be it. William, it seems, was the complete opposite. He brooded, pacing back and forth in the foyer. Even though he wasn't mad at Margaret, judging by his attitude, he very well could have been.

"What was he thinking, sneaking into a house in the middle of the night? I could have shot him!"

Margaret tried to calm him. "This is his home, William. He wasn't thinking…"

"Well it's obvious we need to keep my being an English officer a secret from him."

Margaret agreed with him on that point. "That would probably be a good idea for now." Taking his arm to stop his pacing, she tried to calm him. Standing in front of him, she tried to explain. "William, he's a good man. He may drink too much, but he's a good man." William was still angry and she could see it in his eyes lit by the moonlight shining through the window into the landing.

"I've seen too many men make stupid decisions when they were drunk, and it usually got someone killed," he said angrily.

Looking up at him, Margaret laid her hand on his strong shoulder. She could feel his warm skin under the light cotton of his shirt, and suddenly regretted touching him, realizing how close he was. "We can trust him, believe me."

Reaching up, William laid his hand on hers, trying to collect his thoughts. "I just want you safe." He was concerned, worried, and all too overwhelmed by her presence.

Bravely testing herself, Margaret took a small step forward, her mind only halfway on their conversation. "Patrick would never put us at risk."

William took the next step, closing the distance between them that much more. "I know he wouldn't intentionally, but I…" he stumbled upon feelings he was trying to keep hidden. Closing his eyes, he fought to find the right words. "I just don't want anything to happen to you." When his eyes opened all he saw was Margaret's charming face looking up into his.

"Nothing is going to happen." Margaret smiled. "We're in good hands with you here." She hoped, like all men, flattery would calm him.

William looked down, trying to avoid her eyes. She was too beautiful, too soft. Taking a step back, he needed to get away before he did something that he would regret. "I'll see you in the morning," he mumbled.

He climbed two steps before Margaret stopped him. "May I have my gun back?"

The words brought reality back to him, the strange feelings overwhelming him a moment ago evaporating as William took it from his waistband and handed it to her, a sly smile crossing his lips. "I'll give this back, if I can have mine. If I'm going to protect you, I'll need it."

Margaret nodded. "Tomorrow." she said softly, taking the gun from him. "Goodnight."

"Goodnight," he said.

Margaret waited in the darkness until she heard the door close upstairs. Sitting down on the bottom step, she frowned. Why had she done it? Why had she touched him? Why did she take that step forward? He had been so close, so alive, so much what she needed. She longed for lips to kiss, strong arms to hold her close, to kiss her hair, to love her. Closing her eyes, she saw William's face, felt his muscular arm under her fingers. When she opened her eyes, she stared at the moonlit floor and frowned. She couldn't think that way. She wouldn't do that to Edward.

Margaret walked through the dark to Edward's study. Moonlight filled the room coming in a window looking out into the night. She had taken great care to put the study back in order after the English had destroyed it. All of Edward's papers were back in their proper place, paintings hung, and Reggie had taken care of numerous repairs. The only things missing were the antique sword and the musket that had hung on the wall.

She sat down gently in Edward's chair and ran a hand over the top of his dark, wood desk, copying moves she had seen Edward make a thousand times. She opened the bottom right side drawer, inside were miniatures of her and each of the children from when they were little. She'd even had one made of Sarah, knowing one day she would surprise him with it. Often, when Edward would be working late at night, growing tired and frustrated, he would open that drawer, look at the portraits, and remind himself of what he was working for.

Margaret curled up in Edward's chair, picturing him working, watching him do figures and make plans as she loved to do. He would be charting his next voyage and she would come down after the children were in bed, sneak behind him, put her hand around his shoulders and do her best to distract him. Of course she always succeeded.

She wanted so badly to see him again; just to talk to him would be all she'd need, just for a couple of minutes. To hear his laugh, and listen to him joke with Sam and Patrick after dinner would be enough, just to touch him one more time. Wiping away a tear, Margaret closed her eyes, wrapping herself up in memories.

Joseph woke when one of the horses snickered and pawed the ground. Sitting up on the driver's seat of the carriage, he tried to shake off his sleepiness. It was either very late or very early, he couldn't tell which. The trees surrounding The King's Quarters were silent, but he heard laugher coming from inside the tavern a few yards away. He knew they needed to be going, but didn't know exactly what to do about it. Climbing down off of the carriage, he walked towards the tavern.

Joseph took a cautious step inside, not sure what he was going to see. All the other customers had left long ago and there wasn't even a bartender at his normal place behind the counter. A worn out clock on the counter read four-thirty. A loud burst of laughter came from the corner and Joseph looked over to the crowded table. He recognized the state Sam was in immediately.

Sam was surrounded by four very rough looking men and laughing to the point of tears after one of the men finished a raunchy joke. As Joseph approached the table he could see that three empty bottles were on the table along with one that was still half-full. The laughter stopped as Joseph approached. He tried to smile a little, but kept his head lowered as he walked around to where Sam sat.

"This boy belong to you, Mister? None of us around here are rich enough to have any slaves," one man laughed and grabbed the half-empty bottle.

Turning, Sam looked up at Joseph standing at his side. "Oh, Joseph. I suppose you've come to take me away." Sam pushed his chair back. "I guess if I must return, I must."

Standing, Sam took his first step on his bad leg and fell, catching himself on the table. Sam and the other men burst out laughing while Joseph helped him stand up again.

"Well, gentleman," Sam said, addressing them. "It's been a pleasure."

"Remember what we told you," Pike said from his seat. "You are master, take your place."

Nodding, Sam bowed clumsily to the men. He stood, leaning on Joseph to keep his balance, and made his way out to the carriage.

Chapter Twenty-Two: The Attic

The sun poured through the round window on the wall giving the attic and the old furniture a peaceful, dreamlike feeling. An old baby crib, a couple of chairs, a small table turned on its side, as well as some empty frames and quite a few dusty paintings filled the space as Margaret led William up the narrow staircase. He wanted to get his gun and was curious to see what the condition of his uniform was. After the night before, he wasn't going to go without it again. There was too much at stake in case anything happened and, without his weapon, he wouldn't be able to protect Margaret and the children.

Kneeling down in front of a good-sized trunk, Margaret motioned for William to join her. He held back a yawn, not having slept much after their unexpected visitor had arrived. Besides the fact that he was awake, listening for any more uninvited intruders, all he could see when he closed his eyes was the woman next to him. He remembered the softness of her skin. Wondered what it would be like to gently kiss her lips. Shaking off the thoughts for the thousandth time, he looked into the trunk Margaret had opened. She laid aside some clothes and he saw that, underneath, the trunk was full of papers.

"Are those letters from Edward?" William asked.

"Some of them," Margaret said, moving things around. "Most are ship manifests." Margaret looked up at William next to her. "In Edward's line of work it was very important to have alternative paperwork available," she said the last few words slowly grinning, proud of how clever Edward had been.

"So you knew he was smuggling?" William asked, surprised.

"Of course, and it worried me constantly. I was just glad when he stopped sailing the ships himself. He'd had one too many close calls, so before Megan was born he decided to let others make the dangerous runs south." She gave William a smile. "I have no doubt that his retirement disappointed quite a few English officials who would have loved to be the one to catch him."

William nodded. "Edward had a grand reputation and a long list of violations. They just couldn't find evidence enough to charge him with anything."

Margaret set aside a stack of papers. "Trust me, he was caught plenty of times, he was just clever enough to talk his way out of it," she laughed. "I think he paid as much in fines as he ever made. But, in all honesty, he did it more for sport than for profit. He enjoyed getting something past the English. It was just before he retired that he received his commission from the Continentals."

William grew more curious. "Why didn't he join the navy? I'd think he would have preferred the sea." William had always wondered why his brother decided to join the cavalry.

Margaret gave him a cautious look. "Are you sure you want to know?"

"Nothing could shock me at this point," he said smugly.

Margaret pursed her lips. "Edward always said that if he was going to fight against his fellow countrymen he would do it face to face, not behind a ship's cannon. When it became clear that all trade was going to be reduced because of the war, he lent his ships to the navy."

Nodding, William reached into the trunk and rifled through some of the manifests. There were fake papers for ships from Spain, Portugal, France, even Denmark. Margaret pulled out some more papers and paused, not sure whether to ask him a question that had always been on her mind. Finally, she took a deep breath and decided to ask him.

"Why did Edward dislike England so much? He was already a proud patriot when we met, otherwise he never would have made it past my Uncle Seamus. I just never knew what motivated him."

William sighed. "I suppose things might have been different if our family had been part of the aristocracy. My father was a military man, and even though he made a fortune in trade, we were still considered middle class. Because of that, Edward was exposed to all types of people.

"He loved to walk the shipyards and talk to sailors and craftsmen from all over the world. I remember he became friends with men from Spain, the Colonies, Scotland, even Ireland," he said giving Margaret a raised brow. "I suppose he learned first-hand the treachery that befalls the poor. He also just loved the adventure. Edward was always looking for the next voyage, never considering what it might be doing to others." A hint of anger was evident in his voice, something William couldn't hide.

"It sounds like you didn't agree with his leaving," she said carefully. "Is that why the two of you never spoke?" Margaret asked quietly, watching his reaction in the foggy light of the attic.

William was silent for a minute. "Yes," he finally answered reluctantly. "I was upset that he didn't have more loyalty towards his family. I was only seventeen when he left. Our father had just died, and our mother needed him."

"Is that why you joined the army?" Margaret asked. "Loyalty? Or did you have your own sense of adventure to fulfill?" William looked at her questioning eyes, and didn't know what to say.

Margaret grinned. "It's obvious that you're different from most English soldiers. Not only am I the wife of a Continental officer, but I'm also an Irishwoman. From most Redcoats those offences would have gotten me raped and thrown from my house, whether we were family or not," she added, her blunt honesty direct and to the point.

"You haven't met many decent soldiers if you ask me," William said, trying to change the conversation.

"That's my point," she prodded, not letting him side-step the question. "You treat me, Abigail, Reggie and the children with the same respect I imagine you have for your men. You can't tell me that that's not rare," she said. "I think you share more of your brother's beliefs than you realize."

William was silent. He thought of Timothy, who had been killed for simply standing up to Pearson. He thought of Ginny Welch, who had been used and thrown away. He thought of the many orders he had followed against his better judgment. She was right, and he knew it.

It wasn't his beliefs that made him a soldier. It had been expected, and he followed, trying to prove that he could be loyal, even if his brother couldn't. He wondered how different his life would have been if he hadn't joined the army. Would he have a wife, children, a house in London, or a small country estate? Would he be happy, or bored with his life?

Reaching down, he took hold of a letter. "What are these? Some sort of secret correspondence?" he asked, teasing.

Margaret gave him a couple more. "No, they're from your mother. She wrote all the time. Edward was very upset when your aunt wrote that she had passed away." She sat back on her heels. "I think that was the only time he ever regretted leaving England. He wished he could have been there."

"So do I," William answered somberly, remembering the delusions of his dying mother. He laid the letters down, not wanting to see them.

Margaret finally found the bottom of the trunk and pulled out William's red uniform jacket. "I hid your things up here so that they wouldn't be found easily in case anyone came looking." She handed the folded jacket to William. "I cleaned it as best as I could, but there was so much blood I couldn't get it all out."

William had no words when he unfolded the jacket and saw what remained. Dark red bloodstains covered one side. He ran a hand over the jagged slit where the militiaman's knife had stabbed him and folded it again, laying it aside, the jigsaw memories of that day too disconcerting. Margaret handed him his sash and boots. The sash was covered in blood as well, his boots only in a little better shape.

"This boot had been soaked in blood," she said softly, motioning to the left, remembering all too clearly the night he had stumbled into their lives. Too easily, she could still see the fever in his eyes, the pain he had been in. Quickly putting the thoughts aside, she thanked God that he was alive. "Other than that, though, there's no real damage," Margaret said.

"I think these are beyond repair," he said, amazed at the amount of blood he had lost.

Margaret sat back. "It truly is a miracle you survived."

Feeling William watching her, she turned her attention to the object in her lap. William followed her gaze and saw his gun, stirred by the way she cradled it gently and ran her finger over his name carved in the handle. Desires he had been desperately trying to keep at bay flooded his senses. He turned his head so he wouldn't see her and make the temptation worse.

He had thought it through too many times during his restless nights. Under normal circumstances, he would have made advances to Margaret long ago; nothing would have been able to hold him back. She was only a few years younger, extremely beautiful, kind, and spirited. Unfortunately, nothing would ever change the fact that she was Edward's wife. Not to mention that she was still in mourning which made him all the more ashamed for what was he thinking.

"William?" Margaret's voice brought him back to the attic where she sat too close to him. "Are you all right?"

Her dark eyes, warm and concerned, looked up at him. Leaning closer, she laid a gentle hand on his cheek. "You're pale as a sheet, are you feeling well?"

William couldn't stand it any longer. He could smell the sweet rose scent she wore, feel her warm breath on his cheek, her lips red and tempting. Reaching out, he gently touched a lock of her long hair. He could hear nothing but the frantic beating of his heart, the air so dense and heavy that it seemed thick.

Reading his mind, Margaret leaned forward and kissed him, her lips soft and warm. Holding her head with one hand, he pulled her closer with the other. He kissed her carefully at first and then with more passion, both resigning themselves to the feelings they had been trying to ignore. They parted slowly, but William still held onto her, not wanting to let her go. His skin was burning where she had touched him. Their breath mingled together only inches apart. William went to kiss her again when the attic door swung open.

"Mrs. Margaret? Are you up here?"

At the sound of Reggie's voice, William leapt to his feet. Margaret, kneeling on the floor, put a hand to her mouth, still able to feel his lips there. Coming into the attic, Reggie immediately sensed the awkwardness of the situation. His gaze shifted from William, trying to stand nonchalantly in the corner, to Margaret on the floor, apparently upset about something.

"Abigail said I should come see if you needed any help," he said quickly, trying to give the reason for his intrusion.

Margaret stood. "Thank you, Reggie, but that won't be necessary."

Standing, she took a step forward, the blood rushing to her head, all of the emotions running through her body finally catching up with her. Everything started to go black, and Margaret caught herself on a dresser. William rushed to her side.

"I'm fine," she said in a whisper. "I'm fine." She turned her back on the two men. "I'll be down in a minute." Reggie left quickly, anxious to get away from the uncomfortable situation he had innocently stepped into.

Coming up behind her, William put a tentative hand on her shoulder. "Margaret," he began.

"I'll be down shortly," she said so softly he could barely hear.

Feeling distraught and foolish about what had happened, William left, still desperate to hold her again.

Chapter Twenty-Three: Discovery

Frederick Capshaw had left Charleston in the early hours of the morning. Suited up in his best breeches, stockings, shirt and vest, he opted to forego the coat, knowing he would be riding back in the midday heat. Putting on his best tri-corn, he went to his father's stables. Once there, he selected the fastest horse, a sixteen-hand brown gelding, perfect for the ride. He made certain he had the letter and began the fifteen-mile journey to the Wallace plantation.

His father had made it clear to him that his task was of the utmost importance. Under normal circumstances, his father would have sent one of his clerks or apprentices, but since most of the young men who regularly worked were at war, that left Mr. Capshaw with only one person to make this most important of deliveries…his own fifteen year old son. Frederick took his job very seriously and had listened carefully as his father gave him instructions. Mr. Capshaw had brought him into his office and spoke to him over his gold-rimmed spectacles and a large pile of papers.

"You are to take a letter directly to Mr. Samuel Wallace. There will be no meandering or lollygagging. Do you understand?" Frederick nodded. "This information is confidential." He gave his son a stern look. "Do you think you can manage this, Son?" Frederick nodded again, not really sure he could, but certainly willing to try.

"Get there quickly and deliver the note. You can pick it up at the office." With that, Frederick was dismissed.

He picked up the letter from the skinny, pale-faced clerk named Thomas as ordered. Now he was on his way, doing his first considerable assignment that, he hoped, he would be well compensated for.

The morning grew hot quickly as Frederick made his way through the countryside. Thick trees that lined the road, forcing him to shed his vest, then roll up his sleeves. A large buck ran across the path in front of him, his fingers itching for the musket he had brought with him in hopes of hunting a bit on his return trip.

He stopped twice to let his horse rest and get some water. He needed the break as well in order to relieve himself and make sure he was headed in the right direction. Around noon he reached the Wallace plantation, astonished at the size of it, green fields stretching as far as he could see. He saw the great house in the distance and stopped to put himself back in order, retying hair back and smoothing the fly away hairs into place. Buttoning his vest, he fitted his hat neatly on top of his head, and rode forward.

Approaching the house, he rang the bell and was led into a parlor. While he waited, he helped himself to some pastries a young slave, not much older than himself brought in and laid on the table. The walls were lined with paintings, and mirrors, rich wood trim painted in light peach ran the length of the room. He walked around the room enjoying the pastries and a cup of rich coffee. At home their coffee was always watered down so it would last longer. Finally, after an hour, the door opened.

Catherine woke with a new sense of power. After her confrontation with Sam the day before, she felt that now she had the upper hand. It was around noon and she was planning her next trip to Charleston, waiting for her breakfast to be brought to her room. Colonel Pearson wouldn't be back for a couple of weeks and she planned to be there when he arrived.

A young girl entered and placed Catherine's breakfast on a table by the bed. Walking over to the window overlooking the front of the house and the tree-lined road leading to the stables in the back, she recognized Sam's carriage coming up the rode.

"Where has Mr. Wallace been so early this morning?" she asked the girl curiously.

"Mr. Wallace is returning, Ma'am. He's been out since yesterday afternoon on a business matter," the girl answered, setting out coffee and cream, and quickly leaving.

Catherine nodded to herself. Of course, she thought, a business matter. Adding more sugar than normal just for good measure to her coffee cup, she filled it to the brim. She went to take a sip, but was interrupted by a knock at the door.

"Mrs. Wallace?" one of the young, male house slaves peeked inside. "There's a messenger to see Mr. Wallace, but he said he didn't want to be disturbed. Should I tell him to come back later?"

Catherine glared at him. "Show him to the parlor," she said peevishly. "I'll be there shortly."

Catherine almost laughed when she saw the boy. She assumed Sam would be smarter than to do business with someone who would use a child for deliveries of business documents. Giving the boy an amused, but determined look, she could not believe that she'd gotten herself dressed and made up just for this.

"I hear you have something for my husband," she said with a smile.

Frederick grew uncomfortable, not anticipating on having to deal with anyone other than Mr. Wallace. "Um, yes, ma'am. I was sent to hand it to Mr. Wallace himself. Is he available?" His voice trailed off at the end nervously.

Catherine watched the boy fidget, straighten his vest, than clumsily reach for his tri-corn hat, taking it off to appear more proper. "My husband has just returned from a business trip and is exhausted," she answered. "He left specific instructions that he was not to be disturbed. You can either hand the letter to me, or wait until he wakes which will be I don't know when." Catherine was growing impatient.

Frederick didn't know what to do. He knew he had to give the letter to Mr. Wallace, but he also thought about the musket he had attached to his saddle and the hunting he wanted to do. He didn't want to miss that, and if he stayed too long he wouldn't have enough time.

Catherine could tell the young man was trying to make a decision and decided to help him out. "Young man, do you honestly think that I know nothing about my husband's affairs?" She was using her most commanding voice, hoping it worked. "I can assure you that I will hand it to him as soon as he stirs."

Squirming uneasily, Frederick reached into his pocket. Worry showed on his face as he tried to make a decision. Catherine tried a different approach. Using her most motherly voice, she held out her hand. "You can trust me. My husband and I are very close."

No sooner had the young courier left, before Catherine broke the seal on the note and read.

"Mr. Wallace,

You wrote inquiring about the balance in the joint account under the names of you and Captain Weathers. As it stands, from your last deposit, there is a balance of £70,000. I inquired with our sister bank in Richmond and the amount you would be able to withdraw in cash would be 30,000 up front with an additional 10,000 available every week until the account is dissolved.

I can assure you that the money is safe, even given the current English occupation of Charleston. The account is invested in neutral funds that neither side would be able to seize without proper grounds.

Don't hesitate to let me know if there is any way my staff or I may be of service. We all send our deepest sympathies over the death of Captain Weathers.

Respectfully yours,

Theodore Capshaw

Catherine's knees buckled underneath her and she found herself groping for a chair. "£Seventy-thousand?" she whispered. "Where on earth would he get that kind of…the ships!" Suddenly, she realized why her husband had taken such an interest in shipping over the past years. "I knew they weren't just shipping goods to England under the table." Smiling, she folded the letter and hid it in her bodice, knowing now that she had Sam Wallace right where she wanted him.

Reggie found himself running to the Wallace plantation, wanting to get it over with. He had seen enough and he wanted out. If need be he would beg, plead, whatever he needed to do in order to go home. Now that Mr. Wallace knew about the Englishman, there would be no further reason for him to remain there. He only hoped Mrs. Wallace felt the same way.

Reggie reached the little wood hut his wife and two boys occupied with a smile on his face. On a day like this, they were the only things he looked forward to seeing, figuring he could get in a few minutes with the boys before he had to meet Mrs. Wallace.

Stopping outside, he washed his hot face in the little well that was in between two of the slave houses. Cool and refreshed, he stepped up to the door.

His wife greeted him with a hug. She was skinnier than he remembered, perhaps from worry. Her face was thin and it wasn't joy he saw in her eyes, but anxiety. Not the kind of homecoming he had hoped for. Saying nothing, she let him in the house. Ducking as he always did when he entered, he let his eyes adjust to the dark room, a bit of light coming in through the still open door.

"Where are the boys?" he asked, turning to his wife's dark silhouette in doorway.

The voice that answered wasn't hers, but came from behind him. Turning, he recognized the woman who stood there. "I sent them to help Cecil mend one of the fences near the barn," Catherine said. "Your wife and I were having a chat. We were just discussing the boys' future."

Reggie glanced over at his wife standing meekly in the doorway. It was then he saw the fear in her eyes. She was trembling slightly and he knew she was on the verge of breaking. He knew that now was as good a time as any.

"Mrs. Wallace," he began. "I'm ready to come home. I'm not really needed there. I'm simply in the way. Please, I beg of you. Let me be done with this," Reggie implored.

Catherine thought for a moment as she listened to Reggie pleading his case in front of her. She took a deep, unconcerned breath. "I think that would be a possibility on one condition. I want to know the extent of my husband's relationship with Mrs. Weathers."

Reggie looked confused. "Mr. Wallace? Why he's been over only a couple times since I've been there, I don't know, ma'am."

Catherine rolled her eyes, crossing her arms in front of her. "Come now, I know what's been going on."

Reggie was dumbfounded. "I don't understand, Mrs. Wallace. After Mr. Wallace found out about the Colonel, he and Mrs. Weathers had an awful fight and he left."

Now it was Catherine's turn to be confused. "Colonel? What Colonel?"

Immediately, Reggie realized his mistake. Mr. Wallace hadn't told her about the soldier and, knowing his master's wife, probably for good reason, but it was too late now. "Mrs. Weathers has been nursing a soldier back to health," Reggie began.

"Well, she is just the picture of patriotism isn't she?" Catherine said slowly, feeling the power slipping from her fingers once more.

"That's right ma'am. She is." He regretted the words the moment they came out of his lips.

Catherine watched Reggie carefully. He lowered his head, pretending the conversation was finished, but she knew that wasn't the whole story. "Reggie," Catherine began, talking to him as if he were a child, walking towards him. He was hiding something, and she would find out what it was. "Do you realize that I have the power to take all of this away from you? You would never see your children again. I would work you in the fields until you drop. Do you understand that?"

Reggie didn't look at her, but whispered. "Yes, Ma'am, I do."

"Good, so now that we have that clear, I'm going to ask you again. What Colonel?"

Reggie glanced over at his wife. Her face was ashen. "For God's sake Reggie, think of the boys," she pleaded

Taking a deep breath, Reggie was barely able to find his voice, he spoke. "The soldier is an English officer. That's why Mr. Wallace was so upset."

Catherine nearly dropped to the ground when she heard those words. The woman whose husband had been a well-known Captain, and as she now knew, smuggler, who would do anything to destroy the English, was harboring one in her home. She felt the tide turning once again. Looking straight at Reggie, her eyes dangerous, she ordered. "What else do I need to know?"

Sam woke around four o'clock, tired from making quiet inquiries into the whereabouts of William's regiment all night at various taverns in the regions. After resting for a bit, he ate a hearty meal and asked for his wife to be brought to him. Catherine was let into Sam's rooms by a male servant. Sam, who was finishing his dinner and reading a paper did not stand to greet her.

"Have a seat, Catherine," he said coldly.

Catherine did as she was told. "So, is this your secret little hiding place?" she asked.

Sam put his paper down. "No dear, these are just my rooms. But I wouldn't expect you to recognize them. I had them remodeled a couple years ago." He took a sip of coffee. "That's why I had Thomas bring you. I was afraid you wouldn't remember how to get here."

Catherine smiled, fully aware of the sarcasm in his voice. "If that was supposed to be an insult, Sam, it was a very poor one."

"No matter," Sam said, looking at her. "There's a dinner tonight at General Lambert's. You'll need to be dressed and ready to leave at seven."

"And what makes you think that I'll be attending this…dinner?" Catherine asked cynically.

Standing, Sam went to the mirror to pick out a vest and coat from those his valet had laid out for him. "Because you have no choice, that's why," Sam replied.

Catherine stood. "I have no choice?" she repeated, certain she hadn't understood him.

Sam nodded coolly. "Well, I suppose you could refuse and end up penniless, but I seriously doubt you'll do that."

Catherine nodded in understanding. "Oh, I see. This is the new way you plan on dealing with your miscreant wife. I'm impressed, you thought of this all by yourself?"

Sam turned to her. "This is all your doing, Catherine. You've forced me to take this course of action."

Catherine frowned. "I will not be attending, Sam," she informed him matter of factly.

Sam limped towards her. She had never seen him so determined. For a moment he actually frightened her. "Then I expect you to be out by the end of the week. It's time you start showing your loyalty to America and its citizens, or you will be out on the street. I promise you."

Catherine realized suddenly that he was actually serious. "You're going to regret doing this to me, Sam."

"So what's you answer?" he asked curtly.

Catherine glared at him, disgusted. "I'll be ready at seven." She began to leave, turning back with a smile before she reached the door. "But mark my words, Sam. It's you who has forced my hand."

Chapter Twenty-Four: Either...Or

Sam and Catherine rode silently to the dinner at the Lambert's. General Lambert, retired from the military, was still an important leader in the colonies, and promised to be more so once the country began to take formation after the war.

Without a word to each other, Catherine and Sam exited the carriage and were introduced to the others in attendance. Catherine smiled politely as she shook hands with a Continental Lieutenant, a Captain, their wives, and of course General Lambert himself. All of the men, except Sam, were dressed in their uniforms.

While the men had drinks and talked of the latest defeats and victories, Catherine made polite conversation with the women, discussing the latest fashions, praising the ways in which the officer's wives had found to help the war effort, creating societies of other women who came together to do jobs such as mending uniforms or making meals for the soldiers to carry with them.

Dinner was finally served and they sat down to a magnificently prepared meal. Catherine was seated next to Lieutenant Leix's wife and Captain Dobson, across from Sam who was between Mrs. Dobson and Lieutenant Leix. General Lambert and his wife were seated on each end. After the mindless chitchat with dessert, talk turned to what the new country of America might look like.

"It must be terribly difficult to build a country," Catherine said, venturing to look her best to the other guests. "It would be easier if we were the first settlers here, but since we're not I imagine it makes the job to form a new nation just that much more difficult."

"What do you mean, Mrs. Wallace?" General Lambert asked, setting aside his dessert.

"Well, English law has governed the colonies for over a hundred years. How will you reconcile English laws with the new government? For instance," she explained, "if there was a large sum of money gained by illegal means, say smuggling for instance. Now, under English law, it's a crime to trade with certain countries. What would become of the company's profits if the government were to discover them?" Catherine smiled across the table at Sam, who gawked at her, red faced. She had struck him and he knew it.

"I see your point," the general said as all eyes but Sam's, who had found his dessert extremely interesting, turned to look at him for an answer. "I suppose any illegal profits would have to be frozen until the government could decide how best to use them."

"I certainly don't envy the congress," Captain Dobson said, finishing his cobbler.

Catherine spoke again. "And what about crimes that are new to the country, such as harboring enemy soldiers?" Catherine looked directly at Sam as she spoke, striking home with each word. "How would you carry out punishment for a crime you've never had to deal with before?" Sam grew paler by the minute.

"Now that is something that must be dealt with, and severely." The general gave it a moment's thought.

Lieutenant Leix grew curious. "What would that punishment entail, General?"

General Lambert sat back in his seat. "I imagine seizure of lands, prison time, possibly death. I consider harboring the enemy a very serious form of treason."

Smiling, Catherine watched Sam grow more and more anxious, pulling out a handkerchief and nervously wiping his brow.

"This discussion is far too depressing," Mrs. Lambert interrupted. "Ladies, would you like to join me in the salon while the gentlemen finish their boring conversation?" Mrs. Lambert stood, encouraging the other wives to join her.

Catherine stood proudly, but Sam stopped her from behind, taking her gently by the arm. "Catherine, my dear, would you mind having a word with me outside?"

"Why certainly, Samuel," she said with a loving smile, giving a gracious nod to the other guests. "We'll just be a moment, and I will join you, ladies."

Sam continued to hold her arm, squeezing hard, leading her onto the terrace off of the garden. Once outside he flung her a few feet ahead of him.

"What exactly do you think you are doing?" he said furiously.

"I am simply looking out for my interests," she replied coldly, smoothing her skirt after being thrown about.

Sam came towards her, enraged. He was visibly sweating which made Catherine all the more delighted. "How did you find out? Who told you?" Sam demanded.

Catherine stood up tall. "A lot happened today while you were out. You really should do business with a different bank."

"And the soldier?" he asked, quietly seething.

Catherine smiled again. "I have my sources."

"Reggie," Sam said aloud, realization hitting him. "You weren't being kind sending him to the Weathers'. You were spying on me!" Her ruthlessness amazed him.

"Not on you, my dear, on your Margaret. You were simply an added bonus." Catherine gave him a smug smile.

"You are the most malicious woman I have ever known," Sam said, taking a step back.

"No matter," she said, brushing off the insult, mimicking him, "but I think you will want to listen to my demands," Catherine said, her tone changing. "You will hand over the seventy-thousand pounds to me and divorce me quietly."

"And if I don't?" Sam asked, knowing what the answer would be.

"If not, then I march back in there and tell everyone what your precious Margaret has been up to. Imagine how it would look to have a well-respected Captain's wife on trial for treason. The public would be out for blood."

"That money is not all mine," Sam tried to explain, knowing it was useless. "The vast majority belongs to Edward and should go to Margaret and the children."

"I don't care, Sam. The money goes to me or you'll find yourself guilty of her disgrace."

"Will you give me time to think about it at least?" he reasoned.

Looking up, Catherine sighed, feigning annoyance, thoroughly enjoying herself. "I'm not that heartless, Sam."

"How long do I have?" he asked, resigned.

"Twenty-four hours," she said lightly and waltzed back into the salon.

Chapter Twenty-Five: The Effects of Irish whiskey

William desperately needed out of the house. He was tired of feeling trapped and needed to get away from Margaret so he could sort things out. Unable to face her when she finally came down from the attic, he'd spent the day walking the farm. Partly he wanted to see how long his leg could hold out; knowing the time was coming when he would have to leave. He wanted to know if he would be capable of walking the ten miles into Charleston if a horse wasn't available. Still cautious, he had made sure to bring his gun.

Wandering through the fields, not caring whether he might be spotted or not, he found a field that, at one time, had been full of cotton plants. Now, though, it crunched underneath his feet and half of the ground was charred and black, more evidence of the English. Kicking the ground with his foot, he winced. When he finished muttering a few choice words, something caught his eye, almost glowing with the sunlight reflecting off of it. Bending down to pick it up, he realized that it was the silver button from a uniform jacket. He recognized the English insignia, another reminder of what they had done.

He continued to survey the land and came upon three buildings made of wood boards and clay. They were small but quaint and looked quite comfortable. Peeking inside, he saw that cots lined the walls, and that the one room buildings with wood floors were very comfortable looking. Those Edward hired must have been well treated, he thought.

Walking around behind the lodges, he slowed a bit, the dull ache in his leg becoming harder to ignore. It was getting on towards early evening. William thought about turning around and going back, knowing he would have to face her sometime. If he didn't return soon Margaret might begin to worry. On the other hand, she might be relieved. He turned to go when nearby singing caught his ear.

"O woman full of wile, keep from me thy hand, I am not a man of the flesh, tho' thou be sick for my love."

It wasn't quite an Irish tenor, but it was fair enough and pleasant to listen to. The voice was coming from a cottage on the other side of the cabins. Patrick's place, he assumed.

The Irishman's voice grew louder as he began the second verse. "See how my hair is gray! See how my body is powerless! See how my blood hath ebbed! For what is thy desire?"

Pausing for a moment, William decided to pay a visit to the old drunk. He could at least give a man Margaret held in such high favor a second chance. When he reached the door, Patrick was finishing the song with drama and great flare.

"Every deed but the deed of the flesh, and to lie in thy bed of sleep, would I do for thy love. O woman full of wile!" Patrick held out the last note till he ran out of breath and William tentatively knocked on the door.

Finishing his solo, Patrick welcomed the visitor. "Ah, Mr. Weathers. T'is a fine evenin' for a stroll. Would ye care for a drink?" His face was red and his words slurred, but William entered anyway.

Patrick was surrounded by different sized bottles all ranging in color from pale beige to dark auburn. Stumbling towards one half-full bottle of an amber colored liquid, he held it in front of the lantern on the table. William hoped to God that the Irishman wouldn't knock over the lantern or the whole place would go up in flames.

Patrick smiled as he poured two glasses. "This is a fine bottle, Mr. Weathers. William is it?" he asked admiring the way the amber liquid was illuminated by the light. "Have a seat." He motioned to a chair.

Curious, William sat, somewhat amused at the character in front of him. Unlike Edward, who was used to the Irish drinking and storytelling, William felt that he was in some strange sort of magical place. It was no longer a humid Southern colony, but it wasn't the green island of the North either. For a moment he thought maybe he was trapped in some sort of middle world. More likely, it was the fumes from the strong alcohol that filled the room and was quickly going to his head.

"This here," Patrick said, holding up his glass, "is from 1774, the first year I worked for your brother." He raised his glass to a toast and William tentatively followed. "May he rest in peace."

Patrick and William both drank. Patrick's was down in an instant, but William almost choked, the strong liquor burning his throat. Patrick laughed and went in search of another bottle. "I think ye' need a newer year, lad, perhaps we should try this one."

He poured William another glass. Taking a tentative sip, William set it down, giving Patrick a smile as if it was really good. Patrick was too deep in his cups to notice.

"So, what brings you out tonight, lad?" Patrick asked, his eyes glazed.

"Testing my leg," William answered, swirling around the liquid in the glass, but not wanting to drink it. He'd seen too many under the effect of the stuff and refused to put himself in the same predicament. "I'll have to be going soon."

Winking, Partrick began a recitation. "There is a blue eye which will look back at Ireland; never more shall it see the men of Ireland nor her women," he sang with a wink.

William chuckled uncomfortably. "I'll have to remember that one. Her women, is it?"

"A beauty stainless, a pearl of a maiden, has plunged me in trouble and wounded my heart," Patrick sang quietly.

William frowned. "Is it that obvious?"

Patrick stuck out his bottom lip. "I haven't seen a man so smitten since you're brother took to followin' her 'round the harbor." He lowered his voice and winked. "I could tell by the way you protected her last night. It was like watchin' a mother wolf defendin' her cubs."

William shook his head. "Well, it's over now. I've ruined any chance I had." He slammed the glass on the table, the contents spilling out. Patrick laughed, beginning a new song.

"I am a wand'ring minstrel man, and Love my only theme: I've strayed beside the pleasant Bann, and eke the Shannon's stream; I've piped and played to wife and maid by Baarow, Suir, and Nore, but never met a maiden yet like…Margaret Lara O'Connor Weathers."

He finished with a laugh, proud of his ending. "I've known Maggie a long while, and I tell ye' she doesna give her heart to anyone. But once ye have it, she'll never let ye go." William nodded, staring at the table.

How could he even consider the possibility of being with her, of loving her? But that was all he wanted. If asked, he would give anything to have her. There was nothing more he wanted than for her to love him, to wake next to her in the morning. She had taken care of him, and he wanted the chance to take care of her. He wanted to show her how well he could do that.

Deciding it was time to lighten the mood, Patrick leaned back and raised his glass. "William, lad, do you know why God invented whiskey?" William shook his head. Patrick smiled, anxious to deliver the punch line. "So the Irish wouldn't take over the world!"

William laughed, but it was only half-hearted. He wasn't quite as ready to let their past conversation go yet. "Did you know Margaret when she was a child?"

Patrick shook his head. "No, I met her when she was just a bonny lass. Fresh off the boat she was, and mighty overwhelmed by the new world. How long have you been in the colonies, lad?" Patrick asked.

"Since '74." William replied.

"Aye, well, I'm sure you're aware o' the state of things in Ireland." William nodded. "Things were especially bad for the O'Connor family. There were three brothers and a sister; Sean, Agnes, Seamus, and Michael. Sean, being the oldest when Mrs. O'Connor died two years after her husband, he took charge o' the family.

"As the others grew older, they found their own way in the world. Sean traveled north to find work, and Agnes married a Galway man. Seamus, the man I worked for was busy savin' money for his trip across the ocean, but checked in on his brother quite often. The youngest, Michael, left to his own devices, happened to fall in love with an English lady who just so happened to be the daughter of a Laird. The two of them began courtin' and had plans to elope until her older brothers found out about their affair. Seamus had been very fond of the lady, even offering to take the couple to the colonies with him, but they both refused on the grounds that they couldn't leave their homeland.

"Ye' see the woman had been widowed and was left with a three year old boy. No doubt she was lonely and by the time her family found out about her affair with Michael, she was already with child again. The brother's didna let that stop' em though. Late one night they burned the O'Connor cottage. Michael barely escaped, but he rode after 'em for a ways until he lost their trail." Patrick took another gulp and continued.

"Well, Michael took to livin' under whatever rock he could and tried desperately to see his lover, but her family would have none of it. Late one night one of ladies' brothers found Michael and handed him a bundle of blankets. It was the babe. Her mother had died durin' the birth.

"Michael took the tiny baby girl and started his life over in another village. He built a home and loved the little girl more than anything, naming her Margaret, after his own mother and Lara for hers." Patrick stopped, saddened by the story.

William was silent. "What ever happened to the older child?"

Patrick tried to remember. "The oldest brother took him back to England. He was a lawyer in London, and wanted to give *that* child the best in life."

A nervous knot formed in William's stomach and for some reason he couldn't explain could barely form the words to his next question. "What was the family's name? Do you remember?" he asked in a whisper.

Patrick, forgetting his glass and drinking straight from a bottle, nodded. "That's a name that I'll never forget. Whenever Seamus was angry he would curse the name enough to make the angel's blush. Of course he never mentioned it in Margaret's company. The poor child doesn't know a thing about it."

"What was the name?" William asked again, this time hoping with everything he had that his sense of foreboding was wrong. Taking the glass in his hand, he hoped the action would steady it.

Patrick leaned forward as if someone else might be listening. "Pearson." He said, crossing himself. "The family's name was Pearson."

William's glass fell to the floor with a crash. Amused, Patrick didn't notice how pale William had grown. "Are the spirits too much for ye, lad?" he sat back laughing.

William stood, shaking. "I better be going or I am afraid Margaret will think I left."

Patrick stood. Steadying himself, he walked William to the door. "I'm glad we had this time to chat," Patrick said, holding out his hand. "I hope you don't decide to leave too soon. You could do a lot of good around here." William tried to smile and shook Patrick's hand, needing to leave, but trying to keep some semblance of decency.

The earth spun around William as he stepped out into the night air. It was hot and muggy, but was refreshing compared to the heat of Patrick's cottage. He managed to walk about twenty feet when he had to stop and get sick, unsure whether it was from the overwhelming smell of whiskey, or the story he'd heard.

Recovering, he continued towards the house in absolute shock after what he had learned. How could Hugh Pearson possibly be Margaret's brother? Half-brother, he reminded himself. Why had no one ever told her? Perhaps, given what kind of people the Pearson's were, it was best for her not to know of their existence. He wouldn't want Pearson within five hundred feet of Margaret or the children.

William could see the house in the distance, but something stopped him. In the moonlight, he could make out a carriage sitting in the drive. Figuring it had to be close to ten, and too late for social visits, he picked up his pace and ran towards the house.

Margaret quietly laid the book on the girls' dresser and stood, careful not to make much noise. The girls were finally asleep after an hour of stories, half that time spent convincing them that she could read them just as well as the Colonel. Putting the covers back on Megan, she carefully took Sarah's thumb from her mouth. When she checked on Matthew, he woke as she bent over to kiss him.

"Goodnight, Mother," he whispered.

Margaret smiled at him in the dark. "Goodnight," she said mussing his hair. "You need to go to sleep."

Closing his eyes, he smiled back. "You do too."

Margaret kissed him on the head again. "Always so protective," she said softly. "Don't worry, I will soon."

Shutting the door, she went to check William's room. After the kiss in the attic, he had made himself scarce, and she hadn't seen him since the morning. Abigail said she'd seen him walking the fields. Margaret wasn't too concerned knowing that even though he was recovering well, he wouldn't get very far even if he tried to leave. Finding his door open, she knew he hadn't returned yet.

She stood in the doorway thinking. What would she have said if he'd been there? I'm sorry for this morning? That would be a lie, because she wasn't. She was sorry for her reaction, that much was true, and had surprised herself by how much she'd wanted him. Even more surprising was how much she didn't want him to let her go. In those horrible minutes afterward she had discovered that it wasn't Edward she'd wanted in the attic, but William…him and him alone. That's what had frightened her more than anything.

Turning, she headed back to her room when there was a pounding on the front door. "He's back," Margaret thought, running down the stairs, nervous and excited at the same time. As she reached the door the pounding became louder and stronger.

245

"Margaret! It's Sam, open the door!"

Margaret rushed to the door when she heard Sam's voice. "Sam?" Margaret asked, unbolting the door.

Stepping in the open door, Sam grabbed Margaret by the shoulders. "We have to talk." He was visibly shaken and pale, startling Margaret by his appearance.

"Sam, what on earth is the matter?"

Ignoring her, Sam looked around the dark hallway. "Where's Abigail?"

"Sleeping," she answered.

"The children?" he asked.

"In bed. Sam, what is this about?" Margaret asked, exasperated.

Taking her hand, Sam led her quickly into Edward's study, shutting the door behind them. Going to the top drawer of Edward's desk, he pulled out some matches and lit the lantern on the desk. He closed the shutters on the window in one swift motion and turned back to the bewildered Margaret.

"Sam, would you *please* tell me what is going on?" Margaret was becoming worried.

"Is he here?" Sam finally asked.

Margaret shook her head, a bit of worry crossing her face. No need to ask which 'he' was being referred to. "He went out for some air, why?" Panic overtook her. "What's happened?"

Sam came towards her and gently sat her down. Pulling another chair in front of her he sat down, taking hold of her hand. Nervous, he didn't know exactly how to begin.

"I don't want you to be angry. I should have told you before, but…" He seemed to be at a loss for words. "I just wanted you to be safe, to go where you wouldn't be so alone."

Margaret squeezed Sam's hand tightly. "Sam, please. What is it?"

Concentrating, Sam let the words spilled out. "Edward wanted to make sure that you would be provided for if anything should happen to him, if he was ever arrested or killed. I didn't tell you the whole truth about your finances. There is an account in Charleston where Edward kept most of his profits. Of it, three fourths belongs to you."

"What?" Margaret asked.

"£Seventy thousand total," Sam answered her sheepishly.

Margaret leaned back in her seat. "What? Why didn't he tell me?"

"He didn't tell anyone," Sam responded. "The only people who knew were me, Edward, Mr. Capshaw, and one of his clerks. It had to be strictly confidential so the English wouldn't get wind of it. He couldn't bring it home because, for appearances sake, he had to be a typical farmer who had a couple of ventures on the sea. If not, the English might begin to ask questions."

After the news sunk in, Margaret's eyes brightened. "Then we can fix the farm! We can stay here!" Sam watched her sadly as she stood and walked to Edward's desk. "This is wonderful, Sam!" Realizing that Sam wasn't nearly as enthused as she was, she stopped. "Isn't this good news?"

He hung his head. "Catherine knows," was all he could say.

"She knows?" Margaret couldn't see how that was anything to be upset about. "I would imagine she would be ecstatic."

Sam stood, running a hand over his face. He couldn't bear to ruin her happiness. Shutting his eyes tightly, he spoke again. "Catherine knows about William."

He opened his eyes and saw the joyful expression on Margaret's face dissipate into a mixture of shock and anger. "How could you have told her?" she accused. "Don't you know how much danger this puts him in?"

"I didn't tell her!" he said, raising his voice. "She's been spying on you. She sent Reggie here to keep an eye on you. She thought we were having an affair and he must have told her everything," his voice sounded defeated.

Margaret paled, leaning against Edward's desk as the reality of their situation hit her. All she could see were men coming for William and taking him away, dragging him to the nearest tree and hanging him, or standing him blindfolded in the yard and shooting him.

"It gets worse," Sam said, coming towards her and putting a hand on her arm to prepare her. "If I don't hand the entire account over to her she'll go to the Continentals and report you."

Margaret looked up at him. "Me?"

"It's treason," he said softly. "You would be tried for treason."

"And William?" she asked.

"Prison, or worse."

"How could this have happened?" Margaret asked barely above a whisper. "I understood the risks, but we were so careful. You know why I had to take care of him, don't you? You understand why I couldn't let him die?"

Sam nodded. "I do. I understand completely." The guilt showed on his face. "I'm so sorry, Margaret. I wish I had never married that woman."

Margaret took hold of his hand and attempted a smile. "It's not your fault, Sam. You couldn't have known."

He gave her hand a squeeze. "But I should have."

Taking a deep breath, Margaret pulled her shoulders back. "Well, we'll have to get William away. No doubt, Catherine will have the authorities here soon, but when they find no evidence of any wrong doing I don't think they'll put much faith in the word of a jealous wife and someone she hired to spy on her husband."

Sam nodded. "I can't imagine they would." He grinned slyly at her. "So we've decided. Catherine won't get the money?"

Margaret brushed a lock of hair from her face, determined. "Not if I have anything to say about it."

"I'll have Joseph come back with a horse. It's dark, but Catherine wouldn't notice. Either way, I don't want to take any chances. I suggest you get William away as soon as you can, tonight if possible. I don't expect the Continentals to come until tomorrow afternoon, but the sooner he gets a head start the better. Burn anything that may suggest of his being here."

"That's already done," Margaret informed him.

"Good girl," Sam said with a smile. Taking a step towards her, he put a hand on her arm. "Thank you," he said softly. "Thank you for not hating me. I was so afraid you would think ill of me. I swear the hardest thing I've ever had to do was lie to you that day." He took her hand in his. "You have to know that I was only trying to keep you safe."

Margaret gave him a smile that melted his heart. "Sam, I could never hate you. I love you too much."

Leaning forward, he kissed her gently on the lips. "Thank you," he said again.

"Take your hands off of her," a voice from the doorway said.

Margaret turned to see William standing in the door, gun drawn, eyes glaring at Sam.

"William!" Margaret nearly shouted with relief. "What in God's name are you doing?" she rushed to his side, concerned. "I was getting worried about you. Sam has news. We need to get you out of here."

William continued to aim the gun at Sam. The two men frowned at each other until Sam finally broke the tension.

"I'll be leaving, Margaret," he said. William slowly lowered the gun, but didn't take his eyes off him. "I'm sure there are things you need to discuss." Bowing politely to Margaret, he left.

As soon as the front door closed, Margaret turned on William. "How could you treat him like that? He risked a lot to come here to warn us."

William stuffed the gun in his waistband. "How dare I? You ought to be thankful I got here when I did. I saw the way he was looking at you."

Margaret didn't understand, finding the accusation ridiculous. "Sam is nothing more than an old friend."

"Yes, I kiss all of my *old* friends like that," William said smugly.

Shocked and embarrassed that he had seen, she turned bright red. "Sam has been through a lot," she said quietly. "He wasn't thinking." Margaret was making an excuse for him and she knew it.

"He didn't look confused to me, and you didn't seem to mind all that much," he argued.

Margaret swung a hand up to slap him, but he caught it before she could, pulling her towards him and holding her close. It was as if he wanted something, but couldn't decide whether he should take it or not. Margaret smelled whiskey on him.

"Are you drunk?" she asked short of breath, his closeness going to her head.

William shook his head. "No, just spent time with one. If I had been, I probably wouldn't have been able to save you from that old fool."

Margaret pulled herself away from him, irritated. "That old fool just saved your neck. We'll be receiving a visit from the Continentals tomorrow afternoon. He came to tell me so that you could leave before they came." Her voice trailed off as she realized what she was saying. She didn't want him to go.

"He's even going to have a horse brought by for you." Her voice was strained as she spoke the last words.

William's face was solemn. "Are you sure he just doesn't want me gone?"

Margaret lowered her eyes. "Yes. His wife is angry and very dangerous. She sent Reggie here to spy on me, and he told her everything. She's blackmailing Sam because she discovered an account from Sam and Edward's smuggling ventures." She looked back up at William. "He didn't have to come here, William. He could have just given her the money, but he cared for Edward and didn't want to go against his wishes."

Margaret could hold back no longer. She flung her arms around him, holding him tightly, feeling she couldn't hold onto him hard enough. "I was ready to send you away," she cried, "to keep you safe, but I can't do it. You can hide," she said, clutching onto his warmth and strength. "We can fool them."

Pulling back, William held her face in his hands. He kissed her long and slow, then spoke to her firmly, his eyes focused on hers. "Now listen. We cannot take the chance of them finding me. I won't let you take the fall for this. The English probably think I'm dead by now, but I have to go back. God knows I don't want to, but I have to." He kissed her again. "As soon as I can I'll come back, I promise you."

Margaret ran a hand up his chest and placed her cheek against his. "When will you leave?" she asked quietly.

Gathering her close, he breathed in the scent of roses and vanilla. "Not 'till morning."

Chapter Twenty-Six: By Morning Light

Catherine woke the next morning, enjoying the comfort of her bed a moment before opening her eyes. A gentle rain was falling and she could hear the pitter pat of droplets against the window. Turning over, she saw Sam sitting in a chair next to her bed, her mood becoming triumphant. Just what she had expected, he had finally come to his senses.

"Have you been there all night, darling?" she asked, sitting up with a curious smile on her face and leaning back into her pillows like a queen waiting for her servants.

Sam shook his head. "I've been thinking about our conversation last night."

Running her fingers through her dark hair, Catherine straightened out a few tangles. "Our conversation?" she asked, playing coyly. "Oh, that. I suppose you've come to a decision. You have plenty of time left, Sam. There's certainly no rush."

Sam nodded, resolute. He would give her no satisfaction yet. "Yes, I've come to a decision, and it was a very easy one." Standing, he walked to her dresser inspecting a couple of the trinkets that sat there, setting down one harder than necessary.

"And?" Catherine asked.

"No deal," he answered, turning back to her. "You're not going to get a single shilling of what's in that account. Every penny is going to Margaret and the children."

Catherine stuck her lip out, imitating the pout of a child. Getting out of bed, Catherine pulled her robe around her nightdress. "Oh, Sam, I was afraid that's what you were going to say." She walked over to the dresser and took the hairbrush from his hand. "That's why I sent a letter to the nearest Continental camp yesterday," she sighed. "So, I would guess that a group of soldiers are arriving at the Weathers farm as we speak."

In an instant, Sam had her up against the wall. "How could you!" he shouted. "Do you even realize what you've done?"

Catherine laughed, unfazed. "Do you think I'm stupid, Sam? I knew you would go straight to her."

Releasing her, he stepped back and pointed to the door. "Get out," he seethed.

Catherine straightened her robe. "You see, Sam. I'm not as stupid as you think."

Grabbing a few items, she stuffed them in a small reticule that had been sitting on her dresser. "I know a woman is in a delicate position when it comes to English law, and I may not get very far by accusing you of adultery, but attempted murder?" She leaned her head to the side. "You could deny it, but that's something even the most cold-hearted of judges would find hard to ignore."

Turning back to him, she stopped, reticule in hand. "You'll be hearing from my lawyer." She gave him a calculated smile "Oh, and see that my things are delivered to this address." Laying a card on the dresser she slammed the door behind her.

Sam stumbled to a chair, unable to move, unable to think. She had played him like a fool and he'd fallen into it blindly. Putting his head in his hands he cried, defeated. It wasn't pretty, and it wasn't becoming, but it's what he needed to do. Catherine had destroyed everything, and Margaret would never forgive him.

William was up at sunrise the next morning. He'd fallen asleep on the couch, Margaret in his arms. They had talked until the wee hours of the morning. Smiling, he remembered that he had been telling her about his time in Boston, when he paused and noticed that her breathing had become very steady. Looking down, he'd seen that she was asleep. Not wanting to move her, he had simply made himself comfortable.

Watching Margaret for a moment as she slept, he could see the peace in her face, the way she fit just right in his arms. For the first time in his life he was truly happy. He longed to touch her again, but knew that if he woke her he would never be able to leave. Placing his face close to hers, he listened to her soft breathing.

Moving as gently as possible, he slid her sleeping form onto the couch and stood with a stretch. He bent back down, barely touching her lips as he gave her one last kiss, every cell in his being hoping that she would wake and beg him to stay.

Outside, the morning was fresh from the rain that had just finished falling. Walking to the barn, William opened the door and found the horse saddled and ready to go as promised by Sam, but there was something else William hadn't expected. Petting the horse's soft nose and feeding it some straw was Matthew, speaking softly to his new found companion.

"Aren't you up a little early?" William asked, startling the young boy.

Matthew looked William over, wondering whether or not he was going to be in trouble. "I heard a horse in the barn when I went to get the eggs. Abigail lets me collect them once a week," he explained, and patted the horse on the nose again.

The horse was large and dark brown with a blaze on its nose. "My father used to have a horse like this," Matthew said, "but it didn't have the white spot." It was the most words he'd ever said to William.

Coming up next to the boy, William laid a hand on the horse's back. "You miss your father don't you?" William asked him gently.

Matthew nodded.

William watched Matthew closely. The boy was very much like a junior version of himself, the dark hair, and the blue eyes. "You know," William said smiling, "I knew your father when he was very little."

Matthew eyed him suspiciously. "You knew my father?"

William nodded. "I did."

Matthew mulled over that information for a minute. "If that's true, what was his favorite food?" he asked, challenging him

William knew he was being put to the test. The little boy hadn't trusted him from the first. It was obvious he was still grieving and too scared to see past William's English uniform.

William thought for a moment before answering. "That's a hard one. What if he changed his favorite?"

Matthew shook his head. "You can never change your favorite, that's what my father said. 'A favorite is a favorite…always.'"

"In that case," Williams said, "it's easy, because for as long as I can remember, you're father's favorite food has always been blackberry pie."

Matthew smiled and nodded. It was the first time William had seen him smile in his presence. In that instant William realized what the little boy needed. He needed to talk about his father, to know about him. Again William regretted having to leave and doubted whether or not he was making the right decision. Shaking his head, he could afford a few minutes, Matthew was more important.

"Do you see this?" William rolled up his sleeve and showed Matthew a long, thin scar on his arm. "Your father gave me that."

The child's eyes lit with excitement. "Really? How?"

"Well, one day, the two of us decided that we were going to be great swordsmen, so we snuck into his father's study and borrowed two swords. We found a nice little glen, the kind you see in paintings, and began to duel.

"We did very well for about five minutes, but then his sword slipped and cut my arm. It was just a scratch, but it was bleeding a lot. I was mad because I thought he had done it on purpose so I threw my sword down and ran towards him. He saw me coming, and we took turns pummeling each other for a good half-hour.

"When it was all said and done, I had a bloody arm, a bloody nose and two black eyes. Your father, who was bigger, got by with only one black eye and a busted lip." Matthew smiled and laughed as William tightened one of the straps on the horse's saddle.

When he had stopped laughing, Matthew looked back up at William. "Are you leaving?" he asked.

William turned back to him. Instead of seeing the delight he had expected to see on the boy's face, he saw that the sorrow had returned. Kneeling down so that he was at eye level with the little boy, William nodded. "I just have to leave for a little bit, but I promised your mother that I would be back soon. Is that alright with you?" Matthew nodded enthusiastically.

"I have something you need to do for me, though." William's voice was serious. "I need you to take care of your little sisters for me. Do you think you can do that?" Matthew nodded.

"Good. You might look after your mother too. Make sure she doesn't get herself into too much trouble." He smiled at Matthew and began to stand, but Matthew hugged him tightly, not letting him go yet.

"You're a good boy, Matthew. Very brave, just like your father." Returning the hug with the same intensity, William mussed the boy's hair as he stood, but something in the distance caught his attention…the sound of horses.

Margaret woke up on the couch confused at first, but then realized that she was feeling something she hadn't felt in a long while, loved, protected, cared for. She then remembered falling asleep in strong arms that had held her close all night, a warm heart beating next to hers.

Sitting up, she brushed the hair from her face, knowing he was gone, saying a silent prayer that she could be strong. She closed her eyes, trying to take a deep breath and make his leaving easier for her.

She got up and dressed, fixing herself up, changing into a new dress, brushing her hair and pulling it back. Smiling at herself in the mirror, she tried to push back the pain and loneliness that threatened to return. "He will be back," she told herself over and over, but it didn't do much to ease the ache in her heart. Sighing, she went about her morning routine.

Creeping into the girls' room, she kissed them each on the cheek to wake them, pulling open the curtains, to let in some morning light. Looking out the window she wondered where William was, when he had left, and how far had he gotten. How was he feeling? Was he heartbroken like she was? Suddenly, her stomach dropped as she clearly made out the column of riders coming towards the farm. She couldn't tell how many there were or what uniform they wore, but she had her suspicions.

Margaret ran over to Megan's bed and shook her awake. "Megan," she said, sitting the drowsy five-year-old up in bed. "I'm going to shut your door. I don't want you to open it, no matter what. Do you understand?" Megan closed her eyes again, but Margaret gave her another little shake. "Do you hear me?"

"Mm-mm," Megan whined and laid back down.

Margaret rushed out of the bedroom, shutting the door behind her. She hurried next door to Matthew's room, but the boy wasn't there. She looked all over the upstairs, but he was nowhere to be found. Margaret ran for the stairway. "Abigail!" she yelled, running down the stairs, looking in each room a second time as she headed to the kitchen.

Abigail appeared from behind the kitchen door, wiping her hands on her apron. "What is it Ma'am?" she asked.

"Have you seen Matthew?" Margaret asked, worried, almost frantic.

"No, Ma'am," Abigail answered, not understanding the concern. "Perhaps he was up early to gather eggs?"

Just then there was a knock on the door. Abigail recognized the fear in Margaret's eyes. "Mrs. Weathers?" she asked, hoping for some reassurance, coming fully out of the kitchen. She received none.

There was a knock again. Margaret grew pale and turned to the door. "Stay in the kitchen Abigail, and say nothing." Walking to the door, Margaret took deep breaths, and smoothed out her skirt. Straightening her shoulders, she turned the latch.

Smiling brightly, she opened the door and greeted the soldiers with a "Good morning, gentlemen," nodding to each of the six Continental soldiers standing in front of her. She had plenty to hide, but was bound and determined not to give them the satisfaction of knowing that.

The sergeant in charge of the men nodded and three of his men dispersed, presumably to make sure that no one escaped out the back door and to check the barn and surrounding buildings. The sergeant turned back to Margaret and smiled slightly. "Mrs. Weathers? I hate to disturb you. I know this is going to sound ridiculous, but we received a report that you were harboring an English soldier."

"I'm sorry, I don't understand." Margaret put on her best shocked appearance.

"I know it's ludicrous with your husband being who he was, but we have to investigate." He looked at her sympathetically and lowered his voice a bit. "I served as a private under Captain Weathers for two years. He was well respected."

Margaret smiled back. "Thank you, Sergeant," she said, her appreciation genuine.

"Do you mind?" he asked, motioning inside.

"Oh, no, not at all. Please, come in." Margaret took a step back and allowed the soldiers to enter. Immediately the other two began to check behind doors and in rooms for anything suspicious.

"I do apologize," the sergeant said. "I know this is terribly difficult after everything you've been through." The sergeant gave another silent command to his men and turned his attention back to Margaret. He was very considerate, but extremely shrewd and carried out his orders with skill and authority, while treating Margaret with kindness and understanding at the same time.

"Would you mind showing me upstairs?" he asked politely, although Margaret knew it was an order and not a suggestion.

"Certainly," she said, beginning to worry about Matthew again.

They climbed the stairs and Margaret pointed out the children's rooms. The sergeant took a quick look around Matthew's room.

"Where's the boy?" he asked.

"He likes to get up early and collect eggs from the chickens." Margaret said, hoping that was the case.

The sergeant nodded. "My men will find him if he's outside."

Margaret opened the door to the girls' bedroom. The sergeant poked his head in, careful not to disturb the sleeping children. He was joined by his men as he finished searching Margaret's bedroom. He gave a nod and one of the men went about searching the guestroom. Margaret's stomach was in knots.

The other soldier gave his report. "Nothing downstairs but a slave woman, Sir."

The sergeant nodded. "What's behind this door?" he asked, motioning to the door at the end of the hall.

"That's the attic," Margaret answered.

The soldier opened the door and climbed the stairs. He was back soon, having found nothing.

"I do apologize for all of this Mrs. Weathers," he said as they made their way back downstairs to the front door and the porch. "Again, I am sorry for your husband's death." With that he whistled, gathering the rest of the men together and left the house.

When William heard the horses arriving, he carefully peeked out a hole in the barn door to see who was coming. Seeing the back of a navy uniform, he swore. They were at the front door of the house, and as the door opened the man in charge dispersed three men. Two went around either side of the house, while one headed straight towards the barn.

William rushed to Matthew's side and pulled the little boy to a dark corner of the barn where he was certain no light would hit them. Crouching down in the corner, he pulled Matthew back against him. "Don't make a sound," he whispered to the nervous little boy.

William held Matthew tightly to keep him from panicking and with his free hand took out his pistol and pulled back the hammer, readying himself for whatever might come through the door.

For a long time they could hear nothing. William assumed the soldiers would be checking around the house and the cabins farther out. Then they heard voices outside the old wood walls of the barn and the sound of gravel crunching under boots. The door to the barn opened slightly with a low groan and Matthew whimpered. Instinctively, William put his hand over the boy's mouth to make sure he didn't cry out.

The big wooden door swung open slowly with a creak and William raised his gun slightly. The horse whinnied and pawed the ground. One of the Continental soldiers walked in and slowly surveyed the barn. It was dark and he could see shadows in the rafters, along with old cobwebs. William tried not to breathe, watching the soldier closely to see what he was going to do. The soldier took a tentative step forward, but was stopped by a whistle from near the house. Turning to leave, he looked one last time behind his shoulder.

William and Matthew remained motionless until the thunder of the horses faded away. Finally, William let out a sigh and lowered his gun.

"Are you alright?" he asked the frightened Matthew who nodded quickly, trying to be brave. "Let's get you in to your mother. She's probably worried to death about where you are." Standing, he took Matthew's hand and carefully exited the barn.

No sooner were they back out in the morning sun, than Margaret was running from the house towards them. "Matthew!" she yelled, falling to her knees hugging him, thankful he was safe.

When she looked up and saw William, her voice caught in her throat. "I thought you had left."

"Not yet," he answered. Patting Matthew on the shoulder, William looked down at Margaret as if he wanted to say something. He moved towards her.

"Don't," she said before he could reach her. "It'll be easier if you just go."

Saying nothing, William turned back to the barn to get the horse.

With all her strength, Margaret stood and began to walk Matthew back to the house, her whole being shaking. She was stopped by William's voice.

"I will come back," he yelled to her. There was a pause followed by another shout. "I love you."

Turning, Margaret let out a sob, sending Matthew back to the house in front of her. Unable to stop herself, she ran to William. Catching her in his arms, he kissed her cheeks, her neck, her hair.

"I promise I'll be back soon. I promise," he told her over and over.

Margaret held him tightly. "You had better, because I don't think I could handle losing you as well." She pushed him away. "Now go! Go before I refuse to let you." Margaret turned and ran to the house.

Chapter Twenty-Seven: The Search

Phillip knocked on the door of the farmhouse and took a step back, anxious to see what, or who, would come to the door. After having spent the past week and a half with little or no news of William, he was becoming more and more frustrated. He had stopped at, what he believed, to be every home in a five-mile radius of the site where William and his men had been attacked.

He had started his search there at the site of the attack, but the only evidence that anything had taken place was a tree riddled with musket balls and a rusted knife with dried blood caked on it. Unnerved by the forest, and afraid of suffering the same fate as William and his men, he quickly began his search in more populated areas.

He stepped forward to knock again, but before his hand reached the wood, the door was opened and he found himself looking down at a short, chubby, red-faced Irishman.

"Can I help you, lad?" the man asked.

Phillip grew nervous as the man eyed him up and down holding a large, very lethal looking musket between his hands.

"I'm looking for a friend of mine." Phillip answered, having given up trying to imitate the southern accent used in the area. He had tried it for awhile, but it was not something he had a talent for and only cast more suspicion on him. "We were supposed to meet in Charleston a week ago, but he never came. I am worried about him and was inquiring at any of the houses he might have stopped at along the way."

Before the man could slam the door in Phillip's face, a lovely woman came up behind the man. "What is it, Patrick?" she asked. The woman had the same accent, but it was much less pronounced.

"Please," Phillip said, desperate, looking to her for some sort of information. He took a step forward. "I'm looking for a friend. I'm afraid he may have been injured. His name is William Weathers."

Margaret sighed as loud Irish brogue erupted behind her. "William Weathers! Now why on God's green earth would he be lookin' for the Captain's brother?"

The woman gave Phillip a look that resembled a child resigned to its punishment as the coming tirade ensued.

"You said he was from the North, but…well that explains the accent!"

Margaret winced as Patrick put the pieces of the puzzle together.

"Margaret Lara O'Connor! What have you done? So tha's why the Captain didn'a speak of him. His brother was an English soldier!"

"Officer," Margaret corrected him.

Patrick's face was scarlet and growing redder by the second. "Oh, excuse me, officer. Tha's why the Continentals were here. They were lookin' for him!"

All Margaret could do was nod. "I'm sorry, Patrick. I should have told you."

"Damn right you should'a told me! Oh, the blessed mother protect us," he hollered, and began to curse behind her.

Margaret turned back to Phillip who was watching the scene with curiosity. "William is fine," she said quickly, "He left this morning for Charleston. He was hoping to find a regiment there."

"Thank you," he said. "If I hurry, maybe I can catch him."

Margaret followed Phillip to his horse. "Good luck," he said, motioning towards Patrick standing at the door.

"Keep him safe," she said, and Phillip saw the worry in her eyes.

"I will," he promised, riding off, hoping his search was finally at an end.

William pushed his horse forward through the dense undergrowth of forest. Deciding to stay off the main roads, he opted instead to follow the rode by carefully staying a hundred feet to the side of it. He figured there would be less chance of running into an awkward encounter if anyone would happen by.

The hours dragged on as he rode slowly towards Charleston, stopping frequently to stretch his aching leg and let the horse rest or drink from a stream he had found along the way. More than once, he almost turned back, but decided against it and angrily urged the horse forward.

As it began to grow dark, his leg was hurting so badly he knew he needed to stop for the night. Finding himself a spot on the warm ground under a large oak, he slept, dreaming of Margaret's kisses.

The next morning he woke to the sound of horses snorting. Thinking nothing of it, it wasn't until he heard the whinny of two horses instead of one that he became aware. Instantly, he was on his feet, his gun cocked and ready to fire. It took him a moment to realize who was standing in front of him.

"Phillip?" he asked, still aiming his gun at the figure.

"Good morning," Phillip answered. "I've been looking for you."

Relaxing, William lowered his gun.

"You look good," Phillip told him.

"I've certainly felt better," William answered glumly, limping over to where his horse stood. "Let's go," he said, shaking off his sleep and mounting his horse.

"Do you want to talk about what happened?" Phillip asked.

"No," William said, finishing it.

Lady Dougherty ran a hand over the table. "Molly, look at this. It is unacceptable. I want you to dust everything in this room again and—"

"Madam," a butler interrupted. "Mrs. Catherine Wallace is here to see you."

"Mrs. Wallace? By all means show her in." Lady Dougherty turned back to the servant, Molly. "Go about your chores. I don't want this to happen again." Seeing Catherine being escorted into the hall, she dismissed the girl, turning her attention away.

"Mrs. Wallace," she greeted her friend with a smile, holding out her arms in greeting. "It is so wonderful to see you." She stopped short before embracing her friend. "Why Catherine, what on earth is the matter?"

Catherine had entered with her kerchief out and upon greeting Lady Dougherty collapsed into her arms sobbing.

"It's horrible, Lady Dougherty, absolutely horrible," she said through her bouts of sobs.

"What is horrible, dear?" Lady Dougherty asked, bewildered by Catherine's behavior.

"It's Samuel. He tried to…" she broke off, dabbing her eyes.

"Catherine, you must calm down and tell me what the matter is." Lady Dougherty took her arm and led her to a sitting room. Over her shoulder she caught the eye of the butler and ordered for some tea to be brought for them. "Now, let's just sit down right here, and I want you to start from the beginning." Lady Dougherty sat down next to Catherine and held her hand.

A maid hurried in and set down a tray of tea and biscuits. Carefully pouring a cup for Catherine, Lady Dougherty took a small flask from her bodice and poured a couple of drops into Catherine's cup, knowing it would help calm her poor friend.

"There, dear," she said handing it to her. "This will make everything better."

Catherine replied with a barely audible 'thank you'.

"What did Samuel try to do, Catherine?"

Catherine took a sip. "A rider came to our house," she explained. "Sam had requested not to be disturbed, so naturally I went in his stead to greet the boy." She stopped to wipe her nose. "When I took the letter to his room he went into a rage. He said I had been spying on him. I swore to him that I hadn't even opened the letter because it was addressed to him." Her voice cracked a bit. "He called me a liar and the next thing I knew he came at me with a knife. I barely escaped the house with the clothes on my back."

Lady Dougherty's voice was a mixture of pity and anger. "This is horrendous, Catherine. Lord Dougherty must hear of this. You just sit right here and relax, I will be right back."

Catherine sat back and watched Lady Dougherty storm down the hallway. Sipping her tea she looked out the window over the lush and magnificently trimmed gardens, quite proud of her little spectacle. In a matter of minutes she heard voices echoing in the hall and Lady Dougherty reentered with her husband in tow.

"Deplorable," he said, coming into the room red faced. "The man is a monster." He looked Catherine over as though making a decision and then addressed his wife. "Lady Dougherty, we will see that Mrs. Wallace is taken care of while she is with us. In the meantime, I'll see what can be done about this." Lord Dougherty started to leave, thought about it for another moment, and turned back to her. "Madam, is there anything else you can tell us that may help in our dealing with the man?"

Catherine stood and held tightly to the kerchief in her hand. "Yes, Sir. It has to do with his business. For months-- no, probably for years now-- he has been part of a smuggling party. Evidently they have amassed thousands of pounds. I've been doing some investigating while in the city. It appears that he and Captain Edward Weathers of the Continentals were partners for quite some time. Now it seems that my husb--Mr. Wallace, I should say, has recruited someone else to do his dirty work. He's been speaking with a Colonel William Weathers, evidently the brother of the late Captain and," her voice broke, "an English officer." Sniffing, Catherine held her kerchief to her face. "I can't believe he's been such a beast. I didn't know he was capable of such treachery."

"Good Lord, Lady Dougherty, is nothing sacred? I would expect such behavior from the Americans, but an English officer?" He paced the floor as if he was trying to get his brain around this horrific news. "Pearson must know of this," he announced. "I will go straight to his Majesty if I have to Mrs. Wallace. Rest assured, Madam. We will see to these barbarians." Lord Dougherty

269

marched back down the hall, muttering under his breath, leaving the ladies alone again.

"Well," said Lady Dougherty triumphant from having done her good deed for the day. "That settles it then. Lord Dougherty will take care of everything. I'll take you upstairs and have one of the girls find you a dress for dinner."

Catherine smiled sweetly at Lady Dougherty, tears shining in her eyes. "Thank you so much. I don't know what I would have done without you."

It was late evening when William and Phillip rode wearily into the English camp near King's Mountain. Their arrival created quite a stir around camp and they were taken directly to General Trummel who was as shocked as anyone to see them.

"Welcome back, Sergeant Mitchell," said the General who had dressed hastily.

Phillip nodded. "Thank you, Sir. It's good to be back."

"And Colonel Weathers," General Trummel shook his hand enthusiastically. "We had feared you dead."

"I almost was, Sir. I was wounded badly, but a kind family bandaged my wounds," William answered, leaving it at that.

"Well, we are glad to have you returned to us safe and sound. You were sorely missed, Colonel."

"Thank you, Sir," William said with a nod.

"Get to your tents gentlemen. I have no doubt that you are both extremely weary. We'll speak more tomorrow." And with that they were dismissed.

"General," William called after him. "I am sorry about my men, Sir."

The General frowned. "We all were, Colonel. Rest now."

Chapter Twenty-Eight: Camp

On William's first day in camp, he volunteered to take some men out on a regular morning patrol. The day was hot and as the morning went on the men grew restless and irritable. William rode ahead, unaware of the grumblings behind him.

Phillip, knowing the men were on the verge of mutiny, rode up next to William. "Colonel, the men need to rest for a bit. The horses are tired and I'm afraid a fight might break out if we don't stop." William continued as if he hadn't heard so Phillip spurred his horse forward a few feet. "Colonel!"

Finally noticing him, William reined his horse back. He looked at Phillip, confused.

"The men need to stop, Sir." Phillip repeated.

Looking back at the group of eight soldiers who had stopped about fifty feet behind him, William nodded. "We'll stop at those trees up there. I think there's a stream for the horses." Phillip nodded and rode back to inform the men of the plan.

While the men took a chance to rest and eat a bit as their horses drank the cool water from the stream, William wandered off by himself. Phillip watched his friend sitting beneath a distant tree, physically there, but a million miles away. Asking one of the other men to watch his mount, he walked casually over to where William sat.

William's horse was busy munching on the tall grass, its tail swishing back and forth to keep away some flies. Patting its rump as he walked by, Phillip watched his friend for a moment. Something wasn't right. William was distracted, depressed almost.

Tearing apart a leaf piece by piece, William threw the remains on the ground.

Phillip leaned against the tree. "So, who was the woman?" he asked. "Margaret, I think her name was?"

William looked up at him. "What?" Phillip couldn't help but notice the look of longing that passed over William's face when he'd been caught off guard.

Phillip sat down next to him, trying to avoid a spot of mud, and taking his musket from his back and laying it next to him so he could sit more comfortably.

"I stopped at about twenty farms asking if they had seen you. Little did I know that I would actually find one, and one I might add, with so fetching a mistress."

William remained silent, but Phillip continued. "Well, when I said your name, the old Irishman who was there had a fit. He started yelling about how some Captain was right not to speak to you and, to be honest, I could only understand about half of what he said," Phillip let out a laugh remembering the little man. "He was in a rage about how she should have let you die and that the Captain would never…" Suddenly the same look of realization that Phillip had seen on Patrick's face came over his. "The Captain, your brother?"

William nodded.

"William," Phillip asked tentatively, not sure he wanted an answer. "Did you leave on purpose?"

William shook his head as he played with a stick in his hands. "No," he finally answered. "After I was injured I lost consciousness. When I woke all my men were dead and the horses gone. I don't remember much of what happened after that, probably because of the fever, but I guess I stumbled into their house. I didn't realize where I was until I had been there for a while."

They were silent for a couple of minutes until Phillip finally laughed. "I mean, it's not funny or anything," he said, explaining himself, "but after everything that had happened between the two of you and then his letter, well, it just seems like it was providence."

William said nothing.

"So, what happened to him?" Phillip asked.

"He died," William answered. "At Camden."

"Did you tell his wife about the letter?"

"She found it in my jacket," William said, throwing the stick on the ground and standing.

"What are you going to do?" Phillip asked, sensing William's distress.

"I'll go back when the war's over."

"To England?" Phillip asked, knowing the answer already.

"No," William said, shaking his head. "Not to England."

"Back to her," Phillips said.

William answered with a slight nod, standing to stretch his leg.

"You realize that the English thought you were dead," Phillip informed him bluntly. "You didn't have to come back."

William paced for a bit, and then stopped, the same thought had been tearing at him from the moment he'd left. Watching, Phillip could visibly see William's pain and distress. "I couldn't stay,"

William tried to explain. "If I had, the Continentals would have found me, sent me to prison and done God knows what to Margaret. If the English had found me, I would have been hung as a deserter. Either way, I couldn't win. I could have stayed and lived in happiness, but we would have been constantly on the run, looking behind our shoulder. Or, I could come back, finish the war, and return to whatever is left as a free man."

"Or you could be killed next week and never see her again," Phillip spoke quietly. "Is it really worth it?" he asked. "Or are you scared of how much you love her?" William looked down at him and Phillip smiled. "It's written all over your face." He paused. "It was certainly written all over hers."

There was a shout from the men, and William jumped to his feet painfully. In the distance, he saw the source of the commotion. Coming from the west were about ten dark-coated riders. Quickly mounting his horse, William followed Phillip who was running behind him. The men were scurrying to their muskets as they reached them. They could hear the horses now as they bore down upon them. Dismounting, William hit his horse on the backside, sending it running back to the stream. There wasn't time to escape. The soldiers were coming too fast.

"Prepare to fire!" William yelled to his men.

Hiding themselves behind the trees, they waited as the riders came closer and closer. When they were just feet away, William gave the command. "Fire!" he yelled.

The men came from behind the trees and fired, startling the colonial riders. As his men went to reload, the remaining colonials fired, killing three of William's men.

William's musket was ready and he gave the command again. "Fire!"

Two more colonials fell along with three horses, the peaceful glade erupting into smoke and fire. "Get to your horses!" William ordered, knowing he needed to get his men to safety.

Firing his pistol, he ran for his own animal, pushing one of his men quickly in the same direction. As he did, a bullet tore through his arm, sending him sprawling to the ground. Phillip, seeing William fall, turned. Running back, he dragged William to his horse. Clenching his teeth, William pulled himself into his saddle with his good arm. Phillip turned, a colonial rider bearing down on him. Trembling, he grabbed his pistol and fired, sending the man flying off his horse.

Phillip was frozen, unable to believe what he had just done. He heard a pounding in his head and turned to see another rider, pistol aimed, coming towards him. A shot rang out and the man fell forward.

"Phillip! To your horse, now!" William yelled, shoving his pistol back into place and kicking his horse.

Still shaking, Phillip ran to his horse and followed William and the surviving men back to camp.

William found Phillip that evening relaxing in his tent reading a well-worn copy of "The Odyssey". His arm had been bandaged, but he wasn't injured badly. He'd been lucky, the bullet had just missed the bone and joint as it passed through the flesh near his shoulder. When William entered the two soldiers Phillip shared his tent with excused themselves.

Phillip set down his book. "How's your arm, Colonel?"

William brushed off the question. "It will be fine." He busied himself examining a powder horn on a small table near the tent's entrance until he finally spoke again. "Thank you, Phillip. You saved my life."

Phillip sat forward on his cot. "You certainly returned the favor."

Visibly uncomfortable, William turned to face his friend. "I've written a letter of resignation and plan to give it to the General as soon as he returns later this week."

Phillip nodded, not surprised.

"You were right about everything," William continued. "I can't stay here and live without her. I know it's selfish, but I can't do it. I love her, Phillip, and being away from her is tearing me apart. She is part of my soul. I can't close my eyes without seeing her face. I have to go back to her, and I have to go, before it's too late."

Phillip put his book down with a thud. "That's the first sensible thing you've said in days."

"Do you have proof of what the man has done? No offense meant to the lady, but lawyers hear claims like this all the time."

"Other than her own word, I'm sure we could find a servant or two who witnessed the scene."

"Slave testimony is practically worthless, but it may be useable. I'll speak with some of my uncle's friends here in Charleston and see what I can do."

"There is another matter to discuss, but that can be done tomorrow."

Catherine stood outside the door to Lord Dougherty's study, barely breathing as she listened to the conversation between Lord Dougherty and Colonel Pearson. Lord Dougherty had sent a rider to Pearson soon after Catherine's arrival and Pearson himself arrived within the day.

"It just disgusts me," Lord Dougherty spoke again. "I don't know what the world has become. Gone are the days of respect and decency when people knew their place and understood that those in charge knew what was best for them."

"Yes, the debauchery of mankind is in full force," Pearson added.

Lord Dougherty sighed, "Colonel, I will leave you for the night. All of this excitement has exhausted me."

Catherine moved away from the door and heard nothing more of their farewells. Ducking into a doorway, she waited for the sound of the men's footsteps to fade away. Holding her breath when she heard a pair of boots coming up the hall towards her, Catherine saw the tall, broad-shouldered form of Pearson pass by. He stopped at a door at the end of the hall and Catherine pushed herself further back into the shadows in case he turned and saw her. Pearson entered the door and it shut behind him.

Stepping back into the hallway, making certain no one else was nearby, Catherine crept down the hall, making her way to the door Pearson had entered. Before she could knock, Pearson, dressed in his shirtsleeves, having abandoned his coat and vest, smiled at her.

"Well, well, well," he said, leaning a hand against the doorjamb. "If it isn't the poor, abused wife." Catherine's face reddened a bit at the jibe. "You wouldn't make a very good snoop," he added, allowing her to enter.

Haughtily, Catherine walked into the room. "I've been having a very trying time and I appreciate your speed in seeing to it."

Pearson chuckled slightly. "Yes, I'm sure the trauma has been very difficult for you." He took a seat and surveyed her for a moment. "I'm sure it took all your strength to escape the clutches of that wild husband of yours. I know how quick and agile middle-aged men with war injuries are." Pearson smiled and took a drink.

"So, which did you appeal to first?" he asked. "Lady Dougherty's feminine compassion, or her patriotic spirit?"

Catherine frowned and glared him. "If this is the abuse and thanks that I'm going get from you, I will gladly leave."

"So what drove you here?" Pearson asked, still amused, knowing Catherine wasn't going anywhere.

"Sam received no less than he deserved. Not only did I find out that he had been lying to me for years, but has been hiding £70,000 in a private account. I have been made a fool of." She grabbed one of the posts of the bed as she spoke. "Even when I found out about the money, I was going to make it easy for him. I gave him a choice. He could either give me the money and be done with it, or I would go to the authorities about his lady love harboring the younger Weathers." Catherine's grip on the bedpost tightened. "But he couldn't even take my peace offering. Instead he decided to be noble and ran straight to her. No doubt to warn her so she could get Weathers out of the house."

"Excuse me?" Pearson sat forward, confused. "Did you say Weathers?"

"Yes," Catherine said bitterly. "Did you not know? The saintly Margaret has been nursing an injured Colonel William Weathers back to health. And, I might add, has been caught in the act of…shall we say…finding comfort in the arms of another man, her dead husband's brother to be exact."

Pearson stood. "That lying traitor! He told me he was dead. I knew I was foolish to believe him!" Pearson was shocked at his own stupidity. "So, Weathers is probably on his way back to camp as we speak. The traitor will ride back into camp like some kind of prodigal son returned from the dead, while the whole time he's been rutting with his dead brother's wife. How's that for coveting thy neighbor's wife?" Pearson grabbed his vest and coat and began to dress. Catherine rushed towards him.

"Where are you going?" she demanded.

"King's Mountain," he announced. "That's where Trummel and his men are camped. That's where Weathers will be."

Catherine stepped towards him majestically. "What about me? I'm standing here, and all you can think about is William Weathers?

Pearson shot her a look mixed with caution and anger. "This is important, Mrs. Wallace. I don't imagine you would understand."

"So this really is what it was about all along? I knew it," Catherine spat out. "For a moment I thought, perhaps, that you actually cared for me, but you were only using me to get to him. You just wanted information!" Catherine pushed him violently on the chest, but it didn't move him an inch.

Pearson shoved her to the bed. "Don't shriek at me woman! I know what you are all about, and you knew from the beginning what this was. If you didn't, than you're more of a simpleton than I imagined."

He left the room, slamming the door behind him.

Pulling herself up, Catherine burned with rage, wishing to God that she had a gun, a knife, anything that would make him pay for the anger inside of her. She went to the dresser and took hold of a decanter. With all her strength, she flung it towards the door where the bottle shattered in an explosion of glass.

Chapter Twenty-Nine: Accusations

William went back to work the next morning, not letting the dull pain in his arm stop him. Throughout the next couple days he helped check in supplies and ran drills. He was helping with a horse that had thrown one of its shoes when he was greeted by a staff sergeant.

"The General would like to see you, Colonel," the sergeant said.

Nodding, William handed the horse off to one of the privates standing next to him. They stopped at William's tent so that he could put on his coat and hat. Deciding to look more casual, William placed his hat under his arm and they walked silently to the General's tent. Taking the resignation letter from his pocket, he ducked inside.

William was surprised to see that it was not a private meeting. Besides the General, there were three other officers present and two privates standing guard at the entrance.

Deciding this was not the time to speak with the General about giving up his position, he quickly put the letter back in his coat pocket. It was then that one face caught his attention, Colonel Hugh Pearson.

William's stomach dropped and his hands grew cold. What business did he have there? Pearson was the only one in the tent wearing a smile. That couldn't be good. In an instant, the picture of Margaret's father holding his newborn daughter in his arms, mourning the death of the woman he loved ran through his mind. Just as quickly, he saw a glimpse of Margaret in the face of the arrogant man in front of him. William looked away, pretending that he could care less that Pearson was present.

"General, you wanted to see me?" William said with a bow, tying to remain calm even though his senses were foreboding.

"Colonel Weathers, yes," the General replied, his face grim. Picking up a piece of paper from his desk, he walked around to the front. "I received a disturbing letter that could not be ignored." He gave William a concerned look. "Normally when we receive reports like this we hardly pay them any attention. We look into them of course, but rarely do we find that the accusations have any validity. Unfortunately this one comes from a well-respected member of the peerage who is demanding some sort of action be taken."

"I'm sorry, Sir, but I don't understand," William said.

The General sighed. "You've been accused of treason, Colonel."

William glanced at Pearson out of the corner of his eye then quickly back at the General. "Sir?"

"Lord Dougherty, a prosperous Charleston man, has accused you of being in league with a private shipping firm that has been running a well-known smuggling ring." The General looked down at the paper. "Also listed are Samuel Wallace, a plantation owner; and the former Captain Edward Weathers of the Continentals. Your brother, I've recently been informed." The General looked up at William with disappointment.

"Sir, there has been a mistake," William retorted. "This is absurd."

Pearson took a step forward. "Do you deny, Colonel, that Captain Edward Weathers of the Continental army was your brother?" Pearson asked with arrogance.

"No, but-"

"I don't know about you, General, but that is evidence enough for me to be suspicious of anything the Colonel might have to say," Pearson said, his face proud, almost triumphant.

"With all due respect, General, my brother and I have not spoken in over ten years. Our political beliefs are completely independent of each other."

"Perhaps," Pearson spoke up again. "if the fact that your brother was an officer in the Continental army and a well-known smuggler had been known before now, I suspect his Majesty would have been less generous in bestowing upon you so high an office. The fact that you kept it secret for so long only raises questions to your motives as far as I'm concerned."

"Colonel Pearson, that will do," the General growled at him.

Pearson took a step back, but the triumph never left his face.

"William, I am very sorry, but given the situation, I have no choice," General Trummel said.

The General nodded and two men were at William's side. One was securing his arms behind his back while the other searched his person. The soldier laid William's pistol, sword, and knife on the General's desk. Pulling out the folded piece of paper from William's coat pocket, he handed it to General Trummel.

The General opened it and looked up at William, surprised. "What is this, Colonel?"

"It's a letter of resignation," William admitted with defeat.

"Really!" Pearson said with a laugh. "That certainly tidies things up a bit. Frees up plenty of time for domestic diversions doesn't it?"

William glared at Pearson. There was something about the way he spoke, the way he was gloating over William's misfortune.

Pearson knew more than he was letting on, and that frightened William more than being held as a prisoner.

The General gave Pearson one more disgusted look and turned back to William. "I'm sure this will all be straightened out soon."

William put up no fight as he was led to a wooden shack in the center of camp where his hands were tied behind him around a tall post in the center of the floor. The shack was barren, no cot, no chair, just the dirt floor, the wooden post, and the newest and only prisoner.

For the time being, William wasn't thinking of escaping. He wasn't wondering what he had done to deserve to be in his present predicament, he was only worried about not returning to the one place he wanted desperately to be. He wondered if anyone would send Margaret word of his death if they hung him. He hoped Phillip would tell her, or perhaps Samuel Wallace would see it in a paper and relay the news to her.

That thought was the one that angered him most. He knew the news of his death would drive her to Sam, and he knew the man would use it to his advantage. Hitting the back of his head on the post behind him, William tried to keep out the picture of a distraught Margaret being comforted by the older gentleman.

The door to the shack opened with a creak and in stepped the man William had been expecting to see.

"Stand up, Weathers," Pearson ordered.

William managed to stand, even if it was an awkward attempt. "I should have guessed you were responsible for this," William said, taunting him.

"Oh no, you put yourself here Weathers when you couldn't keep your mouth shut about the whole affair in Boston." Pearson stepped up close to William. "Because of that, I have been unable to advance myself. You've destroyed my life Weathers and disgraced me."

William laughed. "Your life? What about the lives you destroyed? What about Timothy? What about Ginny Welch? Did you care anything for her or was she just another conquest to you?" William shifted his weight to take some of the pain off his leg. "How old would your child be now if it had lived-- six, seven?"

Pearson came close to William, anger in his grey eyes. "I don't think you can lecture me on morality, Sir. How noble is it to take advantage of a widow in mourning? Tell me, how do you think your brother would react if he knew you were bedding his wife?"

William shot forward, wanting to strangle Pearson's arrogant throat, but unable. "You will not speak of her! Do you understand? She is of no concern to you!"

Pearson punched him hard in the face and William's head slammed back against the pole. William almost slid to the floor, but Pearson pulled him back to his feet, grabbing his injured arm tightly. He cringed, but refused to cry out.

"I'm afraid she is of great concern to me," he whispered. "You see, she shot one of my men awhile back, and England looks on those who murder his Majesty's soldiers with about as much respect as traitors."

William was taken aback. "You!" He fought to catch his breath. "You ordered the farm destroyed. Why? That was before I even knew who she was?"

"You may not have known, but one of my--what was the word you used-- conquests in Charleston knew your brother. I had hoped that by using him I would be led to my ultimate prize…you."

Pearson pulled a pistol from his waistcoat and examined it. "I was really hoping that I would get to use this on the mighty

Captain Edward Weathers, and take him down myself, but in the end it wasn't necessary. He was such a poor soldier that a couple other Englishmen took care of it for me."

He examined William. "I believe it was a shot here… and here." Pearson pushed the barrel of his gun into William's chest and stomach before returning the pistol back to its place. "War is cruel, isn't it? So many nameless faces, so many deaths. The innocent are killed along with the guilty." Tipping his hat, Pearson sauntered to the door and left.

William was seething. He tried uselessly to free his hands from the ropes that bound them together. "Don't you touch her!" He shouted, his voice hoarse with the effort. "Pearson! I'll kill you! I swear! I'll kill you!"

Pearson nearly danced his way back to the tent he was being housed in next to the general's. He had William Weathers exactly where he wanted him.

"What's got you so happy?" Balis asked as Pearson entered smiling.

"At last," he said, making a grand sweep to grab a glass, "everything is falling into place. Weathers is in torment, and I am certain to be thanked for apprehending a turncoat." He poured himself a tall glass of whiskey. "I do wish I could stay to see him hung."

"Are we going back to Charleston?" Balis asked, joining him in a drink.

Pearson nodded. "I have some business to attend to. I want you to come with me until we get just out of camp." The expression on his face changed. "Trummel doesn't trust me, and the feeling is mutual. After I'm gone, I want you to come back and quietly keep an eye on Weathers. If Trummel pulls anything and Weathers escapes, you have my permission to kill him."

Balis raised an eyebrow. "Are you sure?"

Pearson set down his glass. "As much as I would love to take care of him myself, I'm at the point that I just want him gone. He's been a thorn in my side for far too long." Pearson raised his glass in a toast and smiled again.

William tried desperately to free his hands. Pulling on the ropes, he tugged for hours until he was exhausted and bloody. His arm was covered in blood from where Pearson had reopened his wound and his wrists were rubbed raw. Cursing, he swore and fought against his bonds again.

Late in the night a tired and restless General Trummel came to visit the exhausted and desperate William. He only needed to take one glance at William to see what torture the man was going through. Giving some orders to the guard outside, the soldier left, returning with a bucket of water. Dismissing him, Trummel sighed as he looked William over.

"William, William, what kind of mess have you gotten yourself into?" He walked behind William and cut the ropes from his hands.

It took all of William's strength to keep himself from falling over. He rubbed his sore wrists and closed his eyes tightly, fighting back the pain and exhaustion. The General brought the bucket of water to him and knelt down close to William, helping him get a drink. After the water quenched him, William wet his face, the cold water reviving him and he could once again think clearly.

"General," he said, his voice hoarse, "it's Pearson, he's—"

"I know," the general said, standing. "The man's a bad seed. He's been ruining the name of good Englishmen for years. It's in his blood I guess. I knew his father ages ago and he was as ruthless as his son. Supposedly, the elder has had a change of heart, but I knew him too well to believe it."

"You knew Pearson's father?" William asked, taking another drink of water.

The General gave William a knowing look. "Not his real father, not much is known of him, but the uncle who raised him. It seems to me, though, that you've known Pearson for some time."

"We were quartered together in Boston," William's voice was still hoarse.

"I heard," the general responded. "I received a letter from General Miller in Boston, not long after you came into my service. He told me about the whole affair. To be honest, we expected something like this. At first, I feared maybe Pearson was behind your disappearance."

William tried to stand, but his legs were still too weak. "Sir, I have to explain. My brother—"

"Is of no concern," he said. "What matters now is that we get the matter of the accusations leveled at you addressed. Under normal circumstances we would expect a visit from an inspector in a few days, but because of the war his arrival could take as long as a month. I'm afraid this is going to be your home for a while."

The general went to leave, but stopped, looking back at his prisoner. "It is unfortunate, though, about the state of things. If you were to escape I wouldn't even have the manpower to go after you." The general shook his head and left.

William sat back against the sturdy wooden post as he took in what the general had said. If he escaped? How could he? He could barely stand, let alone get past two guards without any weapons. Closing his eyes, William leaned his head back and sighed, waiting for deliverance.

Before long, William thought he heard shouts outside and the smell of smoke wafting into the small building. He heard men running, assuming to where the fire was, but he didn't move. He only wished that the fire would grow and take him as well.

Finally, curiosity got the better of him when he heard whinny of horses outside the door. Taking a few feeble steps forward, he almost ran into Phillip who rushed inside, breathless.

"Are you going to stay in here all night? I'm not good at these kinds of things."

Uncermoniously, Phillip handed William his pistol, knife, powder horn, and pouch full of bullets. William took them, bewildered, not sure what was happening.

"Come on!" Phillip urged him. "Everyone's at the other end of camp. It's our only chance to get you out of here."

William followed him outside, his strength returning as the possibility of escape became tangible. Heavy smoke filled the air and he could hear the shouts of men as they tried to stop the fire that lit up the southern end of camp. As Phillip was loading supplies onto the two waiting horses, a loud explosion that startled one of the animals.

Phillip turned to William with a grin. "One of the tents held an extra stockpile of powder," he giggled.

William looked at his friend, amazed. "You did this?"

Phillip shrugged sheepishly. "I had help."

"You surprise me, Sergeant Mitchell. I didn't think you had it in you."

Phillip smiled. "I'm surprised myself, Colonel."

Climbing into his saddle, William forgot about his pain and exhaustion. The red sea had parted and he wasn't looking back.

Chapter Thirty: Departures and Returns

"Where to?" Phillip asked after the glow of the fire had long since disappeared behind them.

"My brother's farm, Pearson has something planned. I know it." William spurred his horse to move faster. "He was the one who sent the English to destroy the farm, and he knows Margaret killed one of the soldiers while they were looking for information on me. That's the only reason Edward died." William shook his head. "Pearson just wanted to get to me. I can't help thinking that if it wasn't for me Edward would still be alive. Even if Pearson didn't pull the trigger, I know if he hadn't been on that battlefield Edward would never have ended up dead."

"Do you think he'll try to do the same to her?" Phillip asked, concerned.

"If he can't do it legally, I have no doubt he'll take the matter into his own hands. That's what scares me."

William and Phillip rode through the night, finally stopping when neither one of them could go any further, and made camp under an old stone bridge that crossed a dry creek bed. William slept soundly for a couple of hours, but woke with his head full of terrible thoughts, fearing what Pearson might do to Margaret. He wouldn't put anything past him. The man could kill without a thought. What more could he be capable of?

He sat up, afraid of what the next days might bring, but there was one thing he knew. No matter what happened, Hugh Pearson would not escape, he was going to make certain of that.

He tried to clear his mind, listening to the chirping of a nearby cricket, but was suddenly on edge. There was a silence in the air he didn't like. Reaching down slowly, he took hold of his pistol. William waited, feeling, more than hearing the threat behind him in the dim firelight.

With precision, he turned, catching his assailant off guard, causing the man to drop the knife in his hand. Instantly, the man was on the ground, William's knee on his chest, his pistol at his throat. Balis coughed, unable to breathe with William's weight on top of him.

"Where is Pearson?" William demanded, not needing to ask who sent the man as he pushed his gun harder on the man's windpipe. "Where is he?"

"He can't breathe, William," came Phillip's voice from behind him. The commotion had awakened him and he now stood behind William with his own musket aimed at Balis.

Dragging Balis to his knees, William moved the gun from his throat to his head. "Now, tell me where he is."

Grinning, Balis spit some blood on the ground. William clicked back the hammer, ready to fire.

"William, don't," Phillip said. Kneeling down, he turned his attention to Balis. "Next time I won't stop him. Answer the question."

"He's on his way to Charleston. Said he had business to take care of there," Balis answered.

"Did he say anything else?" Phillip asked.

"No, nothing," Balis said, sitting back on his feet, his face warped in the darkness.

"He's lying," William snarled.

Balis shot him an angry look. "My orders were to keep an eye on you. Kill you if necessary. Other than that, I can't help you gentlemen."

Phillip stepped close to William. "What do you want to do with him?" he asked.

William examined the poor excuse for a man in front of him. "He's not worth wasting ammunition on," he answered, disgusted. "We'll tie him to that tree and he can hope some hungry animal doesn't find him."

The days after William left were harder on Margaret than those after Edward's death. The knowledge that she had lost not only one man she loved, but possibly two was too much for her to bear. She spent most of her time trying to preoccupy herself with things around the house, but doing a terrible job of it.

While making an effort at some needlepoint one afternoon, she found herself staring into space and accomplishing nothing more than a couple of stitches. Sending the children out to play, Abigail came to Margaret, taking the needlepoint from her hands.

"Why don't you go for a walk? Perhaps it will do you some good to get out. You haven't left the house for almost a week."

Margaret felt stinging tears in her eyes, but tried to blink them back. "I need to tend to the children, take my mind off of things."

Abigail took her hand. "Maybe there are some things that you need to think about, things that you shouldn't hold back. I'll take care of the children's dinner." She laid a hand on Margaret's shoulder. "You go outside and cry as much as you need to. You will feel better." Nodding, Margaret made her way slowly to the door, making an effort to put one foot in front of the other.

Outside, the heat of the summer day hit her like a heavy weight. She made it to the barn, but could hold back no longer in the musty, dim light. Tears ran down her cheeks as she opened up her emotions and let them fall. She had never felt pain like she did at that moment. It was as if her heart was being torn open and she could feel each fragile slice being taken from it. She cried for Edward, for the loving husband, friend, and father that she had lost suddenly without being able to kiss goodbye. She cried for the violent way he died, alone and surrounded by death on the battlefield.

She cried for William, for her guilt, still feeling that she had somehow betrayed Edward, and for the pain of having to face her feelings. She cried for what William might have to go through, and for the fear that she might never see him again. She didn't want him to suffer his brother's fate and she cried, afraid that he might.

Finally, when the tears stopped, Margaret lay in the dirt, numb and never wanting to move again. She then did something she wasn't used to doing at times like this. Instead of surrounding herself with anger, or work, she opened her mouth and prayed. She spoke to God honestly, praying for her heart's deepest longings, telling Him about her deepest fears.

She fell asleep at some point and woke, lifting her arm to her face and, for the first time in hours, felt alive again. The light of the setting sun was dim, a slight breeze in the evening air. Sitting up slowly, her head foggy, she took a deep breath. Trying to regain her composure, and knowing where the strength to carry on came from, she stopped and finished the prayer she had started.

"It's in your hands," she repeated over and over. "It's in your hands." She made it back to the house and when pain gripped her, she simply stopped herself, raised her eyes to Heaven and said the words again.

Feeling hungry for the first time in days she went to the kitchen to find something to eat. Opening the door, the last person she had expected to see was sitting at the kitchen table waiting for her.

Patrick hadn't spoken to her since Phillip's appearance. After swearing for a good hour after Phillip left, Patrick had stormed off to his cabin and had not been to the house since. Margaret could only imagine what Patrick thought of her and of what she had done to the memory of her beloved husband. She had not only betrayed Edward's country, but Patrick's as well. Margaret sat down across from him at the table, not saying a word.

Patrick took a sip of his coffee and sighed. "I'm not goin' to lecture you Margaret. I think I did enough of that the other day, but I'm not goin' to tell ye what a saint y'are either. What you did was a dangerous thing tha' could'a gotten the both of ye killed." Sober as Margaret had ever seen him, Patrick finally looked up at her. "I will say that I'm glad ye did it though."

Margaret lowered her head. "You can be as angry with me as you like, Patrick."

"What you did was a brave thing, Maggie. Edward didn't hate the English. He just didn't agree with their legislation. It is stupidity and pride like mine that has caused our people so much trouble, the same pride that killed your mother and caused your poor father so much heartache."

Margaret looked up. "Patrick, did you know my mother?" It had been a taboo subject for so long, she'd never thought of asking Patrick what he knew.

"No," he answered. "But yer uncle often talked about her. She was a beautiful English woman and loved yer father dearly. She died givin' birth to you. Her brothers, out of dislike for yer bein' half Irish, gave ye to your father."

Margaret sighed, not sure how she felt about the information. "No one has ever told me anything about her. I'm thirty-two years old and I've never even heard her name spoken."

"You have heard her name, Maggie," Patrick said softly. "Ye've lived with it all your life. Her name was Lara and your father named you after her."

Margaret let out what was in between a laugh and a sob. "Lara."

Patrick stood and came to where Margaret sat, pulling a chair close to her. "I'm sure she would be verra proud of you. So would yer father...and Edward."

The tears came again as Patrick hugged her. The weight of guilt and grief lifting as her old friend forgave her and held her in his assuring, fathering arms.

Finally, Margaret was able to put herself to work and she and Sarah, who was refusing to go to bed, helped Abigail fold laundry while Matthew and Megan went to bed. Margaret was glad to be able to do a task and forget about her troubles. Soon Sarah finally grew tired and Margaret took her in to lay her down.

Abigail met her as she was coming out of the girls' room. "Mr. Wallace is downstairs, Mrs. Margaret. He's waiting in the study."

Nodding, Margaret hurried down the stairs to meet him, anxious to see Sam, especially after what had happened after his last visit. She hoped that too much damage hadn't been done to their friendship. Sam was pacing when she entered, his cane gripped in one hand as he carved a path in the floor. He stopped as he saw her, and took a very formal stance, waiting.

"Sam," Margaret said smiling. "I'm so glad you came back." She made a move towards him, but he took an uncomfortable step back, stopping her abruptly when she saw his uneasiness.

Regaining her composure, she straightened herself and tried a new approach. "I do apologize for William's behavior last time, Sam. He was only trying to protect me. He left safely," she told him, watching for his reaction, "a little over a week ago. Never would he have meant to offend you."

Sam spoke with words that were just as formal. Gone was the intimacy and friendliness that they had always shared. "There is no need to apologize" he answered stiffly. "I am glad he left without difficulty."

Margaret nodded, hurt by his coldness, yet understanding the need for it.

"I've also come to tell you that I have decided to move to Philadelphia. I have some friends there who will help see me settled. I have left word with my lawyer that in the event the funds in the bank become available the entire sum is to go to you directly." He finally looked up at her for the first time.

"Sam," Margaret asked. "Why Philadelphia? It's so far."

His expression was blank. "Distance is exactly what I need right now. I need to start over, get back to the law and away from farming."

Margaret took another step forward and again Sam stepped back, putting his cane out with his hand as a barrier between them. This time the hurt was evident in Margaret's eyes and voice.

"Sam, please, we need you here," she pleaded. "You have a wonderful plantation and friends that will miss you dearly. I'll miss you dearly." She watched him with concern. "I don't know how I would have survived the past few years without you."

Sam once again put up his façade. "I do apologize for any trouble my move may cause. I have hired a Virginia man to oversee the plantation and any other land holdings I have here. I will, of course, leave my address so that if you ever have need for anything you can contact me."

"For God's sake Sam, stop this." Storming over to where he stood, Margaret took his free hand, this time refusing to let him escape. "Quit treating me like I'm some sort of client, and talk to me, Sam. Me… Margaret."

"I know too well that it's you," Sam shot back, the emotion returning painfully to his features as he pulled his hand away. "But this was the only way I was going to get through this."

"Then don't go, Sam," Margaret begged.

"I have to." He rapped his cane on the floor with a force that took Margaret by surprise. "It will be best for all of us."

"Best for who Sam? Catherine? Is she the one behind this?" Margaret was getting very tired of the woman.

"No, best for me," Sam admitted and sat down, emotionally spent, into a chair.

Margaret knelt down beside him. "Why would leaving behind all the people who love you, Catherine withstanding, and starting all over again be best?"

Sam shifted uncomfortably and looked away from her. "Because of you," he finally said.

"Oh, Sam," Margaret said with a sigh.

"I can't see you anymore, because, if I do, it will break me," his voice was quiet, filled with remorse. "I love you, Margaret, and have for some time. I believe I can presume with certainty that you don't feel quite the same way for me." He laid a hand on hers. "I have to go, Margaret, because I don't think I could take seeing you with anyone else."

"Sam, I am so sorry," she said in a whisper. Touching his arm, she looked up at him and added. "You have been the greatest friend anyone could ever imagine."

Bending forward, Sam kissed her gently on the forehead. He let a moment pass and then spoke. "But you don't love me do you?" he said, knowing her answer.

Margaret shook her head. "No. No, I don't. Can you ever forgive me?"

Sam pulled her close. "My God, yes, I forgive you. I could never hate you."

Margaret pulled herself back and looked at him, not knowing what to say. "I'm going to miss you so much," she said with a smile.

"I'll miss you too," he kissed her cheek and smiled at her.

Suddenly feeling alone and frightened as the reality of his leaving hit her, she frowned. Just like Edward, Sam could tell what she was thinking, and he tried to reassure her. "You're not going to be alone. You have Patrick and Abigail, and I have no doubt that you'll be hearing from Colonel Weathers again."

Margaret found comfort in his touch as she held his arm and walked him to the door. Stopping, she hugged him, and smiled at him one last time. "Good bye, Sam."

"I'll write you when I get there," he said.

Margaret watched as he climbed into the carriage aided by Joseph. He gave her a wave, motioned to Joseph, and they were off into the dark night.

The night after Sam left, the Weathers family began to fall back into the normal routine that had been interrupted what now seemed like ages ago. Dinner was finished and the windows stood open, letting a warm breeze through the house. Matthew was once again positioned on the floor playing with some wooden soldiers Patrick had found for him, while Sarah brushed a doll's hair, and Megan read aloud from the Bible again. Abigail was cleaning in the kitchen and Margaret was busy at work sewing a dress for one of Sarah's dolls.

Megan read as best she could, without stumbling over any words. "And he said unto him, Son, thou art with me, and all that I have is thine. It was meet that we should make merry, and be glad for this thy brother was dead, and is alive again; and was lost, and is found."

Megan stopped when they heard the sound of horses outside. Margaret put down her sewing, and the children all froze. They heard the whinny of a horse and seconds later boots echoed on the wooden porch. Slowly, Margaret reached for the pistol on the fireplace mantel, tiptoeing to the door and waiting. There was a knock and Margaret slowly opened the door holding the pistol in front of her.

Before the visitors could say anything, the pistol fell to the floor with a crash and Margaret was in tears, holding onto William with all her strength, smothering him with kisses. The girls, realizing who it was, ran to the Colonel and hugged his legs almost knocking him over. Phillip stood back, feeling both uncomfortable and touched at the display in front of him.

When Margaret finally let William free he picked up Sarah in his arms and nodded towards Phillip. "I know the two of you have met," William said smartly to Margaret.

Phillip smiled shyly and nodded. "Thank you again for your help."

Margaret ushered the two men towards a seat. "Abigail!" she called. "We have guests!"

300

Sticking her head out of the kitchen door, Abigail quickly reappeared with a tray of tea and coffee.

"You must be starving," Margaret said, noticing their dusty and disheveled appearance. Both men were without their uniform jackets and their white muslin shirts were brown with dirt.

"How long have you been riding?" she added, too many questions forming in her head. "I'll have Abigail make you something."

"That would be wonderful," William admitted.

The men took their muskets from their shoulders, laying them next to the door leading to the kitchen. Margaret hurried to the kitchen door, but turned quickly back to William kissing him firmly on the lips and smiling. Saying nothing, she hurried back to the kitchen. In another moment she was back, ushering the children up to bed. With many groans and complaints she watched them march up the stairs to their rooms. She then turned back to William and Phillip.

"How did you leave so soon?" she asked sitting down next to William and putting her arm through his.

William lowered his head. "Let's just say I resigned my position."

"Will they be looking for you?" she asked, concerned.

William stopped her questions with a kiss. "Don't worry, all that matters is that I'm here." Margaret couldn't help but notice that he kept his pistol close by his side.

Chapter Thirty-One: By the Light of Day

Margaret stretched in bed as the early morning sun came into the room. She sat up sleepily. Remembering that William had returned she jumped out of bed, pulled on her robe, and rushed to his room praying that it hadn't all been a dream. It hadn't been; there he was standing in front of the window looking outside at the misty morning lost in thought. Margaret came up behind him silently. Putting her arms around his waist, she kissed him gently on the shoulder.

"He's out there somewhere, just waiting," William said softly.

"Who is?" Margaret asked, hearing the fear in his voice.

"Hugh Pearson. He's wanted revenge ever since I was in Boston with him." He turned to face her, knowing it was time. "Margaret, there are things you need to know and be prepared for."

Leading her over to the bed, he sat her down, not quite sure how he should begin. "Pearson was the one who ordered the men to attack the house. He was only looking for information about me. When I was back in camp, he showed up with charges of treason, making claims that I was part of Edward's smuggling."

Margaret had been tracing lines on his hand, but raised her head when he mentioned Edward's name.

"Before I escaped he made some threats. That's why I came as quickly as I could. Unfortunately, he's probably guessed where I've gone, and I doubt he will be very happy about my escaping."

Margaret nodded. "So he'll be coming here?"

"Yes," William said.

"How many men?" she asked.

"It's hard to say," William admitted. "He could come with a whole company, or consider it personal and come himself. Of course he's too cowardly to come alone, so he's sure to have some henchmen with him." William held her hand tightly. "I want you and the children to go stay with Samuel. You'll be safe there."

Margaret shook her head. "I'm not leaving you. I'll send Abigail with the children, that way they will be safe. Sam is going to Philadelphia, but I've no doubt they will be welcome to stay there."

"Margaret, you don't understand. The man is dangerous, evil. I don't want you here." His voice was stern, but Margaret spoke back defiantly.

"I am not leaving," she repeated.

William stood, frustrated, trying a different approach. "Margaret, I plan on killing him, and I don't want you to see that."

"I'm not scared," she said undaunted. "I've killed a man before."

"Another reason you shouldn't be here. That was one of his men. He may come after you as well." William didn't want to tell her the real reason he didn't want her there, but Margaret must have sensed his unease.

"William, what aren't you telling me?" she demanded. Sighing uncomfortably, William stood as she came to him. "You don't have to protect me. Whatever it is, I need to know."

William shook his head. "You don't know what you're asking."

"William, please."

She had to know and William knew it. He couldn't hide the truth from her forever and looking at her standing in front of him, he knew she was strong enough…for most of what he had to say.

William sat back down, fidgeting nervously. "Margaret, how much do you know about your mother?" he asked her.

"Until the other night, nothing. Patrick finally gave me a few details. I know that her name was Lara and that she died giving birth to me. She came from an English family and I can only assume they didn't approve of my father."

William nodded his head, pulling her down beside him. "That evening I spent with Patrick in his cabin, he told me everything he had learned from your uncle. Your parents were never married. When her family found out that she was with child they burned your father's home and kept the two separated. After your birth, one of her brothers brought you to your father."

Margaret, who had sat quietly as he told the story, finally spoke. "Why didn't anyone ever tell me? Was it so horrible for me to know about my mother? To know the truth?"

William looked at her gently. "It was probably because there was more to the story. Your mother had been widowed. She'd had another child before you, a son."

"A son?" Margaret was confused and then something occurred to her. "I remember something my aunt said after my father died. She didn't want me to go to London with her because too many of 'her' relatives lived there. So instead I came here with my uncle Seamus. Do you think that's why my aunt didn't want me to go with her? She didn't want me to ask questions and try to contact my mother's family?"

William nodded. "I can only assume so, but—"

"Did Patrick know anything else? Whatever happened to the boy?" Margaret interrupted curiously.

William nodded again. "Yes. One of your mother's older brothers took him to London."

"Is he still there?" he asked.

"No," William said, looking at the floor. "He's here, in the colonies. His name is Pearson, Colonel Hugh Pearson. The man I have to kill is your half-brother."

"My brother?" A frown passed over her face, but was replaced with a hint of optimism. "Then maybe there's something we could do! Perhaps if he only knew who I was…"

William shook his head. "Don't try to find any good or kindness in him," he warned. "There is none, and trying to will only get you killed. The man was raised in a world of hate and that's all he sees, all he feels. I think that's why no one wanted you to know. They didn't want you hurt. They loved you too much, and so do I. I will not see you hurt by that man."

"William," Margaret said, her voice somber. "I have to stay, and you know that."

William nodded reluctantly. "I do."

"When will we get to come back?" Sarah asked as William lifted her into the wagon, placing a kiss on her cheek.

"In just a few days," Margaret answered, smiling. She gave Matthew a big hug. "In the meantime, I want you to go with Patrick and Abigail and have fun. Joseph will be there and you will have the entire house to run around in."

"Won't Sam be there?" Megan asked climbing up next to Patrick and Abigail on the front seat.

"No," Margaret said. "Sam had to go out of town."

Phillip finished saddling the horses to the wagon. "You're ready, Patrick."

Patrick nodded and Margaret gave each child one last kiss and hug.

"We'll let you know as soon as it's safe to bring them back," Phillip told Patrick.

"Watch yourself," William called to him.

Patrick nodded. "Don't worry, I have precious cargo."

"We'll be fine, Mrs. Margaret." Abigail assured Margaret.

Margaret smiled. "I know you will."

The wagon moved forward as Patrick took the reigns and urged the horses to move. He led the children in an old Irish song, Patrick singing in loud Gaelic and the children making up words as they sung along.

Pearson rode south out of Charleston and found his way to a dilapidated barn where he had planned to meet Jass. Pearson found him waiting, exactly as instructed.

"Is he there?" he asked as Jass approached him.

Jass nodded and took a drink from a flask he had with him. "Arrived yesterday with Mitchell."

"Who else is there?" Pearson asked, lost in thought.

"The wife, a slave woman, and three children. There's an older man who lives a little ways from the house."

"Is he there often?"

"Off and on during the day, but hardly ever in the evenings."

Pearson nodded. "I'll meet you there tonight after dark. We'll create a distraction at the old man's and then make our way to the house."

Jass acknowledged with a grunt mid-swallow, wiping his mouth quickly. "Any sign of Balis?"

"No," Pearson said, irritated. "He must have found a better offer. We'll need two other men." With that he forcefully turned his horse around.

"Tonight, after sundown." Pearson said and rode away.

Chapter Thirty-Two: Diversion and Attack

That evening, with the children gone, the house was extremely quiet. William and Phillip had spent the afternoon gathering together any weapons they could find. So far, besides the two muskets and pistols they'd brought with them, they found one pistol, Patrick's musket, and a mean looking hunting knife. With only a small amount of powder and ammunition they knew they might be hard pressed for whatever was coming.

Margaret laid out a small dinner and the three sat around the kitchen table, no one saying much of anything, each too busy sorting through the thoughts in their own heads.

Margaret finally broke the silence. "What are you thinking about, Phillip?"

Looking up from his dinner, Phillip wasn't sure she had actually addressed him. "Me?" he asked.

"Yes," Margaret said with a smile. "You're so quiet; I wondered what you were thinking about."

Phillip blushed and took a bite of ham. He pushed his plate back and smiled, a look of serenity on his face. "I was thinking about a girl."

"A girl?" William teased. "Don't tell me that the highly educated, man of learning, has a broken heart."

"No, not a broken heart," Phillip replied. "A smashed one. Her name was Gillian. Her family lived a mile away from us when I was a child and I worshipped her."

"How old were you?" Margaret asked.

"Twelve, and very scrawny. That was my downfall," he chuckled. "My older cousins always had a good time making my life miserable. One day they were talking to her and I got jealous. I challenged them to a fight and was soundly beaten…badly. They humiliated me in front of her and she just stood there and laughed." He frowned. "I think she ended up married to one of them. After that, I buried myself in books and thought only of my education. My one satisfaction is that I've heard she did not age well," he finished with a grin.

The table was silent again, neither Margaret nor William knowing what to say.

"It's too bad those cousins aren't here now. You could certainly show them a thing or two," William said smiling, defending his friend. "The only thing more frightening than an English soldier is an educated English soldier."

Laughing, Phillip buried his nose in his glass. Unexpectedly a loud explosion in the distance brought them back to the present. William and Phillip rushed to the porch and looked out into the night. Margaret tried to see, but William held her back. About half a mile away, a bright fire was burning.

"Patrick's still." Margaret cried.

"He has a still in his house?" Phillip asked.

"Yes," William answered, leaving Phillip curious.

Hurrying to the front room, William flung his musket over his shoulder and grabbed his pistol. Checking to make sure both were loaded, he handed Phillip the hunting knife that sat on the table. "Phillip, stay with her. Don't let her out of your sight," he ordered.

"But you'll need help," Phillip protested, sticking the knife in his belt.

William lowered his voice so Margaret couldn't hear. "It's a diversion, we know that, but maybe Pearson will be man enough to face me alone." Phillip nodded, hoping his friend was right.

Pearson, sitting on his horse a few hundreds yards out from the house, watched a figure run out to the fire that had brought an unexpected explosion with it. He motioned to Jass and his partner.

"Get to the house, I want them both dead. No mistakes. I'll follow from behind."

William rushed towards Patrick's cabin, which was enveloped in flames. When he got close enough he could see that one side of the house had been blown out. The heat was painfully intense, but William had hoped he could lure Pearson away from the house. After-all, it was him Pearson was after.

The cabin's walls were in flames. Inside bottles of whiskey were falling, creating small explosions. Putting his sleeved arm over his mouth, William tried to take long, slow, deep breaths, the smoke so thick it was choking him.

There was no Pearson. He turned to leave when a musket ball whizzed by and struck a nearby tree. Immediately, William was on the ground. Taking the musket from his shoulder, he watched the trees beside Patrick's cabin like a trained marksman. There was a flicker of movement and William fired, hitting a man who stumbled out of the trees and fell forward. William stood and went to where the man lay dead in the grass. He had about a week's growth of beard and reeked of liquor.

William reloaded his musket quickly and ducked behind a tree, afraid there might be more. A shot rang out in the direction of the house and William's blood went cold as he broke into a run.

Margaret paced the living room floor, while Phillip stood in the doorway, looking far too young to be in this situation. They could see the glow of fire in the distance and the heavy smoke was filling the sky.

"You have to go help him, Phillip." Margaret's voice was on the verge of panic. "What if he gets hurt? What if Patrick came back and is injured?"

"He'll be fine," Phillip answered, fear threatening him as well. "He wants me to stay here with you and that's what I'm going to do."

Margaret frowned, frustrated. Phillip watched her, not letting her out of his sight as William had instructed. Margaret stopped. She couldn't just stand by while William needed her. She turned to Phillip. "I've nearly lost him twice, and he needs our help. You can stay here if you want, but I'm going to help him."

Something in the darkness caught his eye and Phillip grabbed his gun from his belt. "Margaret, get back!" he yelled.

Turning, Margaret saw the two men running towards the porch. She went for her weapon, but was stopped in her tracks when a gun shot went off.

Phillip had taken down one of the men before he reached the steps, but the second was quick to climb up to where Phillip stood. He ducked as the man fired and came up swinging the butt of his own pistol. Knocking the man in the chin, and sending him staggering backwards, Phillip had just enough time to grab his knife and plunge it into the man's stomach. The man seemed surprised at the attack, unnerving Phillip. Pulling the knife out, he pushed the man backwards down the stairs, wishing this could all be over with.

Standing against the side of the house, Pearson saw two shots fired on the porch. Seeing his men fall, he swore then rushed to the porch.

Phillip hurried to reload his weapon. "There were only two, but I have no doubt more are coming," he said quickly, pouring more powder into his pistol.

Margaret ran to shut the door, but before she could reach it a tall figure stepped inside. She stumbled backwards and Phillip hurried to put a ball in his gun. Pearson saw Phillip from the corner of his eye, cocked his gun, and fired. Phillip was slammed backwards by the force of the bullet and fell to the floor.

"Phillip!" Margaret screamed and ran to him. Blood was pouring from the wound in his shoulder. "Oh, no, no," Margaret cried grasping the young man's hand, trying to use her free one to stop the bleeding.

Phillip squeezed her hand. "It's fine, it's nothing." He started to stand, but Pearson was quicker, hitting him on the side of the head with the butt of his gun.

Margaret let out a moan, watching the man in front of her hit the floor. Kneeling over him, she felt for a pulse. It was there, faint, but steady. Knowing what she had to do, Margaret carefully took the bloody hunting knife from Phillip's waistband and hid it behind her back. Standing, she pushed herself carefully back against the wall, turning so the knife would be hidden in her skirts.

Grabbing Margaret's arm, Pearson dragged her forward. With his free hand he twisted her other arm around. Margaret let out a small cry of pain as he pulled her arm out in front of her, smiling when he saw the heavy hunting knife.

"Brave, aren't you. They told me you were a feisty Irish girl," he mused.

"Not as brave as you, sending others to do your dirty work," she shot back.

Pearson was unfazed by her insult. "Do you really know how to use that thing?" he asked, amused by her attempt at bravery.

"I can't imagine it would be too difficult," Margaret said, hoping her courageous front was convincing.

Pearson slammed her hand against the wall and the knife fell to the floor with a thud.

"William will be back in a moment," Margaret said quickly, trying to unnerve him.

"We'll see about that," Pearson said with a smile. "I was hoping he would send Mitchell to check on the fire. I'm surprised he left you alone with that pathetic excuse." He nudged Phillip's unconscious leg with his boot. "Although, I would love to have him here right now."

Pearson looked over Margaret's body. "I can certainly understand why he's been so taken by you." His eyes lingered a moment on her bosom. "Of course I can't imagine you would be interested in me since I'm not related to your husband." Pearson's eyes flashed and he smiled cruelly.

"Let me go," Margaret begged.

Pearson flung her across the room, but Margaret caught herself on a chair instead of falling to the floor. She felt the fear rise in her throat, but she didn't want to give him the satisfaction of knowing that she was frightened.

"Do you remember your mother?" she asked, trying to catch him off guard.

"Excuse me?" Pearson said, amused.

"Your mother," Margaret repeated, regaining her courage. "Do you remember her? Her name was Lara."

Pearson was confused and annoyed at this turn of events. He strode towards her, but Margaret could tell she'd put him off guard. "My mother was nothing more than a whore who squeezed out a pathetic, mewling child before she died; a gift from her Irish lover."

Pearson grabbed her forcefully by her waist and she was again at his mercy. "I don't quite know what to do with you," he said, brushing a lock of her golden hair from her face. "You killed one of my men and therefore you should be punished, but on the other hand, you're so pretty that I'd like to save you for myself. If only I could have both."

With his free hand he grabbed her chin and leaned over her, his lips inches from hers. The hand around her throat squeezed. "Your husband spoke of you before he died you know."

Margaret looked at Pearson, confusion in her eyes.

"Oh yes, I was there. He was an easy target for the English since he had fallen from his horse. Two shots," he said simply, "that was all it took. The ground under him was so soaked with blood there was no way he could have survived. He was in quite a bit of pain if I remember correctly." Pearson's eyes bored into hers and Margaret could see the events happening as he spoke.

"He kept gasping to breathe and tried to mumble something, but then he seemed to be at peace and spoke about you." Margaret let out a hoarse sob. "He said that it wasn't right. He didn't want to leave you alone because too many people had left you already. I can only assume he was referring to your parents?" Pearson chuckled. "And then he just kind of faded away. It was sad really, alone on the battlefield, no one there to comfort him, not even one of his men nearby. Pathetic. All I could do was watch." His hands squeezed tighter.

Margaret couldn't breathe. She tried to loosen the grip of his fingers, but everything was going dark. A voice somewhere in the distance gave her a bit of hope.

"Let her go, Pearson."

Margaret was thrown to the floor, air suddenly filling her lungs, overcoming her, forcing her to breathe in big gulps of air. She looked up and, amidst gasps for air, saw William, his pistol at the back of Pearson's head.

"Ah, Colonel Weathers, so you escaped death one more time. I'm beginning to think you're not human." Turning around slowly, he drew his own weapon. "But I don't think you'll be so lucky this time."

Pearson swung his arm and knocked the gun from William's hand sending it flying across the floor. Recovering, William punched Pearson squarely in the jaw. Pearson was unmoved and drew a knife from his belt. He lunged for William who ducked just before he would have been stabbed. The two men struggled for a moment until William was finally able to throw Pearson backwards.

Standing, Margaret grabbed Pearson by the arm, ready to do anything to save William.

Annoyed, Pearson threw her back to the floor. "Get back you Irish…" Pearson stopped as if something had occurred to him, the pieces fitting together. He rounded back on her. "O'Connor. Was that your name?" He laughed, partly out of shock, partly out of disbelief. "It's not possible. The irony is too much to handle, trying to catch me off guard with the question about my mother. Now it makes sense, you are the child of my mother's error in judgment." He smiled at her, but there was nothing kind about it.

Margaret stood, shaking. She opened her mouth to speak.

"Margaret, don't." William said from where he stood, trying to draw Pearson's attention back to himself.

Ignoring him, Pearson addressed Margaret. "Well, well, well, wonders never cease. I guess it's too bad you took after your father's side of the family, but I suppose that's why my uncle got rid of you. He knew you would always be worthless trash."

William ran at Pearson and threw him to the floor. Struggling, William tried to get his hands around Pearson's throat, but Pearson managed to stand. Grabbing his knife from the floor, he pulled William up and pinned him against the wall.

Pearson grimaced and smiled. "The family resemblance is extraordinary," he said. "Your brother was just as pathetic the last time I saw him, blood spilling from his chest, knowing he was finished, absolutely worthless."

Pearson pulled his arm back, ready to thrust his knife into William when a shot rang out. Pearson fell forward and William buckled under the weight, but managed to drop him to the floor.

William looked up at Margaret as she lowered the pistol in her hand and dropped it to the floor with a sob. Stepping over Pearson's body, he went to her, catching her in his arms before her knees gave way.

"I was so afraid that he was going to…" she couldn't finish the words.

"I know," William said, kissing the top of her head. "But it's over now." He held her close. "It's over."

Chapter Thirty-Three: Starting Over
December, 1783

The winter morning was chilly and a bit of frost covered the windows as Catherine made her way down to breakfast. While most of the Dougherty's house in Charleston was already packed in crates, ready for the voyage to England, the dining room was the one exception, a place of refuge among the clutter.

Catherine sat next to Lady Dougherty, who was pouring some cream into her tea, while Lord Dougherty read his newspaper.

"This is so embarrassing, Catherine. I simply cannot find a thing to wear. We don't leave for another two days and most of my gowns are already packed away. I shall look like a pauper and not a proper lady if I don't find something to wear." She turned to her husband. "I just don't understand what has happened, Lord Dougherty. It seems that ever since dear Colonel Pearson was killed, the war went downhill." Lady Dougherty shook her head. Catherine took a cup of tea, spilling some of it at the mention of Pearson's name.

Lord Dougherty put his paper down. "Did I tell you dear that Trummel wrote and said it was a small skirmish? He must have rushed into something more than he could handle," he said. "Just something a brave man like him would do."

"Oh, it is such a pity," Lady Dougherty pouted, stirring her tea. "Well, at least we're getting out of this horrid place." She reached over and touched Catherine's hand. "I'm so glad you're going to London with us. It is a pity about your…d.i.v.o.r.c.e, but I'm certain that once everyone knows the circumstances they won't hold it against you. I'm sure they will have some pity once they hear how this horrid country treated you, not giving you barely anything to live off of. You know how society can be," she said, taking a sip of her tea.

"I can't believe the court would not hear the testimony of that slave of yours, giving Mr. Wallace the upper hand…and all the money. Simply because a woman made a couple of wrong decisions, people brand a woman, and she is forced to spend the rest of her life watching from the sidelines, walking down the street hearing the whispers from behind her.

"But don't worry dear, no matter what happens you will always have a place with us. Lord Dougherty and I have agreed upon that. If I speak to the right people we should be able to get you into a…decent place in society. Maybe not the best, but we'll see what we can do. We know that giving charity to others is the only way to Heaven."

"Yes," Catherine agreed, her face strangely unemotional.

The post rider made his way through the city of Charleston and out into the country, making a couple of deliveries along the way. He came to his final stop, riding through frost covered fields before coming to the farmhouse. Dismounting his horse, his attention was drawn to the sounds of cursing coming from the nearby barn.

Seeing two men attempting to coax a mule inside, the rider recognized that it was Gaelic being yelled at the stubborn animal by one of the gentlemen. Laughing to himself, the rider climbed the steps to the porch and knocked. A black woman in a cap and apron opened the door, took the letter, and thanked him, handing him a coin for his troubles.

Abigail found William in his study. "Mr. William, this came by post rider, Sir."

Looking up from his papers, William took the letter from her. He took a look at the address and stood. "Margaret will want to see this. Where is she?"

"In the kitchen," Abigail said, going back to her work with a smile.

William went to the kitchen and found Margaret sitting at the table with the children. Megan and Matthew were both working on slates, trying to do some arithmetic, while Margaret was patiently showing Sarah how to spell her name.

Coming up behind her, William kissed her neck. "I wanted to bring this to you, before I go to help Patrick and Phillip shoe the animals. I'm afraid they are having quite a bit of difficulty. I can hear Patrick all the way in the study. I'm not quite certain if it's the horses or Phillip he's cursing." The children giggled, imagining the things Patrick.

Margaret took the letter from his hand. "What is it?"

"It's from Sam," he said, kissing her again and heading outside, grabbing a piece of warm bread as he left.

Margaret opened the letter and read.

Dear Margaret,

My best wishes on your marriage. I wish the best for both of you. Patrick wrote and told me how well the farm was doing. It sounds beautiful. Things are going very well here in Philadelphia. I have made my new home in the city and have been doing quite a bit of work for the new Congress. It is going to be a long and arduous

319

journey, but we are on the road to forming one of the greatest countries ever known.

It is my hope that soon our constitution will be finished and everyone will see how blessed we have been. The sacrifice that thousands made on the battlefield was not in vain. Their spirits will live on in the words of this document and there they will always be remembered.

I will be back for a couple of weeks next month. Tell the children that I will bring plenty of presents.

Always Yours,

Sam

Epilogue

Margaret listened outside the door as William finished prayers with Matthew. They were planning a fishing trip for the next day and Matthew had prayed to catch a very large fish.

Stepping out into the hall, William let out a low whistle. "According to Matthew, Abigail might need to put fish on the menu for a week."

Margaret laughed quietly, taking her husband's hand in hers. "I'm exhausted," she confessed with a yawn. "I think I will turn in. You?"

William pulled her close. "I can think of nothing better. If I'm going to be lugging home all these giant fish tomorrow, I'd better get some rest."

Once in the bedroom, Margaret pulled William with her to their knees, their nightly tradition. Holding hands, they closed their eyes and Margaret began to pray. "Heavenly father, we thank you for all our blessings. We pray that you watch over us, that you keep all four of our children safe. Keep them under your protection..."

William's eyes opened to see Margaret watching him with a smile.

"What?" he whispered, not understanding.

Margaret closed her eyes again. "God, please help my husband understand that he is going to be a wonderful father. That…"

Her lips were stopped with a kiss before she could get all the words out, and Margaret was nearly knocked over by the force of it. Laughing, she pushed William off of her.

"Mr. Weathers, please. I am in a delicate condition"

William was speechless. He smiled at her, beaming, pulling her close. "I love you, my darling, darling wife."

About the author:

Mary Jeanette Valdez is a writer living outside of Wichita, KS. She has been writing for as long as she can remember. She has a BA in English Literature and BA in English Education from Wichita State University. She is currently working on her next novel, while teaching middle school language arts. She is very excited to finally have her work out there for people to read, and hopes her readers thoroughly enjoy it. You can find her on both Facebook and Twitter.